"You may just have found our first genuine break in this case, Doc," Malloy declared with enthusiasm.

"You're welcome," Kristin murmured as she lowered her eyes back to the partially reconstructed skeleton on the table before her.

Which was why she failed to be prepared for what came next. By the time she realized what was happening, it was too late.

Caught up in the moment, Malloy bracketed her shoulders between his hands and delivered a very enthusiastic and yet innocent kiss to her cheek.

The next second, he had released her and quickly crossed the floor, getting halfway to the door.

"I'll get back to you," he promised half a second before he was gone.

Kristin stared at the opened door, stunned. Half of her was hoping that he would live up to his promise— and half of her really hoped that he wouldn't.

* * *

**Be sure to check out the next books
in this exciting miniseries:
Cavanaugh Justice—Where Aurora's finest
are always in action...**

* * *

**If you're on Twitter, tell us what you
think of Harlequin Romantic Suspense!
#harlequinromsuspense**

Dear Reader,

If I ever write an autobiography, it will be called *Taking the Cacti for a Walk*. My husband began collecting cacti and succulents many years ago. Since he worked in aerospace, at times my husband would be required to keep long hours. Long hours during which time the sun could do undesirable things, like turn the temperature very hot or shift position in the sky. All of which would be fine—if it wasn't for the fact that certain types of cacti and succulents cannot tolerate too much heat, while others need to be in direct sunlight for long periods.

Since I was home (with kids and a laptop, not to mention other responsibilities), I was "free" to move these sharp, prickly things around. So I did. From one spot to another. Now, mind you, we're not talking about a plant or two. At one point, there were close to four hundred plants in a whole host of sizes for me to move—more than once a day. And let's not even talk about the times it rained. I began to think of my life in terms of pockets of time when these nasty plants had to be moved around, thus the title *Taking the Cacti for a Walk*.

This book is a direct result of all the field trips my husband and I took, going to out-of-the-way nurseries, looking for specimens to add to his collection. Hey, I had to entertain myself somehow.

Thank you for taking the time to read my book and as always, from the bottom of my heart, I wish you someone to love who loves you back (and if they don't collect cacti, so much the better).

Best,

Marie

CAVANAUGH COLD CASE

Marie Ferrarella

 HARLEQUIN® ROMANTIC SUSPENSE

Recycling programs
for this product may
not exist in your area.

ISBN-13: 978-0-373-27990-6

Cavanaugh Cold Case

Printed in U.S.A.

HARLEQUIN®
www.Harlequin.com

A12006 825798

USA TODAY bestselling and RITA® Award–winning author **Marie Ferrarella** has written more than two hundred and fifty books for Harlequin, some under the name Marie Nicole. Her romances are beloved by fans worldwide. Visit her website, marieferrarella.com.

Books by Marie Ferrarella

Harlequin Romantic Suspense

Cavanaugh Justice

Mission: Cavanaugh Baby
Cavanaugh on Duty
A Widow's Guilty Secret
Cavanaugh's Surrender
Cavanaugh Rules
Cavanaugh's Bodyguard
Cavanaugh Fortune
How to Seduce a Cavanaugh
Cavanaugh or Death
Cavanaugh Cold Case

Coltons of Texas

Colton Copycat Killer

Coltons of Oklahoma

Second Chance Colton

Visit Marie's Author Profile page at
Harlequin.com for more titles.

To

Reta Renner

Who Can Pronounce

Cacti and Succulent Names

That Make My Tongue Ache

Prologue

Josephine Alberghetti placed an overly generous portion of lasagna in front of her daughter, then sighed as she took a seat opposite her.

"Mom, you've been sighing like that since I walked in through the door ten minutes ago. What's up?" Dr. Kristin Alberghetti asked her mother.

Josephine pressed her lips together, as if hesitating to give voice to what was fairly bursting to come out. The next moment, the hesitation was over, just as Kristin knew it would be. Drama and her mother were best friends.

"When you first came to me and told me that you wanted to be a doctor, I was so proud I thought I would just burst," Josephine told her only child. "I wasn't sure how we were going to pay for it with your father, God rest his soul, gone, but I remember being so very, very proud—and determined to help you reach your dream. I was willing to work my fingers to the bone, putting in twenty hours a day to make my little girl's dream come true."

Kristin knew where this was going. The same place that it had gone before.

"Uncle Gasper lent you the money, Mom," Kristin reminded her mother patiently. "Actually, he *gave* you most of it."

Though her father's uncle had fought her, Kristin had stubbornly insisted on paying the man back. It hadn't been easy, but she did it, taking and holding down jobs whenever she could while going to medical school. Through extreme dedication and concentrated energy, at the sacrifice of her social life, she'd managed to graduate ahead of time, thanks to an accelerated program.

But this wasn't about her mother's sacrifices—of which she would have been the first to say that there were a legitimate number. This was about something else. And Kristin had a very strong feeling she knew what that "something else" was.

Kristin and her mother were seated at the table in the kitchen where she had spent her first seventeen years. She had only a little time to spare and had actually popped in to visit in the middle of the morning—taking a couple of hours of personal time—because her mother had complained about being neglected. Feeling guilty, Kristin had juggled a few things, put a couple more on hold and then dashed over.

Kristin's grandmother, Sophia, a fixture in her life for as far back as she could remember, was also there. Kristin exchanged glances with the older woman now. She knew what was coming, as did her grandmother.

Out of respect for her mother—because she knew how frustrated Josephine Alberghetti felt—Kristin kept her silence. But it wasn't easy.

"But why you took all that wonderful knowledge," Josephine was saying, "and training and practically just threw it out the window to become a medical examiner, poking around inside of dead people, is really, *really* beyond me." She looked at her daughter pleadingly. "Can't you just go into private practice? Think of the good you could be doing."

"I *am* doing good, Mom," Kristin told her mother. This certainly wasn't the first time they had done this dance, but her mother seemed to refuse to remember her good reasons for choosing this route. She patiently repeated one. "I'm bringing closure to a great many families who need answers."

In response, Josephine rolled her hazel eyes dramatically. "Closure," she murmured under her breath as if it was a dirty word.

"Leave the girl alone, Josephine," Sophia told her daughter sharply. The family matriarch smiled at her granddaughter. "She is happy closing things. It is her life."

"And she's *wasting* it," Josephine retorted. "How is Kristin supposed to meet anyone when she's standing in the middle of a morgue, surrounded by dead people, for heaven's sake?" she demanded.

"Did you not hear her?" Sophia asked, the volume of her voice increasing as she made her point. At nearly eighty, Sophia Moretti's voice was as strong and loud as when she first arrived in America at the age of twenty-eight. "She is closing things for families. Maybe one of those families has a son—"

Kristin stared at her grandmother, grappling with a sudden feeling of betrayal. No matter what, her grandmother had *always* been on her side. "You, too, Nonny?"

Sophia leaned over the food-laden kitchen table to pat her granddaughter's hand. "I am just trying to—how you say?—*humor* your mama. Marry, don't marry, it is all the same to me. Just be happy, little one," she said to her youngest granddaughter. "The family has enough small people already."

"Easy for you to say," Josephine pouted, not trying too hard to keep the bitterness out of her voice. "*You* have lots of grandchildren and great-grandchildren."

Sophia pursed her lips together. "We are all family, Josephine. We share. You want some grandchildren? I will let you have some of mine."

"Listen to Nonny," Kristin coaxed. "We all live in Aurora. You need short people to hug, you can go over to Theresa's or Lorraine's or Angela's," she said, enumerating her cousins, all of whom were married with at least two, if not more, children, "and hug one of their kids."

"I love those children," her mother replied honestly, "but it's not the same thing, and you know it," Josephine complained. She looked at her own mother accusingly. "You're supposed to be on my side."

Sophia raised coarse hands that had been weathered by decades of hard work and pretended to push back her daughter's words of rebuke. "I take no sides. I just sit and listen."

To which Josephine responded with a contemptuous "Ha!"

Any response from Sophia Moretti was interrupted by Kristin's ringing cell phone.

Josephine sighed deeply as she watched her daughter reach into one of her pockets and take out the offending electronic gadget. To Josephine phones did not belong in pockets, and they certainly didn't belong at a family meal.

Holding her hand up for momentary silence, Kristin listened to the call. Her boss, Sean Cavanaugh, the chief of the crime scene investigation lab, was on the other end of the line.

"Sorry to interrupt your personal time, Doctor, but I'm afraid we need you at a crime scene," he told her, his deep voice rumbling in her ear. "We've found two bodies so far."

"So far?" Kristin repeated uncertainly, surprised at the way he'd phrased the news. "Are you expecting to find more?"

"Unfortunately, yes," she heard him respond wearily. "It looks like there might be quite a few."

How many were there in "quite a few?" Kristin wondered, a shiver threatening to slide up and down her spine. "That sounds like you've hit some kind of mother lode, sir."

"That's what I'm afraid of," he told her. "I'd appreciate it if you got here as soon as you could."

"Yes, sir. On my way," Kristin told him quietly.

Sophia lowered her voice as she leaned toward her daughter, taking care not to interfere with her granddaughter's call. "What means this 'mother lode'?" she asked.

Josephine sighed as she rose to her feet and began to put away the food she had taken out the minute her daughter had walked through the door. Family mealtimes were treasured, no matter when they took place and how small the family unit at that particular moment might be.

Timing-wise, this had to be a new record.

She transferred Kristin's serving onto a paper plate, then with a minimum number of movements, efficiently wrapped it all up in aluminum foil. "It means, Ma, that Kristin is leaving."

Chapter 1

It wasn't going to be one of his better days.

He could just feel it in his bones.

The road Malloy Cavanaugh was driving on was becoming almost dangerously hypnotic. He'd been on it for close to half an hour.

His eyes felt as if they were burning—always a bad sign—and his eyelids kept threatening to shut on him. Thanks to the rather considerable charms of a young woman he'd met the other night with the not totally inaccurate nickname of Bunny, he had gotten very little sleep the past two nights.

Hence, Detective Malloy Cavanaugh of the department's Cold Case Division was not his usual energized self this morning.

Catching up on a backlog of paperwork would have been far more to his liking at this point. At least, if he fell asleep at his desk, there was no danger of driving that desk into a ditch or off the side of the inclined road the way there was at the moment.

Aurora, California, where he had moved several years ago with the rest of his family, was a work in progress, a city whose council worked hand in hand with its developers. Consequently—and aesthetically— that development progressed slowly.

What that ultimately meant was, according to his uncles, Aurora had taken thirty-five years to go from a rural, two-lane, three-traffic-light town to the major thriving city it was today.

That also meant that there were still large parcels of land that were generally undeveloped. Most of them were located on the outskirts of the southern perimeter of Aurora.

That was where he was traveling right now, on his way to a crime scene, which, it seemed, had the dubious distinction of being both the site of a multiple homicide and the site of a cold case all at the same time.

The bodies, according to the investigators who had been summoned by the first officer on the scene, had apparently been in the ground for years; the exact amount of time—as well as the exact number of bodies—had yet to be determined.

Hell of a way to start a Monday morning, Malloy thought, stifling a yawn before it managed to momentarily make him shut his eyes.

He took in a deep breath, trying hard to rouse himself. A better way to go would have been to drink some of the pitch-black, strong coffee that was riding next to him in his vehicle's cup holder, but unless he pulled over—something, considering the narrowness of the winding road he was on, that was not advisable—he was not about to risk reaching for the tall container.

For that to happen, the split second that his eyes might be off the road could just be enough to send him careening into an accident—or his demise.

Notoriously happy-go-lucky and possessed of what some had referred to as a charmed life, Malloy was still not reckless enough to think himself above any and all accidents. Better safe than sorry had been an unspoken mantra in his family, courtesy of his very wise, late mother.

All things considered, he chose to obey that mantra this morning.

The coffee could wait.

Instead, Malloy did his best to snap his countenance into alert wakefulness by biting down hard on the inside of his bottom lip. He stopped just short of drawing blood.

Just where the hell was this damn stupid nursery he was going to anyway, he wondered grudgingly. Shouldn't he have arrived there by now?

According to the information he had been given just before he'd left the precinct, the bodies had been discovered by the owner of a construction crew while clearing some heretofore unused land that belonged to the nursery. The idea was to extend the nursery and erect several more large greenhouses across the two additional acres.

The greenhouses were to display even more specimens of cacti and succulents, as if four acres weren't already enough, Malloy thought darkly.

At the age of eight, after running through what he thought was an empty field at twilight, he'd tripped and gotten almost impaled on the sharp, near-lethal spines of a small, but menacing saguaro cactus. Since then Malloy had developed an aversion for everything and anything that even remotely looked as if it belonged to the cacti family.

To his mind, it only seemed natural that an aversion to succulents should follow, as well. Though a collector would argue the point, it seemed like one and the same to him.

He was vaguely aware that there were whole clubs devoted to meeting regularly and discussing the care and feeding of various different species of these visually ugly plants, but for the life of him, he could not fathom why.

Then again, he didn't understand why anyone would pay more than the cover price of a so-called rare comic book, either.

It took all kinds, Malloy told himself.

Taking a turn down yet another obscure road whose sign he had almost missed, Malloy breathed a sigh of relief. Apparently, he was almost at journey's end. There was a sign posted up ahead just before a newly installed chain-link fence.

The sign proclaimed Rainbow Gardens. The sign looked new, as well.

According to what he'd been told, the old nursery, which had gone by—to his way of thinking—the far more accurate name of Prickly Gardens, had been sold a little over a month ago. The present owner had come in with new ideas, the first of which had included expansion of the nursery so that even more plants could be properly showcased.

Sorry, no expanding yet, Malloy thought. *There's the little matter of some bodies to clear up.*

Malloy pulled his car right up to the gate. The latter was closed.

There was another sign, an older, weather-beaten one, which told whatever traveler approached it that visitors were admitted "By appointment only." It went on to say that if the visitor did have an appointment, to "Please, honk."

There was what appeared to be a trailer standing some distance away, perched just above a row of several small greenhouses. Surrounding those greenhouses were a great many succulents and cacti planted in the ground and growing at a very prodigious rate.

Malloy assumed that honking was for the benefit of whoever was inside the trailer.

With his engine running as his car stood before the gate's fence, Malloy paused to drain half the coffee in the container he'd brought. Only then did he do as the sign advised.

He honked his car's horn.

When there was no immediate response, Malloy did it again, this time leaning on his horn until he saw movement from the trailer.

A man wearing gray dress slacks and a crisp, long-sleeved, button-down blue shirt approached the gates. He appeared totally out of place in the rural-looking, overgrown nursery.

He also looked extremely agitated.

Unlocking the gate, the man greeted Malloy by announcing, "Finally!" as he pulled the gate back.

Malloy drove down the slope and into the nursery, pulling his vehicle over to the first available parking area. The entire space was meant, he assumed, to accommodate several vehicles, but it looked barely wide enough to house three very compact cars. Planning was obviously not someone's strong suit.

Deliberately taking his time—he didn't care for the man's attitude—Malloy stepped out of his car almost in slow motion, his shoes carefully making contact with the sun-cracked dirt as if he could feel the heat through the bottom.

Looking at the man who made no secret of sizing him up, Malloy said, "Excuse me?"

"I said, 'finally,'" the man bit off sharply. "Maybe now that you're here, you can move this so-called 'investigation' to its conclusion." It wasn't a question but a strongly worded order. Angry, the man contemptuously indicated the four idle fellows standing in the distance. "That construction crew is being paid by the hour to stand around and watch that woman bend over."

Okay, maybe he'd had less than the minimum hours of sleep to be sufficiently operational, Malloy thought, but he had just had a really good jolt to his system, thanks to the coffee he'd imbibed a minute ago, and the scowling man in front of him *still* wasn't making any sense.

"You want to run that by me again?" Malloy requested. "Starting with your name."

"I'm Roy Harrison," the guy grudgingly bit off. "And I just had my lawyer buy this property for me."

There was practically steam coming out of Harrison's rather large ears. In his position, Malloy supposed he wouldn't exactly be thrilled, either.

"I take it congratulations are not in order," he commented.

"Damn straight they're not," Harrison snapped. "I paid for a cacti and succulent nursery, lock, stock and barrel. I didn't pay for some freaking boneyard," he bit off in complete disgust. "Can't you and that dour-faced former cheerleader take these damn bones and do whatever it is you have to do with them somewhere else? I've got a nursery to get ready to open," the man complained unnecessarily.

"I'm afraid nothing's happening on that end until all the evidence is bagged and tagged, and we can determine whether or not this was the actual scene of the crime—or if the victims were killed somewhere else."

Though he kept his expression deliberately neutral, Malloy had to admit that he rather enjoyed putting a pin in the man's balloon. He'd never cared for people who were filled with their own sense of importance—especially if they felt that gave them a reason to throw their weight around.

His answer did not sit well with the new nursery owner. Harrison's scowl became almost fierce as he waved a hand angrily in Sean Cavanaugh's general direction. The latter was standing in the distance, working alongside his team.

"I overheard that old guy say that these bones have been in the ground for maybe two decades. What the hell difference can it make now where you look at them?" Harrison demanded. "They're old."

"It makes a great deal of difference," Malloy told the new owner, his voice deceptively calm. "And that 'old guy' you just referred to happens to be the head of the crime scene investigation lab—and my uncle," he added crisply. "So maybe you could find it in your heart to show a little respect for the man and his considerable knowledge. Who knows?" Malloy added "pleasantly," his obvious contempt for the owner beginning to show through. "You play your cards right and the chief actually might find a way to shorten the time."

Harrison already looked infuriated to find himself stymied in this manner, not to mention that he highly resented being rebuked by someone he obviously felt was beneath him.

The next moment, Harrison took out his wallet, his implication clear as he tugged on a larger bill, having it peer over the top of his credit cards. "What can I do to make this go faster?"

"Not bribing me would be a good start." Malloy flashed a completely phony smile at the offensive nursery owner. "Hang tight, Harrison. I'm going to have some questions to ask you in a few minutes." But before that happened, he needed to check in with the CSI team first. "Now, about that 'former cheerleader' you mentioned—"

A barely veiled sneer curved Harrison's thin lips. "Let me guess, another relative?"

Malloy had just spotted the woman the new owner had to be referring to. She was the only female in the area, and, from what he could see at this distance, whoever she was, the slender blonde was nothing short of a breathtaking knockout.

All memory of Bunny, the woman he'd spent his extremely energized weekend with, completely vanished.

"Lord, I hope not," Malloy commented under his breath. "I'll get back to you," he added without sparing the owner another look.

"Who *can* I call to make this go away?" Harrison asked.

"You don't," Malloy answered with finality, tossing the words over his shoulder.

Putting the abrasive owner temporarily out of his thoughts, Malloy made his way toward what was the only center of activity within the area—if he didn't count a neighbor's rooster.

The lone fowl was housed in an opened coop facing the northern perimeter.

Flapping his wings and moving about in what could only be called an agitated manner, the rooster crowed intermittently despite the fact that the sun had long since been up and the current hour was quickly approaching noon.

Obviously the rooster's inner clock needed some adjusting, Malloy absently thought.

For the moment, his attention was not on roosters, or the dead bodies. It was strictly and exclusively on the attractive woman with the killer figure. Despite her appreciative male audience standing a few feet away, watching her every move, the woman appeared to be absorbed by the bones she and two of the CSI agents were digging up out of the ground and arranging on a long, extended roll of burlap.

The annoying owner had been right, Malloy noted, scanning the immediate area. The construction crew Harrison had hired really were, for all intents and purposes, immobilized, no doubt ordered to remain that way by his uncle.

But the crew definitely didn't appear to be suffering any discomfort because of that edict.

Instead, the idle four men looked to be quite entertained as they took in every nuance, every movement made by the young woman studying the various excavated bones.

Malloy approached the young woman and placed

himself between her and the sunlight that had, until that moment, been highlighting the collection of bones she had been assembling.

"Hi, I'm Malloy," he told her.

The voice and sudden distracting shift of light caught her attention. After a couple beats, Kristin finally looked up.

If the exceedingly handsome, exceptionally confident-looking man with the sexy grin momentarily threw her off her game, Kristin Alberghetti gave no indication of that reaction.

Instead, her eyes met his, and she silently waited for him to explain why he was here blocking her light.

The name he offered nudged at something in the back of her mind. After a moment, recognition set in.

Malloy Cavanaugh. One of *the* Cavanaughs.

His reputation had preceded him.

"Of course you are," she replied, turning her attention back to her work.

"And you are?" he asked after several seconds went by and she still didn't volunteer her name, even though he had given her his.

"Busy," Kristin answered crisply without looking up. "And you're in my light," she added rather impatiently.

"Funny, I would have thought that you cast enough light on your own to brighten up anything you needed to look at," Malloy observed.

The blonde looked up again, her expression telling him that the remark—and his charm—left her more than just merely cold.

"Sorry, no," she replied. Ice chips formed around each word. "Would you mind stepping to the side? I got the impression that the owner of this nursery wanted me to be done before I even got here, so if you move out of the light, I can try to accommodate him."

"Sorry," Malloy apologized, following her request. "My bad."

"I imagine you probably say that a lot," Kristin commented, sounding as if she were addressing the observation to herself instead of to him.

Feisty, Malloy thought. Ordinarily, he probably would have backed away. This was, after all, a case, and he wasn't the type to waste too much time trying to break through a woman's barriers. For one thing, life was too short. For another, he was being paid to be a detective, not a lover. And there were a great many willing women out there to choose from.

But, on the other hand, there was a certain appeal to the concept of "feisty," especially when it was coupled with someone who looked the way this woman did.

Exactly who was she?

What was her official position in the department, and how did he get her to open up to him?

"You're new," he said, hoping to initiate a conversation.

Kristin spared him just the minutest of glances before she went back to her work. "Actually, I'm not," she told him.

"I haven't seen you around," he told her. "And I always notice beautiful women."

"Well, I guess you missed one this time," she responded, carefully separating two bones that looked as if they had been fused together by grit and time.

Rather than annoying him, the flippant way she'd answered what was clearly a line—he hadn't been trying to be subtle—seemed to oddly attract him to an even greater extent.

Crouching down beside the woman, he said, "Let's start over."

The look she gave him would have withered a lesser man.

"Maybe later. I'm working now." Her expression turned impatient. "And you're in my light again."

"Right."

To accommodate her, Malloy rose to his feet, taking care to allow the sunlight to stream over and bathe the bones laid out before her.

This one, he told himself, was going to be a tough nut to crack.

And he couldn't wait to get started.

Chapter 2

But for now, as tantalizing as the woman kneeling over the boneyard was, Malloy knew he had to place his private plans on the back burner.

A really distant back burner.

For now, he had a crime to begin to unravel and, from the looks of it, a number of dead people to identify.

Growing up, Malloy had always loved puzzles, both the mental kind and the kind that came inside boxes that were labeled with intentionally daunting numbers like "1000 pieces."

The older he got, the higher the number of pieces stuffed into the box became. But back then, no matter how many parts the puzzle came in, with enough tenacity on his part, they always wound up fitting into one another to form a unified whole.

He had come to learn years ago that life didn't always imitate art. If he were being honest with himself, "hardly ever" was more the case. But each of these bones now spread out on the cloth went into forming a whole person. All he needed to do was find out who that whole person was, so that he or she could be laid to rest.

All he needed to do.

The words echoed in his head, mocking him. There was no "all" about this job, unless the word referred strictly to the number of bones that were even now piling up next to the medical examiner.

As he watched, the pile just kept growing.

It was like trying to look away from a train wreck. Horrific though it was, he couldn't tear his eyes away. Not because he didn't want to, but because identifying the deceased was his job.

So he watched as the CSI team members continued to find more and more body parts, carefully laying each part on the long, unfurled rectangular cloth beside the somber medical examiner. From all appearances—at least to his limited range of expertise in this particular field—time had been the butcher rather than some overzealous serial killer trying to bolster his sagging self-esteem by hacking apart people.

Rather than walk away and get back to the owner as he'd intended, Malloy retraced his steps to the medical examiner.

"Any chance that those overly observant construction workers ogling you over there might have stumbled across some old Native American burial ground while plowing up the ground with their bulldozer?" he asked her.

Kristin looked up to see if the cocky detective was

joking. But the expression on his face, while exceedingly friendly, was apparently serious.

She turned back to her work. "If that were the case, Detective, it was a pretty exclusive burial ground. So exclusive that I highly doubt it existed."

"Again, please," Malloy requested. "In English this time."

Impatient, Kristin rocked back on her heels. In order to be able to look at him, she shaded her eyes. "The bodies that have been dug up so far all belonged to women. While there were some tribes that were predominantly matriarchal in nature, I've never heard of any of them segregating their dead." And then she shrugged as she added a coda. "Anyway, these bodies aren't really that old."

Malloy's eyes swept over the various piles of bones. They looked dried and, in some cases, splintered. "Could have fooled me," he murmured.

"I'm sure a good many things could fool you, Detective, but I don't have time to discuss that," she said, getting back to work. "I'd like to finish up here before the turn of the next century."

Rather than take offense, Malloy merely shook his head. "That was cold, Doc," he told her.

Kristin felt herself bristling. She didn't like the note of familiarity in his voice. "That was accurate, Detective Cavanaugh."

He didn't back off, the way she's hoped. Instead, he said, "Call me Malloy. All beautiful women do."

At a loss as to how to respond or how to put this man in his place, Kristin retreated. Sighing deeply, she went back to ignoring him. She turned her attention to tagging body parts.

"Are you *sure* they didn't unearth some kind of a cemetery when they broke ground over here?" Malloy pressed. There seemed to be just too many body parts for anything *but* a cemetery.

Kristin raised her eyes to look up at him just for a moment. She didn't bother hiding her disdain. "You have trouble understanding the word 'no,' Detective? Or is it that you're just not accustomed to hearing it?"

He didn't answer her.

He didn't have to.

The grin that found its way to his lips did it for him.

Kristin bit off a few choice words that rose to her own lips. This wasn't the time to get distracted or get embroiled in a verbal exchange that wasn't going to lead anywhere. Especially when what she had before her could very well be the defining moment of her entire career. She didn't have time to get sidetracked by a sweet-talking, sinfully good-looking, dark-haired detective who obviously thought that all he had to do was glance at a woman with those bone-melting, seductive green eyes of his and she automatically became his.

Her bone-melting days were definitely in the past.

Long in the past.

So rather than tell this man what she thought of him, Kristin restrained herself and asked what to her seemed to be an entirely logical question.

"Don't you have work to do, Detective? Or has the department taken to paying its detectives to stand around like obtrusive lead statues that do nothing but get in the way?"

"Is there a problem here?" Sean Cavanaugh asked, coming up behind the unit's newest—and in his estimation, brightest—medical examiner.

He'd interviewed and hired her himself after Jacobs, the department's last medical examiner, felt compelled to accept a better position in the private industry. Outside of proposing to his second wife, he felt it was one of the best decisions he'd ever made.

"Just asking the doc here some general questions pertaining to this boneyard that's being unearthed even as we speak." He flashed a wide grin in her direction. "She's giving me the benefit of her rather droll point of view."

Sean looked from his nephew to the young woman he felt was capable of great things. He knew all about Malloy's reputation. He'd raised several sons like that himself and knew firsthand that it took a while for the kinks to work themselves out. Malloy was a good cop and ultimately an even better human being. The name of the game was patience.

Sean, in turn, smiled at the young woman between his nephew and him. "I'm sure that Dr. Alberghetti will let us all know when she's had time to formulate a scientific opinion regarding this unfortunate treasure trove of death that the construction crew stumbled across."

Easygoing almost to a fault, Brian Cavanaugh's somewhat slightly older brother had just finished his sentence as a teeth-jarring, crowing sound pierced the air again.

The closest thing to a dirty look passed over Sean's face as he glanced over his shoulder. "Doesn't that blasted bird ever just stop making noise and go to sleep? That's the third time he's crowed since we got here. Isn't he supposed to be tuned in to some inner clock or something?"

"I don't know about an inner clock, but it's too bad

that he can't talk," Malloy commented, his eyes sweeping over the immediate area, then taking in the weather-battered trailer in the distance, as well. He had to be getting back to the unfriendly owner. "Maybe then he could give us some insight on what happened here."

"He wouldn't be able to," Kristin said flatly, not bothering to look up. "Roosters live about ten years. Fifteen at most. These bodies all appear to be older than that."

Taken aback, Malloy looked at her quizzically. "You actually know how long roosters live?" He raised his eyes to meet his uncle's. "Wow, she's just a regular font of miscellaneous information, isn't she?"

Sean smiled in response. "She reads a lot in her downtime," he told his nephew. "Although there isn't going to be very much downtime in her immediate future, I'm afraid."

"She also has excellent hearing," Kristin interjected without pausing what she was doing.

"My apologies, Kristin," Sean told her, willingly taking the blame. "That was rude."

This time Kristin did stop what she was doing. When she spoke, her words were addressed only to the older man, who she considered to be her mentor despite the fact that he had no medical degree.

"You could never be rude, sir. He, however," she went on, casting one dismissive glance in Malloy's direction, "is an entirely different story."

"Ouch." Malloy pretended to wince. "Moving right along—"

"Please, do," Kristin murmured just audibly enough to be overheard.

Roy Harrison picked that moment to approach the trio, a dark, impatient scowl all but embedded on his long, thin face. "Hey, when is she going to be finished?" he demanded, irritably waving his hand at Kristin.

Kristin was about to speak up and put the sour-looking man in his place when she heard someone else doing it for her.

"When she's done," Malloy informed the disgruntled new owner of the nursery in no uncertain terms, his tone far removed from his usual friendly cadence.

Kristin looked at the detective in surprise. She hadn't expected him to come to her defense. Part of her waited for Malloy to add, "Just kidding," but he didn't.

"Is she going to keep on digging straight down to the other side of the world until she turns up all the bones from here to there?" Harrison retorted.

"Nope, just the ones that are buried along the perimeter of your property," Sean told him pleasantly. His words didn't match the chief's expression.

Apparently, Malloy thought, sarcasm was wasted on the nursery's new owner, because he took the head of the CSI unit seriously.

"My bulldozer can go a lot faster," Harrison told them.

It didn't take a brain surgeon to realize that the man's only interest in the matter was speed, and that he couldn't care less about any sort of resolution as far as solving the crime went. The abrupt cessation of work was costing him a considerable amount of money for each minute that went by, and not only was money the bottom line, apparently as far as Harrison was concerned it was the *only* line.

"Your bulldozer can also crush a lot of those bones beyond recognition," Malloy told him before Kristin could speak up.

In his estimation, Harrison was clearly a Neanderthal type, and anything that the medical examiner had to say, Malloy knew, wouldn't carry any weight. There was no point in having her hit her head against a brick wall.

"It's not like they're exactly a pretty sight right now," the frustrated nursery owner snapped.

"Mr. Harrison, the less time you spend standing here, talking and tying us up, the faster this'll go and the faster you'll be able to get back to building up your nursery," Malloy pointed out. "Now, if you really want to talk, that's great," he continued cheerfully. "I have plenty of questions I'd like to ask you."

At this point, the scowl on Harrison's face was going clear down to the bone. Second-guessing the detective's question, he snapped, "No, I didn't kill anybody."

The smile that flashed across Malloy's lips was entirely superficial and empty. "That's very reassuring to know, Mr. Harrison, but that wasn't going to be my question."

"Oh." Harrison looked somewhat taken aback. "Well, what was it, then?" the nursery owner asked, trying not to look flustered.

To get out of the medical examiner's way—and possibly on her good side—Malloy began to inch his way up the incline, leading the nursery owner back toward the uninviting trailer. "How did you come to be the owner of this property?"

Following the detective, Harrison looked at him as if he were simpleminded. "The usual way. I bought the damn thing."

"From?" Malloy asked, attempting to coax more information out of him.

Harrison's expression grew even more condescending as he looked at the man asking him these questions. "The person selling it."

Malloy blew out a breath, trying not to let his temper get the better of him. This wasn't anything new. He'd dealt with idiots before. "I need a name, Mr. Harrison. Who sold you the property?"

Harrison stopped walking. "My lawyer handled it. He dealt with some long-time employee who worked here. The guy was acting on behalf of the owner."

The man was definitely a challenge to his patience, Malloy thought. "I still need a name, Mr. Harrison."

"I don't have a name," Harrison snapped irritably. "I already told you. My lawyer handled all that. He does all my transactions."

"All right, then I'll need *his* name," Malloy said, the calm timbre of his voice belying the way he really felt about this verbal square dance.

Part of him would have felt a certain amount of satisfaction if he could have discovered that Harrison was behind these murders. He made a mental note to investigate the man's background and his general whereabouts twenty years ago—although he would have been very young at the time.

"Fine," Harrison bit off. "I've got his card in that tin can of an office up there." He waved his hand contemptuously toward the trailer.

"Lead the way," Malloy said amicably, fairly certain that Harrison wasn't aware that he was being led up to that trailer already.

Harrison frowned at the former owner's living accommodations. "First thing in the morning, I'm having that piece of junk hauled off and getting a real RV set up in its place until I can have a building erected." He aimed a penetrating glare at the detective next to him. "Unless that's against the law, too."

Malloy counted to ten in his head before he addressed the owner's contemptuous statement. "None of it's against the law, Mr. Harrison. There are just procedures that have to be followed."

"Procedures be damned," Harrison snorted. "I'm losing money here."

"And I'm very sorry about that, Mr. Harrison," Malloy responded, his voice almost singsong in tone, even as he deliberately assumed a contrite expression. "You could write a letter to the department, detailing the inconvenience that this investigation is causing you—not to mention the money it's costing you," he added, then approximated a sympathetic tone, saying, "Maybe they'll reimburse you."

Again Harrison stopped walking, wonder written across his dour face. "They'd do that?"

Malloy eased himself out of the corner with the skill of a savvy con artist, something he had picked up by observing the people he tracked down and arrested.

"I don't handle that end of it, but nothing's impossible," he told the nursery owner innocently.

Out of the corner of his eye, he caught the amused look on Sean's face. The latter had come closer and overheard him. It took effort for Malloy to maintain a completely unaffected and neutral expression as he followed Harrison the rest of the way up the incline and into the trailer.

The trailer's interior had a musty smell, thanks to piles of papers that hadn't been sorted and either filed away or disposed of in a long time. Harrison cursed roundly under his breath as he searched his desk.

"Here!" Harrison declared dramatically, finally finding the business card he was looking for. He all but slapped it into the detective's hand.

"You might want to call ahead and tell him I'll be stopping by," Malloy advised. He slipped the business card into his wallet and tucked the wallet away. "Do you remember when you bought this property?"

Suspicion crowded the distrustful brown eyes. "Almost five weeks ago. Why?"

"That was going to be my next question," Malloy told him, his voice deceptively friendly sounding. "Why?"

Harrison's dark eyebrows drew together in a perplexed look. "You mean why did I buy it?"

"Yes." It seemed a simple enough question on the surface, Malloy thought. "Was it a lifelong passion of yours to surround yourself with greenhouses full of exotic plants? Or were you looking for a business write-off when you bought this property? Or...?"

He let his voice trail off. There was still the possibility that Harrison had somehow been involved in these murders that made up the cold case. Maybe the man knew about the bodies buried here and didn't want them falling into the wrong hands. In his haste to make money, he'd forgotten that the bodies were on this side of the property rather than the developed side.

Malloy watched the nursery owner and waited for him to respond.

Harrison stared at him for a few moments, then shrugged. "I just wanted my own business, and I thought that being in charge of a nursery like this would be relatively stress free." He punctuated the sentence with a dry, self-mocking laugh. "How's that for a stupid move?"

"Not necessarily a stupid move, Mr. Harrison. Things'll be resolved one way or another," Malloy assured him. "So, you didn't know the owner before the property changed hands?" he asked innocently.

"Didn't know the owner after it changed hands, either," Harrison retorted. "All I know is what my lawyer told me. The nursery used to belong to this collector who got too carried away collecting. He opened up a nursery and did a fair amount of business. He died some fifteen, eighteen years ago and left the place to his sister. She kept the place going, turning it into a real thriving business. When she got sick, she put one of the employees in charge. Eventually she asked him to sell it for her and then I got it. End of story."

Malloy glanced out of the window down to the site of activity at the far end of the property. From this vantage point, he could see his uncle, the two other members of the CSI team, not to mention the doctor with the killer legs, still working the multiple grave site, all under the entertained eyes of the four construction workers.

The latter group gave no signs of moving, the former gave no indication that they were about to stop. All of which put a decided crimp into Harrison's anticipated opening date.

He turned around to look at the new owner. "I'm sorry, I missed the last sentence," Malloy apologized. "What did you just say?"

Harrison frowned at what he took to be the detective's inattention. "I said, 'End of story.'"

"I'm afraid not yet," Malloy corrected, looking at the man pointedly.

Chapter 3

The Cold Case Division of the Aurora PD was not a very big department. Nor was it a very popular department to work for. Tracking down sometimes decades-old information was definitely not to everyone's taste. Patience was at a premium.

When Malloy had been promoted to the rank of detective and put in his application to join that division, he'd viewed working cold cases as a challenge, a way to prove his mettle and his tenacity. Because of his last name, he knew he had to work harder. Cavanaughs were scrutinized closely and held up to a higher standard. This was his way of proving himself.

But there was just so much of a challenge that a man could be expected to take, and working a cold case that had all the earmarks of involving more bodies than were regularly found on a major league baseball team was, in his opinion, over and above the call of duty.

It wasn't something that he really felt he could tackle alone.

So when Malloy got back to the squad room and saw that his partner was not sitting at his desk, he grew somewhat anxious and testy.

For the past week, Frank Weatherbee had been on vacation, but he was due back today. Malloy looked over toward his partner's desk to see if there were any tell-tale signs of life—like Weatherbee's ever-present bag of barbecue chips—on his desk. But there were no chips. Not a thing was out of place, which Malloy didn't take as a good sign. When Weatherbee was in, *everything* on the detective's desk was out of place.

Malloy scanned the squad room. "Anyone seen Weatherbee?" he asked, raising his voice so it would carry throughout the room.

The detective sitting closest to him, Wade Cooper, shook his head. "Haven't seen Weatherbee since he went waltzing off on his vacation, the lucky SOB."

"Well, he should have come waltzing back this morning," Malloy pointed out, annoyed.

"Maybe he decided to take an extra day," Cooper guessed, a vague, careless shrug punctuating his statement.

"He knows better than that," Malloy said, rejecting Cooper's suggestion. "We're shorthanded in the department to begin with—and he knows I'll kill him."

Cooper shrugged again, his narrow shoulders hardly making a ripple beneath the wrinkled houndstooth jacket he wore. "Hey, I'm just guessing here. Why don't you ask Julie?" he said, referring to the department's administrative assistant. The woman's desk was just outside of their captain's cubbyhole of an office. "Maybe

Weatherbee called her to say he's running late because of traffic."

Malloy hoped that was all that it was, although it was getting on in the day and if his partner was going to be here, he would have already made it in.

It wasn't traffic.

When Malloy asked Julie Myers about his partner, he found out that Weatherbee *had* called in. But the word "traffic" had never entered the conversation.

However, something else entirely had. Something else that Julie went on at length to explain. As he listened, Malloy's mouth dropped open. Talk about rotten timing.

"He did *what*?" Malloy asked, staring at the woman who had been with the department longer than his uncle Brian had been the chief of detectives.

Patiently, Julie repeated—verbatim—what she had just told the annoyed-looking detective. "Weatherbee said he broke his leg and can't come in."

The hell he couldn't, Malloy thought in disgust. He'd seen some of his cousins power through with gaping holes in their sides, not taking a break until the case they were working on was all wound up and closed.

Didn't people believe in work ethics anymore?

"I need him," Malloy argued. "Hasn't Weatherbee ever heard of crutches?"

Julie gave him a sympathetic look. "The detective said he was too banged up to use them."

That had Malloy momentarily reconsidering his re-action. "Was Weatherbee in a car accident?" he asked Julie.

The older woman shook her head. "No, a bike ac-cident. From what he told me, he and his wife collided while they were biking through the Los Angeles Forest." There was a drop of sympathy in her voice as she told him, "Weatherbee's mother is taking care of both of them."

"Biking?" Malloy echoed incredulously, still working with that piece of information. "What's he doing on a bike? The guy's as coordinated as an octopus crossing the Painted Desert." He blew out a breath. It would have been funny if it wasn't so damn annoying and inconvenient. "Of all the stupid, harebrained—"

"Hey, don't shoot the messenger," Julie protested, raising her hands to ward off his words before they became too colorful. "I just took Weatherbee's call. I didn't rent him the bikes."

Malloy nodded, a somewhat contrite expression on his face. He shouldn't be taking his frustrations—or Weatherbee's stupidity—out on her. Julie had nothing to do with the situation. It wasn't her fault that his partner was one sandwich short of a picnic.

"Yeah, sorry, you're right."

Malloy frowned to himself as he looked back out at the squad room. It was small, as far as squad rooms went, with fewer than half the number of detectives that departments like Homicide and Robbery had.

Everyone was up to their eyeballs in caseloads.

He looked back at the older woman. "Hey, Julie, how would you like to get out from behind that desk and go out in the field to work a case with me?" he asked, only half kidding.

Humor quickly dissipated in the face of the less-than-eager look the woman gave him. "I know, I know," Malloy sighed. "What was I thinking?"

Julie answered without even sparing him a glance.

"Probably some illicit thoughts about the hot little number you spent the weekend with would be my guess."

Taken by surprise, Malloy stared at the administrative assistant. "How did you know about that?" he asked, both amused and slightly mystified.

"Because, Malloy, you *always* have a hot little number to spend the weekend with," Julie answered. There was a note of affection in her voice as she told him, "If you were my son, I'd have sent you to a monastery a long time ago."

"No, you wouldn't have," he contradicted with far more blatant affection, "because then you wouldn't be able to see my bright, shining face every week."

Julie shook her head in amazement. "You really *do* flirt with every woman you come across, don't you?"

"Only if they're breathing—" and then he winked "—and lovely, like yourself."

"This is April, Cavanaugh, and way too early for you to be shoveling deep piles of snow. Go work your case before it gets any colder," she advised, waving him on his way.

He had been right earlier, Malloy thought as he walked away. This definitely did *not* have the makings of one of his better days.

Hopefully, he thought as he got into his car again five minutes later, this day wasn't going to get any worse.

It didn't get worse, but it didn't get better, either. The man he had driven over to see, Roy Harrison's lawyer, was not in his office.

"When will he be back?" Malloy asked the inert-looking young woman at the front desk of William James, Esq.'s office.

The young woman, who Malloy assumed was either the lawyer's administrative assistant or his younger sister attempting to work off a debt, mechanically mouthed an answer to his question. "Monday." Then added, "Two weeks from now."

"Two weeks?" Malloy echoed. Was the man representing an out-of-state client? "Just where is he?"

The woman's expression couldn't have looked more bored if she'd rehearsed it for hours in her mirror. "He's on vacation."

Damn, had the whole world suddenly gone vacation crazy? Was he the only one who had missed that memo?

"Can you give me the number to his hotel or wherever it is that he's staying? I have some questions for him regarding one of his clients."

The young woman made no move to retrieve anything. "I'm sorry, that won't be possible," she said in a singsong voice. "Mr. James can't be reached by phone. He said he needed this time to unwind."

Maybe it was his suspicious mind, but that sounded entirely too convenient. Refraining from making a comment, Malloy handed the woman his card.

"If he calls in, give him my number. Tell him to call me, day or night. It's about Roy Harrison. I need to clear up a few things. Tell him dead bodies are involved."

He'd thrown in the last line to get the woman's attention, since she appeared to be half asleep, on her way to oblivion.

He succeeded. Her eyes opened so wide, it looked as if she might have trouble closing them again.

"Really?" she asked breathlessly.

"Really," he confirmed with just the right touch of disinterest.

"You said 'bodies.' Plural." Her eyes were glued to his face. "How many?"

"Many," was the only word Malloy offered. "Make sure you tell him to call me the minute he makes contact with you," he emphasized.

Her hand covered the card he'd given her almost possessively.

When she answered him, her voice had dropped down a level, sounding almost conspiratorial. "The second I hear from him," she promised. "Absolutely."

He wasn't going to hold his breath, Malloy thought, leaving the two-story building where the lawyer's office was housed. But then, maybe he'd succeeded in getting a little movement going in that area, making James's secretary see how important the situation was.

Without anything tangible to go on, Malloy decided to pay the ME's office a visit to see if the sexy medical examiner had gotten any further with her examination of the mound of body parts.

Hopefully she could offer him something more to go on than she had in their last encounter.

It felt like he was spinning his wheels. While he had always been a fan of road trips, they involved real wheels and an actual physical destination. Spinning his wheels figuratively while trying to get somewhere on a case had the exact opposite effect of a real road trip. It only succeeded in making him feel exceedingly frustrated.

Malloy took a chance that the good doctor had returned to the morgue and had gotten started on making heads or tails out of the collection of bones she and the CSI team had gathered together. This was his first stop when he drove back from the lawyer's office.

Getting off the elevator in the basement, he followed the signs leading to the morgue. Malloy was faintly aware that there was music being piped into the building's corridor. It wasn't classical music, the way he might have expected—something soothing to quiet any unsteady nerves or a queasy stomach—after all, this was where the morgue was located—but something twangy.

Since he listened to music only occasionally and then to just whatever was currently on the pop stations, it took Malloy a moment to place just what genre he was listening to.

Country.

And whose idea was that? he wondered. Was that supposed to be some subtle commentary on the great circle of life? Down-to-earth folks returning to the earth, or some such circular reasoning?

Well, it didn't really matter one way or another. He didn't care for the music, but he wasn't here to indulge his aesthetic sensibilities. He was here for some sort of answer, or at the very least, a hint of a direction to go in. Right now, he had nothing, and he found that incredibly frustrating.

The door to the morgue was closed. For a moment, he debated leaving it that way and coming back later. He didn't want to disrupt anything that might be going on behind those closed doors.

But then, maybe it was business as usual and the medical examiner was just working with a giant, life-size jigsaw puzzle. In that event, he could even be of some help.

Anatomy wasn't his thing, but jigsaw puzzles were. With that in mind, he knocked once, then turned the doorknob. When he found it to be unlocked, Malloy entered the room.

There was only one living occupant in the room. A bright overhead light illuminated the main exam table. There were other tables, with other overhead lights, but they were turned off. In general, other than the one bright light, the oversize, somewhat chilly room was somberly in the dark.

Engrossed in trying to recreate just one body out of all the various parts that had been dug up and were now available to her, Kristin hadn't heard the knock on the door.

She wasn't even aware that anyone had entered the room until Malloy was less than a foot away from her. At that point, he cleared his throat to get her attention and very nearly caused her to knock over what had taken her over an hour to assemble—a less than half completed body out of all the bits and pieces that had been carefully laid out on all the other unlit tables.

Stifling a shriek, Kristin spun around and glared accusingly at the man who had very nearly caused her heart to pop out of her chest.

The cocky detective.

She might have known.

"What the hell are you doing here?" she demanded angrily.

She didn't like losing her poise that way, especially not in front of an audience—and most especially if that audience was comprised of a man she found to be unimaginably irritating for oh-so-many reasons.

"I'm interested," Malloy told her simply, looking at the progress she'd made with the body parts. He was definitely impressed. This woman had serious jigsaw puzzle skills.

"I'm not," she retorted coldly, her eyes narrowing as she continued to glare at him, hoping he would get the blatant hint and just go away. "I thought I made that clear this morning."

When he raised his eyes to hers, Kristin instantly realized she'd made a gross mistake in her assumption. He wasn't here seeking her out for her company. He was here looking for her expertise.

The first words out of his mouth confirmed it.

"I was referring to your professional opinion."

Embarrassed—and hating it—Kristin could feel heat traveling up both sides of her neck as well as along her cheeks. She struggled, snatching up various unrelated thoughts to get herself focused on something other than what an idiot she'd just been.

"I knew that," she murmured.

At any other time, he would have probably taken the opportunity to tease her a little. He liked the way her blue eyes flashed when she got angry.

But he was short one partner and his competitive nature wouldn't allow him to remain stuck in the mud, not making any headway whatsoever, for long. Solving cold cases was what he was being paid for. He wasn't about to drop the ball now.

But in order to keep from dropping it, he first needed to *get* a ball not to drop. And right now, he had nothing to grasp on to except for the bare bones—pun intended, he thought—of a mystery. He had all the questions without a clue as to where to even begin looking for some of the answers.

"So," he began as if they were having just a friendly conversation, "what have you learned?"

Kristin made no reply. Instead, she just looked at him suspiciously. The detective wasn't being cocky, he was actually asking the question. Was this just another tactic, or was this the genuine Malloy Cavanaugh beneath the jaunty bravado?

She couldn't tell.

When in doubt, go on the offensive.

"Are you asking me to spoon-feed you answers?" she asked.

"Yes, please."

He saw the skeptical look on her face intensify. Maybe he needed to play on her sympathies—provided she had any, he qualified. Right now, the jury was still out on that one.

"I'm down one partner, and the only possible lead I have is on vacation in some unknown location that apparently doesn't have cell phone signals, internet or any kind of telephone service. I need something to go on," he told her truthfully, then began with the most logical question. "Did you get a final count on how many bodies were in the ground?"

"At last count, there were ten. The CSI team uncovered ten skulls," she told him. "But they're not finished digging yet."

That must be making Harrison happy, he couldn't help thinking.

"Ten," he repeated, digesting the idea. "That means—if we're lucky—there are ten missing persons flyers to go with those skulls."

She inclined her head, as if agreeing with him. But

it wasn't a wholehearted gesture. "*If* the reports were filed."

Malloy laughed dryly. "Not much for positive thinking, are you?"

"Give me something positive to think about," she countered, challenging him.

He would if he could, but he had nothing yet. "What else can you tell me?" he asked, then quickly qualified, in case they were still on the wrong foot, "About the case."

"Of the ten people, nine of them are female," she told him.

"And one male?"

Kristin bit back a few choicer comments and only said, "I can see why you'd be so sought after as a detective."

He ignored the sarcasm, focusing on what didn't jibe for him. "Don't you find that kind of odd?"

"What, you being sought after?" she asked. "Actually, yes, very."

The woman had a smart mouth, and he found himself wanting to shut it in the most effective way. Later, he promised himself. He'd get to that later. It would serve as a reward for a job well done. "I was talking about the fact that there was a male in the group," he told her.

Kristin shrugged. He had a point—not that she would say so to him. "Maybe our one male was a transvestite and managed to fool the killer. Oh, and there's one more thing," she said, leaving the best for last.

"Go ahead," he urged gamely.

"The bodies weren't hacked apart." At least, not the ones she'd had time to assemble. She'd examined those sections very closely.

"So they weren't murdered in a fit of rage."

Waiting a beat, Kristin gave him the second part of her findings. "They were broken apart—while the victims were alive."

"Then they *were* murdered in a fit of rage," he said, amending his previous statement. And then he looked at her with a touch of impatience. "Well, which is it?"

Her eyes met his, and just for a split second, Kristin caught herself losing her train of thought.

Rousing herself again, she went on to tell him, "I just present you with the facts as I find them. It's up to you to do the speculation."

With that, she lowered her visor and got back to the business at hand, putting together ten dismembered Humpty Dumpties.

Feeling almost as if he was experiencing whiplash, Malloy watched her work for a moment. This case was definitely *not* going to be easy—for a hell of a lot of reasons, he told himself.

Chapter 4

Kristin could feel the detective's eyes on her. Ordinarily, she could block out her surroundings and work under any conditions, adverse or not. But she had this distinct impression that the detective wasn't watching her work, he was watching *her*, which was something else entirely.

And she didn't much like it.

"Why are you still here?" she asked, not giving the man the satisfaction of looking up at him as she posed the question.

Malloy's voice was mellow and easygoing as he replied, "I thought I'd broaden my education. You know, you can really learn a lot about a person by watching them work."

Obviously the man's supply of lines was endless, Kristin thought reprovingly. Since ignoring him was obviously not working, she decided to put Cavanaugh on the spot instead.

"Oh?" she said skeptically. "And what is it that you've learned by watching so intently?"

"That you're precise and meticulous—and you don't like being observed."

"I don't mind being observed. What I mind is the person doing the observing—especially when he should be working." The look she gave him left no doubts about how she felt about his standing there.

Rather than backing away because he'd been rebuked, Malloy smiled engagingly. "Do I make you nervous, Dr. Kris?"

"You make me irritated, Detective Cavanaugh," Kristin corrected. "Now, if you want me to come up with some answers for you to work with, you're going to have to let me do my job," she said, then added with finality, "alone."

But rather than leave, the way he had initially begun to do, Malloy looked around at the other exam tables. There were six in all, brought in during the rampage of another serial killer several years ago. Now the tables were covered with bones that might or might not be part of the person whose skull rested at the top of each table.

As he glanced around at the various clusters of remains, a thought occurred to Malloy. "Do you think this might be related to a sex trafficking ring or something along those lines?"

Kristin stopped working and looked up. "Excuse me?"

"You know, sex trafficking," he repeated, then went on to elaborate in case she missed his drift. "Unsavory types smuggling young women from around the world for the single purpose of making money by turning them into sex slaves."

"That would be more profitable if they were alive," she pointed out dryly as she got back to sorting. "For most men, dead women are not a turn-on."

"Very true," Malloy agreed amicably enough. "But maybe something went really wrong, and whoever was in charge of this group decided he or they had no other recourse except to kill all these women."

Under normal circumstances, she supposed that the sexy detective's theory was plausible enough. But not in this case. "There's just one thing wrong with that," Kristin said flatly.

"I'm all ears."

No, he wasn't. He was a great deal more than that, Kristin thought grudgingly. Malloy Cavanaugh was all broad shoulders, a quirky, sexy smile and whimsical green eyes that she found vastly disturbing when they were turned on her.

Her unbidden observation came out of nowhere, and she tried to banish it back to the same location, but without much success.

This whole case was making her tired.

"These women weren't smuggled in from outside the country."

The facts, Kris, deal with the facts. The scientific ones. It's the only way you're going to get him to go away.

"How do you know that?" Malloy asked, rounding the exam table in order to see what she was talking about.

Kristin drew in a breath. Cavanaugh was standing way too close to her, but telling him to back off might start him thinking the wrong thing—or the right thing, as was the case. She decided it was best to keep silent on that score. The sooner she got him to leave, the better.

"Their teeth," she pointed out. "The ones who have had dental work done show that whoever worked on them did a decent job. The others just have good teeth. That isn't usually the case for those whose backgrounds include poverty and malnutrition."

He had an adequate enough imagination, but it was hard for him to envision the remains that were arranged on the exam tables once being living, breathing women.

"So it's your opinion that this little band of not-so-merry women was homegrown?"

Kristin bit back a comment about his choice of descriptive words. Instead, she forced herself to make a dispassionate comment. "Appears that way."

Okay, so far he had that the women were most likely from somewhere in the immediate area—or at least this country rather than somewhere out of the country, and that all of them, except for one, were women. It was something, he granted, but still not very much to go on.

"Can you give me a rough estimate of when they were killed?" he asked.

She really wished he'd take a few steps back and stop crowding her. But since he apparently wasn't moving, as casually as she could manage, she did.

"Well, it wasn't all at the same time," she told him. "My preliminary judgment would be that this happened between twenty and twenty-five years ago."

"So this wasn't a mass grave," he speculated.

His wording made her think. "More like a grave of opportunity," she said. "The guy would keep coming back to bury his latest victim because apparently no one had discovered his previous transgressions."

The medical examiner's conclusion interested him. He had no problem adjusting his own thinking to factor in good points. Ego had never been a problem with him. "What makes you so sure it's the same guy?"

"I'm not sure," she admitted. "But judging from appearances—by that I mean the way he dismembered them—it looks that way," she theorized. As if she suddenly realized what she was saying, Kristin stopped working and raised her eyes to his. "Are you through picking my brain, Detective?"

"I haven't even gotten started," he told her honestly, flashing a grin that held a great deal of promise, as well as sizzle.

Kristin found she had to struggle to ignore the unwanted effects he was having on her. How did she get rid of this man?

"That wasn't really a question," she told him. "Let me be more clear. You're *through* picking my brain."

"What's the matter, Doc?" he asked her good-naturedly. "Haven't you ever heard of teamwork?"

Her eyes narrowed to two blue lasers. "I have, Detective. Are you familiar with the concept of carrying someone?"

He cocked his head, as if that would somehow help him get into her thoughts, and asked her innocently, "Is that an offer?"

"*That* is an observation," she informed him tersely. She was telling him that she was aware he was looking to her to do all the heavy thinking here and he was just absorbing her answers without contributing. "Obviously too subtle for you."

His smile only grew more engaging. "I'm really not the subtle type."

"Yes, I noticed," she bit off. She didn't know how to make it clearer than this. "Now, this might get you to first base or whatever base you're aiming for with someone else, but I like to feel that I'm earning the money I'm being paid, so unless there's something else you either want to ask me or share with me, please, leave," she underscored.

Instead of going the way she would have expected any normal male to do, he stayed exactly where he was, as if she'd just given him a choice. "Well, the idea of sharing doesn't sound bad to me," he began.

She'd set herself up for that one, Kristin silently reprimanded herself. "Please, leave," she repeated, and this time she made sure that there was nothing in her tone to leave any wiggle room for him to misinterpret her words.

Malloy inclined his head, as if he'd finally gotten what she was telling him. "Until the next time," he told her as he began to take his leave.

"Heaven forbid," Kristin muttered under her breath just loud enough to be heard.

Opening the door, Malloy wound up all but walking into the two CSI agents who had been in charge of digging up the area where all the body parts had ultimately been found.

Ryan O'Shea and Jake Reynolds were pushing a gurney with what looked to be a black body bag between them.

"Where do you want this, Doc?" O'Shea asked.

Kristin didn't need to ask what they'd brought in.

The sinking feeling in the pit of her stomach told her the answer to that one.

"More?" she groaned, temporarily forgetting about the annoying detective who had invaded her turf and was still in it.

O'Shea nodded. "It's the gift that apparently just keeps on giving."

"How much more giving?" she asked warily as she eyed the body bag.

"We found two more heads," Reynolds told her, aligning the gurney with one of the exam tables and unzipping the bag.

Kristin closed her eyes for a moment, as if trying to center herself before she spoke. Opening her eyes again, she looked at the body bag. It didn't look full, but it didn't appear to be empty, either.

"Just the heads?" she asked.

O'Shea had the good grace to look a little apologetic. "And a handful of miscellaneous bones that might or might not belong to the heads."

"In other words, just like the rest of it."

"Exactly like the rest of it," O'Shea told her, then added quickly in a far more positive voice, "The good news is that I think that's it."

"The bad news is that there are twelve of them." Malloy offered up that observation. Three sets of eyes turned toward him as he continued, "Twelve people without their entire bodies, without names and without a clue why they were unlucky enough to join this exclusive boneyard."

He studied the piles that were already out. Because of his upbringing, to him, bodies meant families. "And twelve families waiting for some word about one of their own who is never coming home again."

Kristin glanced in his direction, wondering if the detective had just said all that for her benefit, or if Malloy Cavanaugh actually did have a sensitive side to him.

The next moment she decided that she was probably giving the man way too much credit. Someone who looked and acted the way that Malloy Cavanaugh did didn't have to have a more sensitive side to him. From what she had heard about him, he did just fine with what genetics had given him to work with. There was no need for sensitivity to enter the picture.

She was partial to sensitivity, responding to that far more than the good looks the man was so generously endowed with. No matter how gorgeous a person might be, looks only went skin deep. Sensitivity went clear down to the bone.

"So you're not digging any more?" Malloy asked the CSI agents.

"Nothing left to dig," O'Shea replied. "Not unless we want our heads handed to us by that maniacal nursery owner, Harrison, because we're burrowing under his greenhouses and destroying those butt-ugly plants that the guy's got everywhere for no reason. We finished digging up the perimeter."

"You do realize that there might be more bodies on the property," Malloy pointed out, turning toward the men. "It's probably less likely," he allowed, "but there is still that possibility."

"We realize, Detective," Reynolds replied with a hint of annoyance. "We didn't just start working crime scene investigations yesterday."

"Good to know," Malloy replied matter-of-factly. "So, what's the plan?"

"Come morning," O'Shea answered, "we're going to use the GPR—the ground penetrating radar machine that X-rays what's beneath the surface," he explained for Malloy's benefit, "so if there are any more bones buried somewhere on the property, we'll know where to dig."

Malloy looked at the two men, surprised. He knew from conversations around Andrew's table that department funds were tight. "When did CSI get that?"

"It took a bit of juggling," Sean Cavanaugh said, answering his nephew's question as he walked into the morgue's exam room, "but I managed to appropriate the funds for it six months ago." He nodded at Kristin as he continued talking to Malloy. "The last annual fund-raiser we had, after the department finished funding its usual widows and orphans charities, the rest of the money was allotted for new materials for the crime scene investigation lab." He looked rather pleased as he added, "I thought this was a good way to utilize the money. This way, manpower isn't needlessly wasted.

"Once the boys sweep the property," he concluded, this time addressing his words to Kristin as O'Shea and Reynolds left the morgue, "we'll know if there are any more bodies to put together and identify." He looked at the different tables. "You've been busy." There was admiration in his voice. "How are you doing?" Sean asked her.

She smiled ruefully at the table she was next to. It contained the body she was presently trying to reconstruct. "Not exactly like the jigsaw puzzles I used to love putting together as a kid, but I think it's coming along."

It was obvious that Sean was pleased with the progress her efforts were making.

"If anyone can do this," he told her, "you can." He glanced at his watch. "Well, I've got to get back to the lab. Call me if you need anything," he told her, then added, "Good job," just before withdrawing.

Kristin turned back to her work and saw that, unlike the others who had come in, Malloy was still in the room. "Wouldn't that be your cue to leave, too?" she asked. By her count, he'd started to leave at least three times. Why was he still here?

Something she'd said to his uncle had caught his attention, and he wanted to ask her about it. "You worked jigsaw puzzles as a kid, too?"

Too.

The word was a warning. She gazed at him warily, wondering where he was heading with this. Was he going to turn this around somehow and use this to his advantage?

Instead of answering his question—a question she knew that he obviously had the answer to—she stated defensively, "That doesn't bond us."

"No," he agreed. "But it does give us something in common." He moved closer to her, not to crowd her but to get a better view of the various bones that were spread out on the exam table in front of her. "Want any help?"

Kristin scrutinized him, trying to determine if he was being serious. "You're joking."

He raised his eyes to hers. "Not at the moment."

Rather than tell him outright what she thought of his offer, she pointed out the obvious. "You don't have a medical degree."

His shrug was dismissive. "I have an excellent working knowledge of anatomy, and from what I've read, you actually don't need a medical degree to do this kind of work. It's preferred, of course, but smaller towns make do with laypeople as long as they're familiar with that old song."

"Song?" she questioned. "What old song?" What the hell was this self-centered, conceited man going on about?

"You know the one," he told her, trying to coax the title out of her.

She had no time for games. "No, I don't," she told him sharply. "If I did, I wouldn't be wasting my breath, asking you, now would I?"

Rather than tell her the name of the song, he took her totally by surprise and began to sing it. "The leg bone's connected to the knee bone, the knee bone's connected to the thigh bone…"

Was he crazy? If he wasn't, he was a completely loose canon. Either way, she wanted him out of her morgue. He was just too utterly distracting.

"Stop," Kristin cried, holding up her hand to reinforce her point.

Abruptly ending the song, he looked at her with complete innocence. "Something wrong?"

"You're actually going to sing that to me?" she asked incredulously.

"Sounds better than just saying it," he told her. "And anyway, it was written as a song, so I just thought I'd get the point across better if I sang it to you. I was told I have a decent singing voice," he added as if that might make her reconsider letting him finish the tune.

"Then go sing to whoever told you that." She closed

her eyes, trying to pull herself together. "You're giving me a headache, Cavanaugh, and I need peace and quiet to concentrate."

"What part of 'peace and quiet' does that country and western song fit into?" he asked, indicating the music that was being piped in. "The peace, or the quiet?" His expression was the face of innocence—annoyingly so.

She blew out a breath and, with it, just possibly the last of her patience. "I just like listening to it. It reminds me of my dad—and why am I bothering to explain myself to you, anyway?" Kristin demanded, stunned as she realized what she was doing.

"Because that's how people get to know each other," Malloy said simply.

This was getting really out of hand now, and good-looking or not, this arrogant SOB was wasting far too much of her time.

"We're not supposed to get to know each other, Cavanaugh. We're just supposed to work together on this case—for now," she emphasized.

"Friends work together better than strangers," Malloy told her.

That did it. Kristin glared at him, biting back choice phrases. *Keep it professional, Kris. Keep it professional*, she told herself.

"I have enough friends." The statement was delivered through gritted teeth.

"I don't," Malloy countered, then added, "You can never get enough of a good thing, don't you agree?"

"Ordinarily, yes," she replied icily. "But not in your case."

Rather than take the cue she was so blatantly giving

him, Malloy grinned, humor sparkling in his eyes. "I'm wearing you down, aren't I?"

"What you're doing," she retorted, "is wearing me out."

His grin just grew broader. "Same difference in the long run," he assured her. Then, before she could resort to anything drastic, he left the room, promising, "I'll get back to you."

He heard her release a guttural sound that amounted to a stifled shriek of frustration.

Yup, Malloy thought as he closed the door, he was definitely getting to her.

Chapter 5

She lost track of time.

After a point, Kristin began to feel as if she had always been doing this, trying to ascertain which bone went where and if the right number of bones were on any given table.

In essence, what she was attempting to figure out was if more bones had been dug up than were needed to comprise twelve bodies—because, in that case, it would mean that there had to be *more* than twelve bodies buried on the property, even if only twelve heads were found.

Twelve bodies, all murdered, was a difficult enough number to come to terms with. The idea of there being even more victims brought a more pronounced chill to her soul.

The morgue's part-time assistants who had been rendering some aid had all gone home for the night, leaving her to work alone.

Thinking he might still find her in the morgue, obstinately working despite the fact that he had told her to leave more than an hour ago, Sean looked in on Kristin just before he left for the night himself.

"You're still at it," he observed as he peered into the room.

"Just a couple of minutes longer," Kristin replied, removing one shin bone and putting another one, this one measuring a more appropriate length, in its place.

"The bones aren't going anywhere, Kristin," Sean quietly pointed out. "They'll still be here in the morning. And reconstructing all these poor victims one day sooner is not going to change the ultimate outcome of what happened to them. Go home, Kristin," he told her a tad more sternly.

"I will," she responded in all sincerity. "I just need five more minutes and then I'm gone. Honest."

Sean shook his head. "Uh-huh." He'd heard that before, including similar words from his own lips more often than he'd like to recall. He understood now his wife's frustration when he'd put her off with them. "Well, I've got a wife at home who gets out of sorts if I'm late for dinner without an active citywide crime wave as an excuse." He paused just before leaving, adding significantly, "It's important to have a life apart from here, Kristin."

Sensing he was waiting for her to acknowledge his words, Kristin looked up, her eyes meeting his. "I know that, sir."

"I hope you do," he told her earnestly. "Good night, Kristin."

"Good night, sir." Kristin picked up an instrument that looked like oversize tweezers. "See you in the morning."

"Hopefully, not in the same outfit," he told her.

Kristin glanced up again and grinned. "I've got a change of clothing in my locker."

Sean sighed, temporarily surrendering. "I had a feeling," he said as he walked out.

He knew it served no purpose to order her home; she was a tenacious young woman who listened politely and then quietly did exactly what she wanted to, making up her own rules. In a way, he admitted to himself, she reminded him of his daughters, all as stubborn as the day was long.

Kristin had meant what she'd said to the head of the CSI lab. She really did have every intention of going home in the next few minutes.

But matching up "one more bone" led to doing "just one more," and then one more after that.

Time continued to dribble away.

The next thing she was aware of, Kristin heard the door to the morgue being opened again. Sean Cavanaugh had returned to make sure she'd kept her word, she thought, chagrined.

"I'm really going to go home right after I make sure that this one last tibia belongs to the body I'm working on, honest," she promised, then confessed almost sheepishly, "It's just that joining these parts together is almost addictive."

"Puzzles can do that to you."

Kristin's eyes widened as her mouth dropped open. That was *not* the voice of the man who had told her to go home earlier.

She swung around.

Surprise turned to annoyance as she looked at the man who had walked in. "I thought you left."

"Apparently, whoever you were just talking to thought the same about you—I filled in the blanks in your conversation," he explained, taking the liberty of reading between the lines and answering the quizzical expression on her face.

"Never mind who you *thought* I was talking to," she retorted. "What are you doing here? Did you lose your way?"

There was no missing the sarcasm, but Malloy responded as if she'd asked a legitimate question.

"Not since I was a kid and my father had the entire family scouring the whole forest, looking for me," he said matter-of-factly. It was an event that had taken him years to live down. "After you mentioned your thing for jigsaw puzzles, I had a feeling you might get too caught up in all this—" he nodded at the table in front of her "—and forget to eat."

"What does that have to do with anything?" Kristin asked testily.

She didn't like being second-guessed or anticipated, at least not by a hotshot who felt that all he had to do to get any woman into his bed was to crook his finger at her. She'd heard the stories, and Malloy Cavanaugh had two strikes against him before they'd ever exchanged a single word.

"Well," he began in an easygoing manner, "I'm trying to tell you that's why I came back with your dinner."

She scowled at him. "I don't have a dinner."

"You do now," he told her, producing a bag from the local sandwich shop and placing it on the only empty corner of the exam table. "I didn't know if you liked your hero sandwiches hot or cold, so I took a chance and had them heat it. If you'd rather have it cold, let it stand for a while. Just don't forget to eat it," he added as a reminder.

She felt herself getting defensive. Where did he get off lecturing her? Or acting like her mother, for that matter? She got enough of that every time she visited home.

"I didn't ask you to bring me back any food," she informed him as if she was disavowing any responsibility for his so-called act of kindness.

"I know."

The simple response effectively took the wind out of her sails and succeeded in making her feel like a bad-tempered ogre.

"Thanks," she muttered grudgingly. "What do I owe you?" Kristin walked over toward the small desk that butted up against the back wall to get her purse.

Following behind her, Malloy shrugged indifferently. "A lead when you come across one."

He knew perfectly well what she was talking about, Kristin thought irritably. "I meant what do I owe you for the sandwich."

Malloy's smile slipped through all the layers she had wrapped around her to keep her safe from people like him. "So did I."

She took out her purse from the drawer, then pulled out her wallet.

"I like paying my own way," she insisted. "Now, what do I owe you? Seriously," she emphasized, her tone indicating that she wasn't going to stand for any more of his snappy patter.

"Okay," Malloy replied gamely. "How does your firstborn sound?"

She stared at him. "What?"

"It's a large sandwich," Malloy deadpanned. "And I had the kid behind the counter throw in two giant chocolate chip cookies."

"How did you know?" she asked. When he made no answer other than to raise an eyebrow, she said, "About chocolate chip cookies being my favorite?"

"Lucky guess," he admitted, "Besides, who doesn't like chocolate chip cookies?"

"My mother," she answered before she could think to stop herself. "She thinks chocolate chip cookies are a cop-out. She's into much more complicated baking," she explained, even though she just wanted to distance herself from the topic—and mainly, from talking to him, period. Malloy was definitely messing with her ability to think.

"Sounds like an interesting woman," he commented. "I'd love to meet her."

Yeah, and she'd probably love to meet you, Kristin couldn't help thinking. If she knew her mother, all the woman needed would be one meeting with the handsome detective and she'd be ordering wedding invitations and reserving a church.

"Why did you do this, really?" Kristin asked him, unwrapping the foot-long sandwich laden with three kinds of meats and two kinds of cheeses—melted together. Since it was heated, the aroma seemed to ambush her, tantalizing her saliva glands. "I mean, I haven't exactly been friendly to you."

His shrug was careless—and absolving. "I figured it was because you were hungry."

"And?" she asked, waiting.

"And I drugged the sandwich," he answered matter-of-factly. He glanced at his watch. "In exactly thirty-three minutes, you'll be unconscious, in my lair and I'll be having my way with you. Or, you'll have your way with me, whichever way you'll want to play this," he added with a disarming wink.

Kristin silently regarded the sandwich, now un-wrapped, on her desk. "I guess I had that coming to me," she admitted almost reluctantly.

Malloy offered her a pseudoinnocent smile. "Mine is not to judge. By the way, don't forget to go home," he told her as he began to head for the door.

"Cavanaugh," she called after him. When he turned around, she asked, "which is the real you, the hotshot or the nice guy?"

"Yes," he answered with the same seemingly inno-cent smile.

And then he left.

Malloy consumed a twin to the foot-long sandwich he'd picked up for Kristin on his way home, finishing it just as he pulled up into the driveway.

After parking his car and letting himself into the townhouse, Malloy began stripping off his clothes as he made his way to his bedroom. He kicked off his shoes, fell facedown on his bed and was asleep within ninety seconds of contact.

Possibly less.

He remained that way until six thirty the following morning when a pronounced ache in his neck penetrated his dreams and woke him up. He'd spent the entire night on his stomach, never a good idea, he silently lectured. He felt like one end of a parenthesis.

Wincing, he stumbled into the bathroom, took off the last of the clothes that had remained on his body and showered. The ache in his neck kept him under the hot water an extra three minutes.

Mindful of the long-running drought that was very much still a part of California's long-term forecast, guilt finally had him turning off the hot water and reluctantly getting out.

This wasn't the weekend, he reminded himself. He didn't have time to indulge himself.

Approximately nine minutes later, Malloy was in his kitchen, eating what was left of a four-day-old pizza that was practically the last thing still sitting in his almost empty refrigerator.

He was going to have to remember to stock up on new leftovers, he told himself.

Eventually.

The thought was gone by the time he'd locked his front door a few minutes later.

Getting in early, Malloy fired up his computer and spent the next two hours going through twenty- to thirty-year-old missing persons flyers.

The number he found was nothing short of daunting. If he was strictly going by the database, it seemed as if at one time or another, close to half the population under the age of fifty had gone missing. Because of the information he'd managed to get out of the closed-mouth medical examiner, for now he ignored the one male victim who had been found on the property and restricted his search to women, but even that number turned out to be overwhelming.

He sat back at one point and just shook his head. In this day and age with all the various methods of social communication that were open to his generation and the one that was even younger, Malloy couldn't help wondering how anyone managed to fall off the grid this way and stay off of it.

Even those who had gone missing twenty years ago should have turned up by now—provided, of course, they weren't dead, he reminded himself. Which was what this was all about.

It took him all that time just to compile a secondary file of missing women from within the area who would have been between the ages of eighteen to thirty at the time, which, according to Kristin, was the approximate ages of the bodies. He'd decided to widen both ends of the spectrum.

Even that number felt incredibly overwhelming. Not because he would have to go through them one by one and make decisions, but because there were so very many people who had never been found, alive or dead.

How did families live with that sort of uncertainty, day in, day out? he marveled.

Malloy thought of his own family. Every last one of them would have moved heaven and earth to find a missing relative whether or not they had the resources of the police department to aid them.

Which, fortunately in their case, they did.

But what if they didn't?

Malloy shook his head. He had to block unproductive thoughts like that. If he dwelled on that aspect to any extent, he might not be able to get any further in his investigation than he'd already gotten—which was not very far at all.

He wondered if Kristin had progressed with her work. If connecting hip bones to the right pelvic bones had in any way moved the process of possible identification along, or if all those dismembered young women they'd found were going to be designated as "Jane Does."

The idea haunted him.

Normally, working cold cases involved finding out how—and why—a specific person had been killed. He'd never had a corpse remain unidentified before, much less an army of them.

Malloy reached for the phone on his desk a couple of times, wanting to call Kristin to ask her if she'd found anything on her end. But after several false starts, he never picked up the receiver.

Although patience wasn't his strong suit, he decided that perhaps the good doctor deserved a breather, at least from him. Maybe she actually did work more efficiently when she was alone, just as she had maintained.

He could only hope that once she did come up with something—and she looked far too intense not to—she'd give him a call if only because she was the type to "pay her own way" as she'd maintained, and after all, the sandwich had been a form of a bribe.

To his frustration, the phone on his desk remained silent.

But just as he got up to get himself a third cup of really bad coffee, a catchy pop tune from the last decade faintly filled the air. The phone in his pocket was making its presence known.

"Cavanaugh," he announced after he'd swiped the screen, sending it into its receptive mode.

"Is this the annoying Cavanaugh who's handling cold cases?" he heard a melodic female voice ask.

Malloy smiled broadly to himself. "Ah, Doc, you kept my card."

"I forgot to throw it away," she countered, deliberately deflecting any hidden meaning the act of retaining his card might have for him.

"So you decided to call the number on it?" he guessed. "Did you call to hear the sound of my voice, or do you have something to tell me?" he asked, allowing just a shade of hope to filter through his words.

"Oh, I have a lot to tell you," Kristin answered. "But if you're specifically asking me about all these body parts that are currently surrounding and haunting me, yes, I called about them."

"I'll be right there," he promised.

"I can tell you what I have to say over the phone," she said, trying to save him a trip—and herself from having to deal with him face-to-face. His presence was difficult to factor into the sum total of her day and still remain entirely unaffected—no matter what she attempted to pretend to the contrary.

"Yes, but I can't see you over this phone," he pointed out.

"It's not necessary to see me in order to get this information," she told him almost defensively, really hoping she didn't sound that way.

"Maybe it's not necessary to you," he allowed, "but it is to me. I'm a very visual man," he explained. "I need to see things before I can retain them."

"You're not serious."

She supposed there could be a grain of truth to what he was telling her. Kristin had to admit he'd gotten her to the point where she was beginning to doubt the most normally acceptable concepts.

"Frequently," he told her. "And twice on Sundays. Hang on, I'll be over before you have a chance to regret calling me."

"Unless you've found a way to travel back into time, Detective, I'm afraid it's too late for that," Kristin responded.

Malloy could have sworn, as he terminated his call, that he had heard a smile in her voice as she said the last line.

That was enough for him to actually envision one in his mind's eye. It was also enough to spur him on and have him make his way down to the morgue in a record amount of time.

The fact that he used the stairs rather than wait for an elevator didn't hurt, either.

Chapter 6

"What did you do, run all the way?" Kristin asked, surprised to see Malloy turn up so quickly when he walked through the morgue's door less than five minutes after she'd spoken to him.

He'd had his own reasons for hurrying, but he refrained from saying so. Instead, he told her, "A magician never divulges his secrets."

"A magician? You've quit the force?" Kristin deadpanned.

Malloy laughed. "Ah, so you *do* have a sense of humor," he commented appreciatively. "Even if I were tempted to make that happen, I couldn't." When she seemed confused, he explained, "Quit the force. I'd have everyone in the family hunting me down. Like it or not, this is the family business and it's become a tradition handed down through three generations."

"You obviously must like it," she observed. He didn't strike her as the type to do anything he didn't want to do, family tradition or no family tradition.

"What makes you say that?" he asked, curious.

She set aside the camera she'd been using to photograph the end results of one of the bodies she'd reassembled on the table to the left.

Kristin wasn't about to flatter him and inflate Malloy's ego, so she kept her assessment down to the bare minimum.

"Otherwise, you wouldn't have said 'even if I were tempted,' which means you're not tempted. You're on the force by choice."

"Busted," he answered with a grin. The woman made a fair detective herself, he thought in admiration. "How about you?"

She'd lowered her visor, not wanting to waste anytime. "How about me what?"

"Why are you doing autopsies—or whatever this practical phase of it is called—" he waved a hand at the tables of bones that were throughout the room "—instead of working in a hospital or a doctor's office?"

She hadn't even told her mother about the little boy who had died on her watch, or how she'd felt as if her insides were gutted because he had done so despite her best efforts to save him. What she said was, "Because the dead don't talk back." And then her voice became cooler as she said, "I'm sorry, but when did this suddenly turn into a therapy session?"

Malloy pretended to be taken aback by her question. "I'm sorry, I thought we were sharing."

"We are—we're sharing information," she said pointedly. And then she realized that her response still left it wide open. "*Work* information," she emphasized, then added, "Unless you're not interested in ID'ing one of the bodies."

Excitement entered both his voice as well as the expression on his face. Everything else was pushed into the background. "You actually managed to identify one of the victims?" he asked.

She couldn't help thinking that he sounded like a kid at Christmas. Kristin was beginning to think that Malloy Cavanaugh was far more complicated than the image he liked to project—or the reputation that had preceded him.

"No," she answered honestly, "but I found a way for you to do it."

He'd really thought that this was going to take *weeks* of chasing after imaginary leads that eventually led nowhere. The prospect that it might be otherwise filled him with hope.

"I'm listening."

"One of the women had a hip replacement—"

He immediately jumped on the morsel she'd held out. "Those things are numbered, aren't they?" he asked, anticipation echoing in his voice.

She nodded. "The prosthetic has an ID number. If we can track that down, we have the name of one of our victims."

"Wait," he said as his thoughts were coming together. "Did you say a hip prosthetic?"

"I realize you probably would rather work with a breast implant," she said dryly, "but—"

"That's not it," he told her, waving the suggestion down and for once not making a wise crack about said body part. "But I thought you said that the victims were all between the ages of eighteen to thirty."

"That's what it looks like," Kristin confirmed. "What's the problem?" she asked.

"Well, wouldn't she have to be older to warrant a hip replacement?" he asked. Senior citizens got hip replacements, not girls right out of high school or college.

"No." Kristin shot down his assumption. "There are a lot of reasons for a young woman to get a hip replacement." To convince him, Kristin ticked off only a few of the ways the need might have come up. "She could have been in a car accident, or just been unlucky enough to fall and break her hip. There's also juvenile arthritis. Then there are some dancers who have the grave misfortune of wearing out certain joints and body parts way before their time—want me to go on?"

Yes, he did, but not about hip replacements. He would have preferred a far more intimate subject to be up for discussion.

"No, you've convinced me," he told her. "Did you happen to write down the number of that prosthetic?"

"No, I thought that I'd transmit it to you by mental telepathy," she answered dryly, reaching for a piece of paper she'd placed on the next table. "Here."

He glanced at the numbers she'd written down as she handed the lined paper to him.

"Too bad. I was looking forward to our minds melding." When she said nothing, he felt the need to explain the comment. "That's a term out of—"

"*Star Trek*, yes," Kristin said, cutting him off before he went on needlessly. "I know."

Her response stunned him, and he looked at her with renewed respect. "You're familiar with *Star Trek*?" Before she could answer him, Malloy laughed, obviously tickled by this newest piece of information he'd learned about her. "First, jigsaw puzzles, now, *Star Trek*. It's like we were separated at birth."

Photographing another segment of the body she was beginning to reconstruct, she shook her head, doing her best to maintain an emotional distance between them— which was becoming harder to do.

"A lot of people like jigsaw puzzles and are familiar with *Star Trek*, Detective," she replied. "Don't get carried away."

Despite her best efforts to block it, there was something boyishly appealing about the expression on his face as he told her, "I've brought you food after hours. Call me Malloy. And, trust me," he added with a wink, "you'll know when I get carried away."

That grin of his was going to be her downfall if she wasn't careful, Kristin silently warned herself. She forced herself to talk facts, keeping a tight rein on her thoughts.

"Those numbers are all cataloged in a database, along with the physician's name and the patient's name," she told him crisply.

She wanted to get him moving and on his way out of the morgue. The space in the area was definitely growing smaller somehow.

"You may just have found our first genuine break in this case, Doc," Malloy declared with enthusiasm.

"You're welcome," Kristin murmured as she lowered her eyes back to the partially reconstructed skeleton on the table before her.

Which was why she failed to be prepared for what

came next. By the time she realized what was happening, it was too late.

Caught up in the moment, Malloy bracketed her shoulders between his hands and delivered a very enthusiastic and yet innocent kiss to her cheek.

The next second, he had released her and quickly crossed the floor, getting halfway to the door.

"I'll get back to you," he promised half a second before he was gone.

Kristin stared at the open door, stunned. Half of her was hoping that he would live up to his promise—and half of her really hoped that he wouldn't.

And both sides were for her best interests.

"I'm not any good at this," Malloy confessed in what came across as his attempt at refreshing honesty.

He was standing in the computer lab, pleading his case in person to his youngest sister. Detective Valri Cavanaugh split her time between the division where she usually worked and crime scene investigations' computer lab.

Usually she filled in if they were shorthanded. But along with this access she'd gained to the police department's intranet, she'd also acquired miscellaneous requests from her siblings whenever they needed to avail themselves to her expertise and her considerable computer wizardry.

"I'm fine with the everyday, routine stuff and plodding through things that I can find in the department's regular database," Malloy went on to tell her, laying out his case, "but this special stuff, hell, I don't even know where to begin. Help me out here, Val," he asked, putting on his most contrite face. "I just can't work magic with computers."

The inference was that she could. But Valri saw through her brother's flowing rhetoric and his golden tongue.

"No, that's a talent you work with women. I'm not one of those women," she pointed out. "I'm your sister, which makes me immune to all the golden words that come out of your mouth."

"Val, I have no idea how you come up with these fanciful thoughts," he said, pretending to be grievously hurt. "I just need my little sister's help."

Valri laughed, turning away from the computer monitor to look at him. "You're slipping, Malloy. You need to do a little brushing up on your acting."

"I'll brush up on anything you want if you just help me out here," he told her. Then, his expression lighting up, he added, "I brought food," before she had a chance to put him off. To prove his point, he shook the bag he held in front of her so that its contents made a noise. "Hear that? It's calling to you."

"Donuts do not call. They make noise hitting the sides of a paper bag as their glaze flakes off, but they definitely do not call."

Opening the bag, Malloy looked inside it as if he was checking out the contents. "I'd say those crumbs have your name on them."

"And I say you're pushing it. You know, between you and Kelly and Moira, not to mention Duncan, it's a wonder I ever get anything done for the department at all."

He pretended to lower his voice so he could whisper in her ear. "Don't look now, baby sister, but Kelly,

Moira, Duncan and I *are* part of the department, so technically, your complaint doesn't hold any water."

She raised her eyes to his. "You want me to find that database or not?"

"Your complaint holds lots of water," he told her with feeling, backtracking quickly.

"Better," she approved, nodding her head. Looking at the numbers that he had handed her from the medical examiner, she paused, thinking. "Give me a minute— this was for a hip prosthetic, right?" she asked, double-checking that he'd given her the correct information so that she logged on to the right database.

"Right," he answered. With that, he turned his back to her and stared at the opposite wall.

The redhead at the next desk saw him and smiled right at Malloy. But for once, Malloy's attention was not captured. It was focused on getting the information he needed from Valri.

Looking at his back, Valri asked, "What are you doing?"

"Letting you work," he said, still looking at the opposite wall. "The medical examiner told me that a watched pot never boils."

"Since when did you start thinking of me as a pot?" Valri asked.

The sound of her fingers flying across her keyboard, making the keys click, brought a satisfied smile to Malloy's lips.

"I don't," he assured her. "I'm just trying my best to be accommodating and unobtrusive."

"Well, stop it," she told him sharply. "You're frightening me. The Malloy I grew up with was not accommodating *or* unobtrusive."

"Sure I was," he insisted good-naturedly. "You're probably confusing me with one of the other brothers you have. You know, the ones who were always dragging their knuckles on the ground and playing pranks on you."

He heard her announce, "Done," with a flourish as the sound of the portable printer beside her computer coming to life underscored the word.

"You remembered which brother you confused me with?" Malloy asked innocently as he turned back around to face her.

Valri held out the information she had printed for him. "No, I was referring to having found the number you were looking for in the database. And I didn't confuse you with anyone. That was definitely you. You, Malloy, have always been one of a kind."

"I'll take that as a compliment," Malloy told his sister, accepting the paper from her.

"No comment," Valri replied prudently, her expression giving nothing away.

Malloy glanced down at the page. He had a name and information, which in turn might lead to more identifications.

"You're the best, Val—and if that fiancé of yours doesn't treat you like the queen that you clearly are, tell him he'll have me to answer to. He makes you so much as frown, I'll beat him to a pulp," he promised.

It was no secret that she was all but walking on air these days. "Alex makes me very happy and you know it."

"Well, just in case," Malloy told her, doing his best to maintain a dead serious expression. "You know where to come."

"Uh-huh." She was already back to the search she had been conducting when Malloy had walked in with his request.

"And thanks for this!" he called out, raising the sheet she'd handed him in the air on his way out.

"Just go!" Valri ordered her brother. "I have work to do."

"Like I said, you're the best!" Malloy told her just before he crossed the threshold.

"Glad you finally figured that out," Valri answered, talking half to herself under her breath. "Certainly took you long enough."

He lost no time getting back to Kristin with the victim's name.

"Doesn't your phone work at all?" she asked him when he came bursting into the morgue. She silently upbraided herself for not being more annoyed to see him invading her space again.

The problem was, she wasn't really annoyed at all— and that sincerely worried her.

"Sure," he told her, crossing over to her. "You called me on it earlier, remember?"

Her eyes narrowed. "That was a rhetorical question, Detective."

"Malloy," he prompted. "We agreed that you'd call me Malloy, remember?"

She needed to hold on to her bearings at all times, because the man had the ability to completely bury her in rhetoric. "Technically, *you* agreed. I didn't agree to anything."

He flashed her that same smile she was positive had

undone many a woman and was steadily getting to her, as well.

"I figured you were just being shy, Doc." And then he got back to the reason he'd hurried back so quickly. "This is the kind of thing I figured you'd want to hear in person. We've got a name," he told her, taking the paper Valri had given him and holding it out to Kristin. "A name to go with that prosthetic you discovered."

She surprised him by not immediately reaching for it. Instead, she said quietly, "The first person to transition from 'Jane Doe' to an actual person."

He caught the note of sadness in Kristin's voice. So, she wasn't as removed from all this as she was trying to appear.

"Makes it more real somehow, doesn't it?"

"You do surprise me, Detective—Malloy," Kristin corrected herself. She felt that since he had brought this back to share with her rather than just running off and claiming the breakthrough as his own, she owed him that much.

"How's that?"

"You're insightful as well as sensitive." She was getting carried away. Kristin admonished herself and walked her comment back a little. "Both very good traits for a Boy Scout."

Malloy laughed and shrugged. "I wouldn't know."

"Didn't make the grade?" she guessed. He must have been one hell of a handful as a boy. Tom Sawyer on steroids. No scout master in his right mind would have taken him on.

"Didn't bother to apply," he told her simply. "So, do you want to know her name," he asked, once again offering her the printed paper, "or just go on thinking of her as Jane Doe number seven?"

He was right. Knowing the woman's name took the victim out of the realm of the anonymous and brought her into the real world. Once she had a name, there was a very good possibility that the broken-up skeleton on her table became someone's daughter, someone's wife, sister, lover, mother, a person who had once had a life that had been cut terribly short by some maniacal monster who fancied himself a god with the power of life and death over some unfortunate victim.

It was a lot to take in. But it had to be done.

"Her name, please," Kristin requested.

He glanced down on the paper in his hand. "The hip belonged to an Abby Sullivan, and you were right. She was seventeen when she had the operation. The last known address her doctor had for her, according to this, was in San Francisco." He planned to verify that himself right after he left the morgue.

"San Francisco," Kristin echoed. "That's a bit of a ways from here."

"She might have just been living there at the time and moved on after she was back on her feet." His words echoed back to him. "Forgive the pun."

Kristin gave him a knowing look. "The pun is probably the least you have to be forgiven for."

He placed his hand over his heart. "You wound me, Doc."

Her smile was quick and fleeting. "I try my best," she commented. "Now what?"

He regarded the sheet of paper that she had handed back to him. "Now I see if I can track down Abby's family and explain to them why she hasn't been home for dinner for the last two decades or so."

"After you track their address down..." she began just as he started to leave.

Malloy stopped and looked at her, waiting for the rest of her sentence. "Yes?"

"Let me know," Kristin told him. "I want to go with you."

Chapter 7

Malloy eyed her uncertainly. He was too young for his hearing to be going. Kristin couldn't have said what he thought she had.

"I'm sorry," he apologized. "I don't think I heard you correctly. You didn't just say—"

"Yes, I did," she told him. "I want to go with you when you notify the family that Abby Sullivan's body was found."

That didn't make any sense to him. Why would she actually *want* to be there? *He* didn't want to be there, but it was part of his job to deliver the notification once the victim was identified. To a person, this was deemed to be everyone's least favorite part of being a detective on the police force.

"Don't you have enough work to do?" he asked after a moment had gone by and he was able to subdue his surprise over her request.

Kristin sighed as she looked back at the tables littered with bones. "Oh, more than enough."

Malloy was still waiting for this to make some sort of sense to him. "Then why...?"

He saw the medical examiner raise her chin at the same time that she clenched her jaw. She looked as if she was bracing herself for an argument. He didn't want to argue with her, he just wanted to understand her reasons.

"Because," she answered, "something like this, notifying a family about the death of a loved one, needs to be conveyed by someone with a sympathetic heart."

"And I don't have a sympathetic heart?" Malloy questioned, then said in all seriousness, "No offense, Doc, but you really have no idea what my 'heart' is like."

"Okay," Kristin relented, backtracking. "Maybe I used the wrong word. Something like this needs to be conveyed by someone with an *empathetic* heart," she corrected. "In other words, someone who's been through it, been on the receiving end of possibly the worst news they have ever heard and most likely the worst news they will *ever* hear in their lives.

"There is no 'right' way to do it," she allowed. "But there are so many wrong ways to break that kind of news, it's frightening. And, if it is done wrong, it can wind up scarring someone, if not forever, then for a very long, long time."

He regarded her thoughtfully, reading between the lines. "This isn't just an abstract theory that you're spinning, is it?"

Her demeanor became impatient. "Do I have to give you a lengthy explanation for everything that comes out of my mouth?"

"Not lengthy, but a few succinct words that drive the point home wouldn't be unwelcomed." He didn't think what he was saying was unreasonable. "Work with me here, Doc. I'm not a bad guy. I'm on your side, but I can't just take you on as a sidekick for this house call for no good reason. I do have people I have to answer to."

Her expression was nothing short of skeptical. "I really doubt you answer to anyone if you don't want to." He kept watching her, obviously waiting for something more. Kristin blew out an impatient breath. "Okay, you want a reason? I'll give you a reason. The person who notified my mother and me that my father wasn't going to be coming home to us anymore, that he had died on the job, did it so matter-of-factly, so *badly* that it took my mother an entire year to crawl out of the depression she had sunk into.

"There were times that I thought she was never coming back to me and that I had lost not one parent but two that day, one to the ravages of a fire and one to the aftermath of that fire."

As she spoke, it was hard for Kristin not to relive the absolute horror of that day. The only thing that had kept her from folding up herself was that she knew her mother needed her. Granted, there were her aunts, her uncle and, of course, her grandmother, who was stronger than the lot of them put together, but Kristin had felt, at least back then, that she and her mother had a special connection and that it was up to her to bring her mother around.

"A fire," Malloy repeated. "Then your father was a—"

She filled in the word for him. "A firefighter, yes. It was that summer that felt as if the whole state was on fire. His company was called in to help battle a fire that some pyromaniac started in the Los Angeles Forest. Three of my dad's friends got trapped while fighting the worst of that blaze, and my dad, being my dad," she said with a touch of unconscious pride, "tried to save them. He died trying."

She paused for a second and took a deep breath. Malloy made no effort to hurry her. He knew how hard this had to be to talk about.

"The man who came to notify us said, 'Alan's dead,' the second my mother opened the door. No words of preface, no words to try to soften the blow in at least some way, just bam! 'He's dead.' And then, because he hated being the messenger, he left." Kristin's eyes met his, and there was a fierceness in them as she made her point. "I don't ever want anyone to go through what my mother did."

"How about you?" Malloy asked. "Didn't you have to grapple with the same abruptly delivered news? How old were you?"

Kristin realized she'd opened up far more than she'd wanted to. "I think I've explained enough to earn the right to come along."

Malloy nodded. "I'll let you know as soon as I find out."

Because she had no choice, Kristin had to assume that he was a man of his word, so for now, she accepted what he told her.

"I appreciate that," she answered.

Kristin sounded rather stiff, but he knew it was because she was trying her best to retreat from what she had just told him. He could tell that it hadn't been easy for her to share something like that. He was rather open and easygoing himself, and he knew a couple of people who couldn't keep a secret even if they got to carry it around in a box.

But the thing about coming from an extended family as large as his, there was always someone in the family whose personality was a perfect match for someone he had encountered. And there were more than a few in the Cavanaugh family who not only kept their own counsel, but had to be all but dynamited out of their shell to render any sort of extraneous information.

The thought of getting the gorgeous medical examiner out of *her* shell presented itself to him. He found the idea rather appealing.

Dynamite didn't always have to be used to get the job done, he mused.

The following morning, Malloy was waiting for her in the exam room.

He had spent the rest of the previous day checking out his various sources. That eventually led to his finding an address for their only identified victim's family. By then he'd been pretty much wiped out. He didn't think that the medical examiner would have been thrilled to be woken out of a dead sleep no matter what news he was bearing.

So he'd decided to bring it to her in person, first thing in the morning.

Except that she wasn't here first thing in the morning. Given her dedication and single-mindedness, he found that rather surprising.

He decided to wait.

Kristin was running late—and she hated that.

After all but baring her soul to the intrusive, not to

mention pushy detective, when she'd closed up shop she'd given in to a sudden urge to spend a little quality time with her mother. Her mother had quizzed her to make sure nothing was wrong. Satisfied that there was nothing dire on the horizon, Josephine Alberghetti had gone into overdrive.

One thing had led to another, and Kristin had given in, spending the night. That, in turn, had led to her being behind schedule.

Which was why Kristin came rushing in five minutes late and trying to juggle holding on to a huge container of coffee from the local coffee shop with one hand as she opened the door to the morgue's exam room with the other.

"So you don't sleep here."

Stifling a shriek, Kristin swung around toward the source of the voice. When their eyes met, there were daggers coming out of hers.

This was getting to be a habit. One she really didn't appreciate in the slightest. She hated being caught off guard, especially by him.

"Is it your mission in life to sneak up on me until you succeed in giving me a heart attack?" she asked Malloy accusingly.

"Actually, my mission is more along the lines of granting your request," he told her, each word slipping out slowly and almost seductively from his lips. Not to mention that his eyes seemed to be saying things to her that should have been censored.

Or maybe she was just reading things into it, Kristin told herself in self-defense. Maybe he was just talking to hear himself talk. The fact that his voice could create goose bumps was her problem, not his.

"I don't have a request," she informed him coldly. "And you almost made me spill my coffee."

"I would have paid for it if you had," he assured her. "I'm good for it." A sparkle entered his eyes. "I'm good for a lot of things," he couldn't resist adding.

It was fun to tease her because he knew what she thought of him, and although he had enjoyed a very happy love life over the years, a large part of it—and his appeal—was discretion.

"I can't think of a thing that would interest me," she informed him crisply. Okay, enough was enough. "Is there a point to all this?" she asked. "Or have you decided to become my personal albatross?"

"You said you wanted to come with me," he said simply, after taking a leisurely sip from his coffee container.

"No, I—" Her automatic denial dried up instantly as the puzzle pieces suddenly sprang together. "You found Abby's family," she guessed. That had been fast, she couldn't help thinking. Maybe the man actually *was* good at his job.

"What's left of it, yes," he told her, getting up and following her to her desk. "I was going to head out first thing this morning to give her father the news and ask some questions, but I did give you my word that I'd let you know. So this is me, letting you know."

She didn't want to just know that he was going to see the woman's family. The deal was that she would accompany him when he broke the news to Abby Sullivan's family. She doubted if he'd forgotten that.

But in case he did, she had no problem reminding him. "The deal was that I'd come with you."

"You actually still want to?" he asked uncertainly.

"A good night's sleep didn't clear your head and make you see that this was a good thing to avoid?"

"You can't live your life avoiding things—because then you're not living," she told him in no uncertain terms.

"Did you get that out of a fortune cookie, or the inside of a greeting card, or…?"

Was he trying to get her angry enough not to go with him? Or did he have something else up that sleeve of his? She found that she was having trouble reading him.

Kristin sighed. "You are not an easy man to like," she informed him.

Rather than daunt him, her retort amused him. There was also no lack of confidence in Malloy's voice as he said, "Sure I am. Just give yourself half a chance, Doc. I'll grow on you."

"Like fungus," she responded. "Not an experience I'd even remotely look forward to or want. How far away is this?" she asked, referring to the house. Malloy wasn't much on doling out details. For all she knew, the dead girl's next of kin lived in another state.

"Not far in miles," he assured her. "Emotionally, however, is another story." He'd done his homework on Abby Sullivan's family. It didn't make for warm storytelling. Something protective stirred within Malloy. He didn't really think that Kristin should be subjected to the ordeal she seemed so willing to take on. "Seriously, are you sure you want to do this?"

"I *have* to do this," she told him, avoiding directly answering the actual question.

He noted the evasion and decided to leave it alone. "Okay, you asked for this," he said. "Let's go. The sooner we get out there, the sooner we'll get you back to those bones."

"You'll be happy to know that our count stands at twelve bodies. O'Shea and Reynolds used that GPR—the ground penetrating radar—on the surrounding area and didn't come up with anything," she told him as they made their way to the elevator.

"I know what a GPR is, Doc," he replied. "You don't have to spell things out for me."

"Funny, I had the impression that I did," she quipped as they got in the elevator car.

Malloy merely laughed to himself.

Abby Sullivan's father still lived in the general vicinity where she had spent her childhood and adolescence. Her mother had died ten years earlier, succumbing to the grief of having a child who had suddenly vanished without a trace, leaving behind no clues.

It was the not knowing that had killed her, Abby's father had maintained. Alone now, he had remained living in the area, afraid that if his daughter did someday return, she wouldn't know where to find what was left of her family.

Age and anxiety had not only stooped the retired college professor's shoulders, but his entire countenance as well, making him look much older than his years.

When Henry Sullivan opened his front door in response to the doorbell, he looked at the two people on the other side of the threshold. It was obvious by the way he stared at them that he was trying to place them.

Peering over rimless glasses that kept insisting on sliding down his nose, he asked, "Yes?"

"Professor Sullivan?" Malloy asked.

"Yes?" This time the word was uttered a bit more emphatically.

Malloy took out his badge and his ID. "I'm Detective Cavanaugh, this is Doctor Alberghetti."

For a moment, the introduction seemed lost on the older man, and then a sudden understanding washed over the lined, drawn face.

"This is about Abby, isn't it?" Each word he uttered was more anxious-sounding than the last. "You've come about Abby."

"Yes, sir, we did," Malloy replied in as calm a voice as Kristin had ever heard him use. She glanced in his direction as he asked Abby's father, "May we come in?"

The older man all but stumbled as he backed up. Kristin couldn't tell if it was because the professor was trying to give them some room to enter, or if he'd stumbled like that from the impact of the words he'd just heard.

Belatedly, Sullivan answered, "Sure. Come in. Come in. I'm right, aren't I?" he asked nervously, looking over his shoulder at the two people even as he led them to his living room.

Every flat surface within the partially darkened room had a framed photograph of a bright-eyed, smiling young girl with long blond hair. It was a panorama that began with a photograph taken straight out of the hospital the day she was born and abruptly stopped with a photograph of her standing before a building that was clearly on a campus. Abby appeared to be about nineteen.

"It's about Abby, isn't it?" Sullivan asked again, his voice sounding raspy as the question clawed up his throat.

"We're very sorry, sir," Kristin said, taking the man's hand between hers as she made eye contact with the professor.

His eyes filled with tears—as did hers. "Then she is dead," he said sadly, murmuring the words almost to himself. And then he looked at Malloy for his answers. "How did it happen? How did my little girl die?"

"We're not sure yet, Mr. Sullivan," Malloy told him. "Her body was found buried at the perimeter of a cacti and succulent nursery in Aurora. It was called Prickly Gardens. Would you have any idea why she might have been there? Did your daughter work there or know anyone who worked there?"

"A cacti nursery?" Sullivan asked, clearly mystified. He shook his head. "She hated those things. What was she doing there?" he asked.

"That's what we're trying to find out," Malloy told him gently, not bothering to point out that he had asked the man the same question. He tried something easier. "When was the last time you saw your daughter?" The man made no response. He clearly looked shell-shocked. "Mr. Sullivan?"

Kristin took the man's hand again, closing hers over it and doing her best to get him to come around. "Mr. Sullivan, this could be very important and help us get whoever did this to your daughter. Please think. When was the last time you saw her?"

He didn't have to pause to think. It was obviously a date that had been stamped on his heart. "August eighteenth of '95. She was driving this old Corolla back to college." He pressed his lips together to keep them from quivering. It took him a moment to pull himself together. "She was a headstrong girl, and we'd had an argument just before she left." He let out a shaky breath.

"Margaret thought she just ran off because I'd yelled at her."

"Margaret?" Kristin questioned as unobtrusively as possible.

"My wife," he explained. "She blamed me when we didn't hear from Abby." For a second, he sounded like a man reliving his worst nightmare. "When she didn't come home anymore," he all but whispered. And then there was confusion mixed with high anxiety as he looked at them. "You said someone buried her? Do you know how long ago they did that?"

"We don't have anything even close to exact yet," Malloy told him, "but since you told me when you last saw her, going by what we do know, I'd say it was approximately shortly after she left home that August."

Sullivan scrubbed his hands over his stubbled face. "Oh, God, all this time I've been hoping, praying that she was all right and that she'd come around eventually. And all this time, she was in the ground—lost to us." His voice hitched.

"If you're up to it, Mr. Sullivan, we'd like to ask you a few more questions," Malloy prompted as gently as he could.

"Anything," Henry Sullivan said. "Ask me anything. I don't have anything to live for except catching the bastard who did this to my little girl." He grabbed hold of Malloy's arm. "You will catch him, right?"

"We'll catch him," Malloy promised.

Chapter 8

"Why did you tell that man you were going to catch whoever killed his daughter?" Kristin demanded in a hushed whisper when they walked out of Henry Sullivan's house nearly an hour later. "You can't make a promise like that in good conscience."

"I damn well am going to try to catch whoever killed his daughter," Malloy told her, and then his mood lightened just a little as, approaching his vehicle, he asked her, "Why are you whispering? Sullivan's inside the house. He can't hear you from there."

Kristin realized that she'd overreacted. She shrugged, feeling somewhat foolish. "For a minute, I thought he might come out and follow us."

She hadn't really thought that, but it was a good enough excuse to give the detective.

Opening the door on the passenger side, Kristin got

in. "That poor man's been through so much. He clearly holds himself responsible in some way for his daughter's death."

"Lots of girls have arguments with their fathers and they don't go running away—or wind up dead." Malloy got in on his side. "Besides, he said she was going back to college after summer break. It's very possible that whatever happened to her might have happened either on the way back, or after she got to school."

"Her father said he never spoke to her again," she reminded Malloy.

He put his key into the ignition and started up the car. "Typical teenage stuff. She held a grudge, didn't want to talk to him until she cooled off—or Sullivan apologized. Either way, that doesn't point to her running away."

"What makes you such an expert on teenage girls?" she challenged.

"Three sisters—and I have the scars to prove it," he added with a grin.

Kristin deliberately looked out through the windshield, avoiding eye contact for the moment. He had a way about him that was getting to her, and she really didn't want that happening.

"Maybe you should look up some of the teachers she had at the time. One of them might be able to give you some insight into what her on-campus life was like."

He glanced at her with amused admiration. "You know, if you set your mind to it, you might make a pretty good detective, Doc."

"What makes you think I'm not one already?" she said, forgetting her promise to herself, and glared at

Malloy. "You put together crime-scene clues. I put together the clues that a dead body gives me."

Instead of offering an argument, Malloy nodded. "You have a point."

Kristin frowned. That wasn't the response she'd expected from him.

"Stop being so agreeable," she told him. "It makes it hard for me not to like you."

"Good, because that's one of my goals," he told her amicably. "To get you to like me."

She wasn't about to ask him about his other goals, and she definitely wasn't going to let him get to her, Kristin thought. She wasn't about to become just another name in a long list of women in his past. "Don't get any ideas, Detective."

"It's Malloy, remember? And it's too late," he told her. "Those ideas have already gotten 'got.' By the way," Malloy said, switching subjects before she had time to get worked up, "you were right."

"About?"

He took a turn down a side street. "I think you being there for Professor Sullivan when I broke the news about his daughter actually helped him process it."

He spared Kristin a glance as he was forced to stop at a red light. "I have to admit I'm surprised. I wouldn't have pegged you for a hand-holder. Especially since you're a medical examiner."

"It's not always a patient's bedside where bedside manner comes into play. I've had to be there for my share of identifications," she told him.

He'd seen her with Sullivan, and it certainly seemed as if she felt the man's pain. But if that was the case, something didn't make any sense to him.

"If you have all this bottled-up compassion, why *is* it that you choose to cut up dead bodies instead of ministering to live ones?"

She thought they'd already gone through this. Obviously not to Malloy's satisfaction. His question reminded her of her mother's oh-so-frequently voiced lament. "Now you're beginning to sound like my mother again."

"Then I guess it's a lucky thing for you that we're back," he announced, pulling up into the precinct's rear parking lot.

Kristin got out of the car while the engine was still running. To her surprise, it continued running. When she looked back into the car, she saw that Malloy hadn't unbuckled his seat belt.

"Aren't you coming?"

"I thought I'd take your advice and take a ride to UCA," he told her, referring to the local university. Abby Sullivan had attended the Aurora branch of the University of California. "Maybe I can find a few answers that might lead us to her killer—and if we're really lucky, to the killer of all those other young women. I'll check in with you later to see if you've managed to identify any of the other victims," he said, putting the car into reverse.

"Something to live for," Kristin cracked, stepping away from the car.

The window on his side of the vehicle was rolled down. Malloy craned his neck in order for her to hear him through the open window on the passenger side.

"It could be," he told her, underscoring his sentence with that same smile that was beginning to twist into

the recesses of her mind like a swiftly boring cork-
screw, unsettling it.

In order to negate the effect, she waved a hand at
the detective without even bothering to turn around as
she headed to the stairs and away from the parking lot.

And away from Malloy.

She could have sworn she heard him laugh as he
drove away, but maybe that was just the sound of the
wind. At least she could hope it was.

Malloy had always had an easy time of getting whatever he needed by managing to effortlessly utilize his
charm. Thus, what might have taken another, more
abrupt detective several hours, if not days, to get his
hands on, took Malloy next to no time at all.

After just a minimum of well-selected words on his
part had been exchanged with Elizabeth Reid, the dour-
looking administrative assistant who had put in more
than thirty years in the registrar's office, she was only
too happy to track down Abby Sullivan's classes and
the names of the professors who had taught them. The
fact that the schedule was twenty years old didn't seem
to be daunting to her.

"I'm afraid more than half those educators have either retired or moved on," the woman told him after she
had returned from the archives. Elizabeth Reid had disappeared for a full half hour and had emerged with the
former student's schedules for the two semesters that
she had attended the university.

She held up the fruits of her labor. Two photocopied
sheets, one for each semester she had attended the university. "I've taken the liberty of checking off the ones
who are still teaching here."

Taking the schedules from her, Malloy smiled appreciatively at the older woman. "You are a real lifesaver, Ms. Reid."

The woman seemed almost lighthearted as she responded, "Elizabeth, please." And then her smile wavered for a moment as she obviously thought about the reason behind the request. "Anything to help find that poor girl's killer. I know that these kinds of things happen all the time, but you'd like to think that it will never touch *your* life," she said with all sincerity.

"Unfortunately, I don't have the luxury to think that way," Malloy told her, taking the two sheets of paper she'd put together.

"No, of course not." Elizabeth was quick to agree. "It must be very hard for you to deal with this sort of thing on a regular basis," she speculated. "How do you stand it?"

Malloy had never dwelt on that part of it. If anything, he always thought himself past the ordeal.

"It comes under the heading of 'protect and serve,'" he answered. He glanced at the two pages that the administrative assistant had handed him. "If I could bother you with just one more question—"

Elizabeth stifled what sounded suspiciously like a giggle. "You're not bothering me at all, Detective," she assured him with an encouraging smile.

His eyes indicated the names on the schedules. "Could you tell me where I could find the teachers that you've checked off?"

"Of course, of course," she instantly agreed. The next moment she was writing in the information beside each of the marked names. Handing the pages back to him, the woman said, "If you need anything else, please, don't hesitate to ask."

"I won't," he told her with feeling. When he took her hand, it was as much to caress it as it was to shake it. "And thank you."

"My pleasure, Detective Cavanaugh," the woman said, addressing his back with a heartfelt sigh. "My pleasure entirely."

The name Abby Sullivan rang no bells for the teachers he subsequently questioned. None of the five instructors he spoke with could remember anything outstanding about the young woman. They were all equally dismayed when they were told why he was questioning them about a run-of-the-mill undergraduate who had left no impression to mark her passage.

In an attempt to jolt their memories, Malloy showed each of them a photograph he had gotten from the victim's father.

Only one of the teachers, Roman Ward, a professor of English lit, recalled her at all.

"Yes, I think I do remember her," Ward said, after studying the photograph on Malloy's smartphone. "She had a nice smile. The kind that was both shy and managed to pull you in at the same time." He handed the smartphone back to Malloy. "You say she was killed?" he asked in subdued disbelief.

"Yes." Malloy tucked away his phone. "Sometime in the fall of '95," he added, studying the professor's expression for any telltale reaction that might give something away.

There was none.

But Malloy noted down the man's name just in case. Not everything was black and white.

So far, the professor was the only one who even recognized Abby Sullivan.

"Could mean absolutely nothing," Malloy allowed. "And then again, he could have said he remembered her to hide the fact that he had reacted when I showed him Abby's photograph," he told Kristin when he got back from the college campus.

It was after five, and the morgue seemed eerier somehow the closer it was to nighttime.

"So in other words, you're telling me you have nothing to tell me," Kristin concluded, putting down the small digital recorder she had been talking into just before Malloy's unannounced arrival at the morgue.

She was becoming oddly accustomed to having him just pop up, and this disturbed Kristin to no end.

"More or less, yes," Malloy agreed. He was about to add a playful coda that he just couldn't make himself stay away, but decided to table that for the time being. With someone like Kristin, unless he was mistaken, less was more.

"Well, lucky for you," she told him with some self-satisfied pride—an emotion she wasn't accustomed to having, "I've had a more productive afternoon."

"Regale me," he told her, happy that at least one of them was getting somewhere with this.

"I wouldn't dream of it," she countered, not quite sure where Malloy wanted to go with his invitation. "But I did verify my hypothesis."

"Which is?" he asked, trying to remember. Since

nothing occurred to him immediately, he requested, "Refresh my memory."

For once, Kristin obliged without prefacing it with a cryptic comment. "I told you that all those bodies we found were killed when they were between the ages of around eighteen to thirty."

"And now you're sure?" he guessed. It wasn't exactly much of a stretch, given her lead-in.

"As I can be forensically," she replied.

"And that verification came in the form of—"

"Their teeth," she told him. It was obvious that she was very pleased with this turn of events.

She might have been pleased, but Malloy had no problem making it known to her that he didn't understand the process.

"But wouldn't you have to have someone's dental records to attempt a match?" he asked.

"Yes, I would," she agreed. "*If* it was for a specific ID. However, figuring out a person's age at the time of death in general depends on the development of the enamel on the person's teeth. Technically it's called a C-14 analysis and when conducted on people who were born in the last fifty years—"

Malloy held up his hands in blatant surrender. "You don't have to go into the particulars, Doc. I believe you."

He paused to look around at the various exam tables, not to mention any available flat surfaces, that were covered with the disjointed but fairly neatly arranged skeletal remains that had been dug up.

"So on the surface," he theorized, "it looks like we're dealing with a serial killer who had a thing for females between the ages of eighteen—and Abby Sullivan was nineteen—and thirty, during a killing spree that ended, what? Twenty years ago, right?"

Kristin nodded.

There was still that one sticking point that nagged at him. "That doesn't explain the presence of the lone male skeleton that was dug up."

She reminded him of what she'd said the other day. "Like I said, he could have been a transvestite and our serial killer did away with him in a rage when he found out he'd been duped. His limbs weren't hacked, so this killing doesn't appear to have been thought out like the rest of the murders. It was spur of the moment," she added. "Or," she went on, thinking out loud, "the male victim could have just been in the wrong place at the wrong time."

Malloy saw what she was getting at. "You mean he could have witnessed the killer in action, doing away with one of the girls, and got killed himself so that he wouldn't tell anyone."

"Yes," Kristin agreed with enthusiasm. "That's exactly what I mean."

Malloy rolled the thought over in his head. "Could explain why the male victim was buried near the others," he said.

"Not near," Kristin corrected. "On top of."

He looked at her quizzically. "Come again?"

"I asked O'Shea for details on how he had found the victim, and he said that all the other bodies were in separate graves, but they found the male skeleton on top of one of the female skeletons."

"Well, that's definitely something to think about," Malloy said, rolling this new piece of information over in his head. "Anything else that you think I should know?" he asked.

"That's it for now," she said.

He thought he detected a note of weariness in the medical examiner's voice. The woman had definitely put in a long day.

"It's after hours," he pointed out. "Why don't you knock off for the night? I'll buy you a drink to celebrate."

Kristin's guard was immediately up. "Celebrate what?"

Malloy shrugged. "Making progress on the case. The end of the day. Whatever you like."

"What I'd like," Kristin told him evenly, "would be for you to stop hitting on me."

If she was annoyed, her voice gave him no indication. He had the feeling she was saying this just out of habit, for form's sake.

"This isn't me hitting on you," he told her. "This is me, offering to buy a colleague a drink."

"Well, 'colleague,' I've still got a few loose ends I'd like to tie up before I leave. But thanks for the offer. Maybe some other time."

"Maybe," he allowed, letting it go at that.

For now.

Baby steps, Malloy told himself. Some things have to be reached using baby steps. And she hadn't told him to get lost or to hold his breath. She hadn't really said no at all and that, in his book, was progress.

"See you tomorrow, Doc," he said as he walked out her door.

"Same time, same place," he thought he heard her mutter to herself.

Malloy grinned to himself as he went down the hall to the elevator.

Chapter 9

Before leaving for the night, Malloy stopped off at his desk. He wanted to get copies of several of the missing persons flyers he'd pulled off the database earlier. If he wasn't going to be taking the lovely medical examiner out for a drink, he reasoned, then he might as well be doing something useful. He had to admit, this case had him more intrigued than most of the cases he had handled in the past year.

Gathering together the papers he wanted, Malloy folded them in half, slipped them into the pocket of his jacket and locked his desk.

Just as he did, he heard what was the unmistakable crack of thunder. It sounded as if it was close by. This was *not* the time of year for rain, at least, in his experience, not here in this part of California. While the rest of the country was familiar with the clichéd rhyme about the relationship between April showers bringing May flowers, there were no April showers in Aurora.

At least, hardly ever, he amended.

But obviously, whoever was in charge of the weather out here hadn't familiarized themselves with the area's bylaws recently. Rain was supposed to be relegated to falling between November and March, with the concentration of rain happening in the middle of that range.

However, it seemed that all bets were off.

By the time Malloy reached the first floor and walked through the precinct's rear glass doors, rain had definitely arrived.

With a vengeance.

Malloy owned an umbrella, but as to even its general location, well, he hadn't a clue. So, raising his jacket up over his head, he made a run for it to the rear parking lot.

Most of the cars in this part of the lot had cleared out, so there was no momentary hesitation as he tried to find his car. It was right out in plain sight.

Hitting the security button on his key ring, he heard the familiar squawk that told him the car had unlocked and was waiting for him to get in.

He did the latter posthaste.

Brushing the stray drops of rain from his hair and his clothes, Malloy allowed himself a moment to bless CSI's efficiency. The perimeter of the nursery had been swept in its entirety, and all the data that *was* data had been tagged, collected and brought to the lab. The heavy rainfall wouldn't be interfering with his case or washing out what could have been a possible crime scene. That was an immense relief.

Buckling up, Malloy put his key in the ignition and

turned on the lights at the same time. Time to go home and see if there was anything he could scrounge up in his refrigerator. He knew he could swing by Andrew's house and find a meal waiting for him. The man always had something ready to put on the table, no matter what time of day or night someone arrived on his doorstep.

But as tempting as that was at the moment, Malloy knew it would be taking advantage of a very good thing, and he really didn't want to be seen in that light. He genuinely liked the spur of the moment—as well as the planned—get-togethers that his newly acquired grand-uncle held, and the last thing he wanted to do was show his appreciation by becoming a moocher.

Rain suddenly began lashing at his windshield, as if to somehow make up for all the time that had been lost this past year.

Too much rain was as bad as not enough. No one wanted to find themselves caught up in a flash flood without warning, or to have—

Malloy's thoughts suddenly evaporated as he squinted at something that was smack out in the middle of the front lot. Drawing closer, he saw that it was a stalled car. A stalled car with a very wet driver, despite the um-brella the driver was juggling in one hand. The wind had decided to whip up the rain, and it was falling not just down, but sideways, as well.

The umbrella was just two steps away from being totally useless.

The driver was circling the trunk and taking out what appeared to be a jack.

What a time to get a flat tire, he couldn't help think-ing.

Even as the thought—and sympathy—crossed his

mind, he began slowing down. Malloy was close enough to the scene now to see that the person dealing with the flat tire was a woman.

No sooner had he noted that than he realized that he was slowly driving by Kristin's car. He'd already intended to stop and help the driver, but this really cinched it. The next moment, Malloy came to a dead stop right beside Kristin's two-door compact.

Rolling down the window on the passenger side, he leaned over so she could hear him more clearly and asked, "Need help?"

Kristin would have loved nothing better than to say "No," that she had it covered and then to wave him on his way. But as much as she loathed to admit it, she *did* need help. She'd never changed a flat tire before.

Not only that, but just standing out here had made her look as if she was the first cousin of a drowned rat—despite the umbrella she was holding.

To stay dry, she would either need the wind to cooperate—or to be encased in a bubble.

The distress Kristin felt was because she'd never been in a situation like this before, and because she had to *admit* that she'd never been in a situation like this before. She didn't like not being in control. She liked being perceived that way even less.

"Yes," she was forced to admit. Then after a beat, she added an almost unwilling, "Please."

Malloy grinned when he heard the inclusion of the second word. Rolling his window back up, he turned off the engine—leaving the car exactly where he'd stopped it—and got out. Kristin immediately shifted over to him, holding her umbrella aloft just enough to cover both of them.

"Lucky for you that I was looking for a damsel in distress to save," he told her, then indicated the front seat of her vehicle. "Why don't you get into the car and I'll take care of this?"

Kristin shook her head. "You can't hold the umbrella and change the flat."

Malloy grinned. "Guess you've got a point," he agreed. "I left my second set of hands at home." And then he said more seriously, "I'm already wet. More water won't hurt." He nodded toward her vehicle. "Get in the car," he repeated.

"But you don't have to get any wetter on my account," Kristin argued, refusing to give an inch. Instead, she went on holding the umbrella over his head.

Malloy opened the driver's-side door. "Nobody's keeping score."

Her eyes met his. In that moment, he knew she was not about to budge, no matter how long or persuasively he argued.

"I am," she countered.

He shook his head, surrendering. "You are by far the stubbornest woman I've ever had to deal with—and I come from a family of stubborn, pigheaded women. Congratulations, you are now the queen of stubborn women." He took out the car jack as well as the torque wrench. "My sisters will be by to pay homage later."

As he moved back to the front tire, she moved with him, holding the umbrella over his head as much as possible. The wind still refused to cooperate.

"From what I've heard about the Cavanaugh women, I'm in very good company."

Getting the jack under the car on the side with the flat, he began to slowly raise it up.

"And what have you heard about the Cavanaugh men?" he asked, curious.

"To be very careful around them," she answered Malloy seriously.

"Well, they were right," he said as he removed the last lug nut from the tire.

Putting all four down next to the jack, he went back to her trunk to retrieve the spare. Moving aside the plastic mat that was covering it, he loosened the tire so that he could lift it out.

"About the *other* Cavanaugh men, not me," he assured her, hefting the tire out. He had to wait a second until she got out of his way before he could start to put the spare on.

"Oh?" she asked, trying not to laugh despite the fact that she could now feel water making the inside of her shoes soggy. "You're different?" she questioned, playing along.

"Absolutely," he said with feeling. Slipping the lug nuts into place, his forearms strained as he made sure that each one was securely tightened before moving on to the next one. "I'm just a pussycat," he informed her, looking up and winking.

Kristin deliberately ignored the corresponding flutter in her stomach. "That certainly wouldn't be my description for you."

Malloy tested each lug nut one last time to make sure he hadn't missed tightening one of them. "Oh? And just how would you describe me?"

She paused for a minute as she chose her words. "Pushy, persuasive—and dangerous," she concluded even as she felt her pulse speeding up with each word. Damn it, she should have more control over her reactions than this.

"Dangerous?" he echoed incredulously. "Me?" And then he laughed at the very idea. "Only if you're a bad guy. The innocent and pure have nothing to fear from me," he assured her.

His smile went clear down to her bone. "Oh, I think the 'innocent and pure' have a great deal to fear from you, Cavanaugh," she told him. "Mainly that they wouldn't remain that way."

"You do have one hell of an imagination, Doc," he told Kristin.

Finished, with rain and a reasonable amount of dirt clinging to his slacks around the knee area, Malloy rose to his feet and carried the tools he'd used back to her trunk.

Closing it, he turned to look at her. "You're ready to roll," he told her, then qualified, "Although I wouldn't roll too far. Those tires are only good for about fifty miles at best. They're thinner and smaller than the real thing, but they can get you to a gas station where you can buy another tire—or two to keep them balanced and equal," he added. "By the way, that last part was free," he tossed in.

Immediately alert, Kristin braced herself. "And the first part?" she asked. What would he want for that? "You changing my tire," she prompted.

"That'll cost you," he answered. Then, seeing the wary look on her face, he couldn't find it in his heart to tease her and draw this out any longer. "That drink I asked to take you out for earlier," he told her.

"You want to buy me a drink?" she asked, not all that certain that she believed him.

"Unless they're giving them away," he added. "Or someone's buying rounds for the house. Yes," he confirmed, "I'd like to buy you that drink."

"But I'm wet," she protested, looking down at her clothes. Because of the umbrella, she wasn't completely drenched, but she was a long ways from dry.

He spared her a glance and tried not to let himself linger over the way her blouse was provocatively clinging to her upper torso. His imagination was in danger of running away with him at any second, so he reined it in but not without some effort.

"Don't worry about it," he assured her. "Everyone else will be wet, too. No one'll notice."

Especially if their eyes were sealed shut, he added silently. The woman was impossible not to notice, but saying so was not going to get him what he wanted— just a quiet drink with her to start to break the ice between them.

Kristin chewed on her lower lip as she weighed the pros and cons of the situation. Malloy didn't have to stop to help her. If he had driven away, she wouldn't have even known that he'd seen her or the dilemma she had found herself in. If he'd just gone home, she would have been none the wiser and he would have been dry.

She owed him.

And she always paid her debts.

Kristin made her decision. "I guess I can't say no."

"You can always say no," he contradicted, surprising her. She found herself warming to him far more than she wanted to or was comfortable with. "But I'd really rather that you didn't."

"Okay," she agreed, even though a part of her felt that she would regret this. "But we'll each drive."

"Wouldn't have it any other way," he told her. He had an exact location in mind. "Do you know where Malone's is?"

Malone's was a bar owned and run by a retired police officer, and it was where all the off-duty law enforcement agents went to try to shake off the stress of the job. They did so by exchanging stories, picking each other's brains about particularly baffling cases and just spending some time in the company of people who knew what they were feeling without their needing to say a word.

"I'm familiar with it."

The way she said it, he had a feeling that Kristin might have driven past the place once or twice without really taking any note of it.

So this would be something new for her, he thought, enjoying the idea.

"Tell you what, you follow me. Malone's isn't far from here." Then, to encourage her to come, he said, "The drinks aren't watered down, neither is the conversation— and Sal makes a mean cheeseburger if you're hungry," Malloy added as he felt his stomach rumble in protest that it had been neglected.

"Sal?" she repeated. *Was that one of his girlfriends?* Kristin couldn't help wondering. "Is that short for Sally?"

He laughed, thinking of the feminine name being affixed to the barrel-chested, balding man he'd just mentioned. "It's short for Salvatore," he told her. "Salvatore Vincenzo. A great cop," he told her. "Caught a bullet, retired and lasted four months before he was looking for something to do with himself. Eventually, he bought the bar."

Kristin was trying to connect the dots. "But you just said that the bar's name was *Malone's*, not Vincenzo's."

At least she was paying attention. "The guy who originally owned the bar was Tim Malone. His widow sold the bar to Sal. She wanted it to be 'in good hands,' she'd told him, which was why she'd sold it to another cop."

Although Malloy had to admit that there was something intimately isolating about standing out here in the rain with this woman, he decided that it might be a better idea to go where catching pneumonia wasn't a viable option.

"Why don't we continue this inside Malone's?" he suggested. "Where it's dry," he added so that she understood why he'd said what he had. "You can ask me anything you want then."

His teasing comment made her realize that she was still standing out in the rain with her less-than-effective umbrella, listening to his every word.

What was the matter with her?

She knew better, and she definitely had enough sense to come in out of the rain. So what was she doing here, getting soggy, talking to someone she had just recently been trying to get away from?

She had no answer for that, which bothered her even more.

"Right," she murmured. "Sure." Neither word sounded very convincing to her ear. "You lead the way," she added unnecessarily as she slid behind the wheel of her car again, doing her best to simultaneously close her umbrella as she did so.

She still managed to get wetter. Muttering to herself, she tossed the umbrella on the floor of the passenger side.

Malloy pretended to take no notice as he got into his own car.

A minute later, he was leading her out of the parking lot and onto the main drag in front of the precinct. From there, it was a very short trip to the bar he had invited her to.

Despite the weather, the parking lots behind and in front of Malone's were more than three-quarters full. They had to find spaces that weren't next to one another or even in the same row.

He saw a spot closer to the building and, flashing his rear lights to catch her attention, directed Kristin to it. Once she understood and eased her car into the parking space, he went looking for one of his own.

After finding one, he parked his vehicle and then hurried over toward the rear entrance.

He was surprised to find Kristin waiting for him outside the building, right under the eaves.

"Why didn't you go inside?" he asked her once he was close enough for her to hear him.

"I thought if you didn't see me, you'd leave, and the whole idea of coming here was because you wanted to have a drink together. I didn't want to sit in there, waiting and wondering how long I should give you before I gave up and went home."

"You wouldn't have had to wait at all," he assured her. Malloy opened the door. Flashing a smile, he took her lightly by the arm and guided her into Malone's. "I wouldn't have kept you waiting. Takes less than two minutes to hurry across any corner of the parking lot to Malone's entrance."

He was being charming again, Kristin thought. Right now, he had far more going for him than against him—which was bad. She'd do well to get away from him as soon as possible.

"Just one drink," she reminded him.

"And a cheeseburger," he added.

She supposed there was no harm in that. "And a cheeseburger," she echoed a second before the warmth generated by the bodies within Malone's hit her, welcoming her as if she were an old friend instead of a stranger.

Chapter 10

While not overwhelmingly loud, the atmosphere within Malone's was definitely boisterous. It took a moment for Kristin to orient herself before she moved forward.

As she walked just slightly in front of her unofficial guide, Kristin saw that more than a few of the bar's occupants smiled and nodded in his direction. It certainly wasn't in hers, since she had never been here before and, for the most part, hadn't interacted with all that many members of the police force. Only a few faces of those patrons present now were vaguely familiar to her.

"Beer okay with you?" Malloy asked her, bending to get closer to her and posing the question right next to her ear.

Kristin fought back a shiver that came shooting out of nowhere.

"Beer'll be fine," she answered stoically.

She half turned to see if Malloy had heard her and saw that he was looking at the man behind the bar, holding up two fingers.

"Coming up," the bartender replied, then proceeded to fill two mugs with the amber liquid, placing them on the counter.

Malloy put several bills on the counter beside the beer mugs. "Cheeseburger still sound all right to you?" he asked Kristin.

That would mean waiting for the cheeseburger to be made, not to mention the time it would take to eat it once it was brought out. None of that pointed to making a quick getaway. But she had to eat something, she reasoned, and although her refrigerator was filled with meals her mother had made and loaded her down with the last time she'd visited home, Kristin felt like having something different.

So, after a minute's worth of mental wavering, she answered him.

"Yes."

Malloy picked up the two mugs from the counter and handed the first one to her. "And two of your world-famous cheeseburgers, Sal."

"Gotta be a real small world, then, Detective," Salvatore noted dryly. "Haven't seen you here," the bartender went on, addressing his words to Kristin this time.

"There's a reason for that, Sal. It's her first time," Malloy told him. Then, after slanting a significant look toward Kristin, he added, "here."

"Let her speak for herself, Cavanaugh," Sal told him, then asked Kristin, "You can speak for yourself, can't you?"

She shot a reproving look at Malloy before answering the bartender. "Yes, I can. Very well, as a matter of fact."

"See?" Salvatore said to the man who had ushered her in. "I had a feeling. By the way, since this is your first time here, the first drink's on the house." So saying, he slid a bill back toward Malloy. "Save it for the next time," the bartender told him.

It was on the tip of Kristin's tongue to protest that there wasn't going to be a "next time," but that seemed rude somehow, so she decided to keep those words to herself.

"About the cheeseburgers, Sal?" Malloy prompted patiently.

The smile Salvatore offered was for Kristin alone. "Coming right up. Oh, a word to the wise." He leaned over the bar, getting closer to her. "Watch yourself with this one, honey."

She was quick to set the man straight. This was a bar, and she had no doubt that misinformation could take off like wildfire. There was no way she wanted that to happen. "We just work together—temporarily," Kristin told him in no uncertain terms.

Salvatore merely smiled at the information, obviously discounting it. "Uh-huh. That's what a lot of them say," he said as he went to fill the order.

"Let's grab a table before they're all gone," Malloy advised, taking his beer and leading the way.

"Salvatore doesn't have a very high opinion of you, does he?" Kristin noted as she sat down at the table Malloy had staked out.

He shrugged indifferently. "Probably has me confused with one of my cousins."

Setting her mug down on the table, Kristin looked around at the room. Because of its reputation, the customers in Malone's were all men and women who were associated, in some capacity, with the police department. A number of them, she was fairly certain, were related to the man who had brought her here.

Turning back toward Malloy, she studied him for a moment before abruptly asking, "Just how does that happen?"

He assumed she was referring to his being confused with one of his cousins. "Well, most of us have the same hair color, more or less, and if you look quick, we've got roughly the same build, give or take a few inches, so if you're only—"

"No," she said, stopping him before he could really give her an involved answer. "I mean how does it happen that practically every member of your family and your extended family winds up being on the police force?" she asked.

"I'd call it luck," he told her.

He said the words so effortlessly, he sounded as if he believed them—but then, she also had the impression that he could sell fur coats to people in the middle of an unending heat wave. There was just something about the man that won people over to his side—hence his reputation.

"The city's lucky to have so many dedicated members on their police force," he went on to tell her. "I'm not talking about myself, but when it comes to Andrew and Brian and Sean, well, they're the personification of dedication. Only reason Andrew 'retired' was because his wife disappeared and he had five kids to raise—all of whom, by the way, are now on the force."

"Andrew," she repeated a little uncertainly. The name was familiar, but she couldn't go beyond that at the moment. She tried to remember which one that was. "Was that—"

"The former chief of police," Malloy prompted, filling in the void for her. "He's a pretty remarkable guy in a lot of ways. When everyone thought that his wife was dead, he didn't. He refused to give up. It finally turned out that she was in a car accident, one she managed to walk away from—but because of the whole trauma she went through, she got amnesia.

"Uncle Andrew kept working the pieces, looking for clues whenever he could—and he found her eleven years later." Malloy looked at her, driving his point home. "*That's* what I mean by dedication."

"Is Malloy bending your ear, recounting all his heroics?"

Kristin turned around to see who was talking to her. At the same time, the owner of the resonant, slightly mocking voice came around to face her. There was an engaging smile on the man's lips as he placed himself between her and the man he'd just referred to.

Holding a mug of beer in his hand, he crouched down at the table, his attention completely focused on her. "Has he told you about the time he dove into the water, fully clothed, to save that little boy who'd gotten dragged out by a riptide?"

Kristin stared at the other man for a moment. At first glance, she could have sworn he and Malloy were identical—but that wasn't possible, was it? Malloy hadn't mentioned anything about having a twin, and she was fairly certain that he would have said something if he had a twin brother.

"I've had one sip of beer. I can't be seeing two of you," she protested.

"Oh, but you can," the man bending next to her assured Kristin with a wicked grin. "Because there *are* two of us. I'm the better-looking one, of course. Or should I say the best-looking one?" This time, the question was directed to Malloy.

"You shouldn't be saying either," Malloy told him matter-of-factly, "because you're not. You're lucky Dad didn't drown you when you were born. Legend has it that they used to do that with the ugly ones."

"See," his brother said, his attention back on Kristin, "if he doesn't have a story to fit the occasion, he'll make one up. That's always been a failing of his, that sad sense of competition." He shook his head, as if he actually felt pity for Malloy.

"You're his brother, aren't you?" she concluded. It wasn't a guess, but she had yet to hear a name, or any indication that they weren't just identical-looking cousins.

Bryce Cavanaugh lifted his mug in a toast to his brother. "Found yourself a bright one this time I see. Good work, little brother."

She should have gone with her first instincts. Maybe coming here was a mistake after all. "He didn't 'find' me. We just work together."

Bryce looked around the room, his implication clear. They were here after hours. Under no circumstances could Malone's fit under the heading she was citing.

"Nice work," he pronounced, the same wicked smile tugging his lips.

Since his brother wasn't leaving, Malloy knew he had to make introductions. "Doc, this annoying character is my brother, Bryce. Say goodbye to the nice lady, Bryce," he ordered his brother.

Bryce rose back up to his feet, holding his beer mug remarkably steady. "Want to keep her all to yourself, do you, little brother?" Bryce gave her one final once-over. "Can't blame you, but good luck with this crowd," he advised.

Turning, he saw the bartender approaching with the two cheeseburgers that Malloy had ordered. "Hey, if that's your idea of wining and dining, she's going to bail on you, little brother, and I couldn't blame her." He bent over to get in closer to Kristin and advised, "Hold out for something better, Doc."

With that, Bryce made his exit.

"Sorry about that." Malloy managed to get in the simple words of apology just as Sal placed a plate in front of each of them.

"My cheeseburgers are nothing to apologize for," Salvatore said, pretending to be indignant.

"I was apologizing for my brother," Malloy told the older man.

Sal nodded his head knowingly. "Hey, can't pick your family. But if I could, I'd take yours in a heartbeat over some of the other families I've come across. At least yours isn't dysfunctional. You don't get to really appreciate that," he told Kristin, "until you get to experience it firsthand.

"Okay, I'll leave you to your dinner." And then the bartender looked at Kristin as he said, "Enjoy."

The next second, he was hurrying off to get behind the bar again.

Malloy's attention shifted back to the woman he'd

brought here. She'd been a pretty good sport so far, but he didn't want to push it if Kristin felt out of place.

"Look, we could get that to go if being here is making you uncomfortable," he offered.

It was an offer she hadn't expected him to make, and she wondered if he'd said it just for show, or if he actually meant it. If it was the latter—and she had to admit she was leaning toward that—she would have to reevaluate her opinion of Malloy. He wasn't nearly as self-absorbed as she'd first thought.

"Not uncomfortable," she corrected. "Shell-shocked, maybe, but not uncomfortable."

"Shell-shocked?" Malloy questioned, not really sure what she meant.

Kristin nodded. "I don't think I've ever seen so many Cavanaughs gathered together in one place before. Takes a bit of getting used to," she confessed.

For one thing, a great many of them looked more than just passingly similar, both in build and in coloring. It would take being around them for a while to begin to tell them apart—and she had no intention of doing that.

Her comment had Malloy looking around himself, as if seeing his siblings and cousins for the first time. And then he laughed.

"This is nothing. You should see what it's like at one of Andrew's parties. There's nothing but wall-to-wall Cavanaughs then—if you don't count the civilians."

"The civilians?" The term gave her pause. "You mean people who don't belong to the police force?"

"No, people who don't officially belong to the family—yet," he added with a smile, thinking of the last two men that had gotten tangled up with his sisters. It was only a matter of time before they, too, were family.

"Is that your way of saying that the people in your family are just irresistible?"

"No, that's my way of just stating facts." Thinking it safer, he switched topics. "How's your cheeseburger?" He nodded at what was left in her hands.

She hadn't realized that she'd picked the cheeseburger up and had started eating. The problem was that when she was nervous and there was any food around, she ate it. Ate it without really even tasting it sometimes.

Kristin raised her eyes to his, startled by the realization. He made her nervous enough to eat. This was a *real* problem.

He kept watching her. And then she remembered he'd asked her a question. He was probably waiting for some kind of an answer. Being here like this with him made her feel as if her brain was sleepwalking.

She'd graduated high school a year early, graduated from medical school on an accelerated program and she knew for certain that she was at the top of her game when it came to her work. But being around Malloy Cavanaugh scrambled her brain for some reason, making her feel as if she had the IQ of an under-watered potted plant.

Get a grip, Kris. So he's sexy and good-looking, so what? Just skin and genes, no big deal. It's not like he did anything special to get to look that way.

"Good," she heard herself saying, referring to the cheeseburger. "Actually, better than good."

Malloy smiled, satisfied. "Told you."

Well, she couldn't very well deny that, Kristin thought. After all, he had recommended the fare. "Yes, you did."

Malloy made no effort to hide his pleasure. "Since

you're being so accommodating, maybe the next time Andrew throws a party, you'd like to come by to see what it's like for yourself."

She had heard stories, good-natured, feel-good stories, about the parties thrown by the senior Cavanaugh. And one of the driving forces behind those stories.

"Malloy," she began pointedly, "I'm not some lone wolf that has to be socialized. I have a large family that is forever trying to fix me up with someone. I love them dearly, but, well, there are times when even the morgue isn't quiet enough for me. Does that make any sense to you?"

Not that it mattered, she silently added, because whether or not he understood, she had no intentions of becoming some kind of a cultivation project for him or any of the other Cavanaughs. If she wasn't willing to be one for her mother, she certainly wasn't going to be one for one of his family.

"That makes infinite sense," Malloy told her honestly. "I know exactly what you're talking about. It's like every wedding that takes place in the family just makes them hungry for another one. I'm surprised that Uncle Andrew hasn't started looking for someone for my dad." He laughed, knowing that the motivating factor, at least in his family, was love. His entire family meddled, and it was all due to a sense of love. Which made it just that much harder to fight. But he intended to. "It's as if there's some unwritten law that no Cavanaugh can remain single indefinitely."

Kristin suddenly laughed.

"What?"

"Maybe your Uncle Andrew thinks of himself as a modern day Noah, sending everyone off two by two."

So saying, she thought about what Malloy had told her about his family earlier. "Does your dad like being single?"

Though he came from a close-knit family, his father wasn't the type for long, soul-baring talks—or short ones, either.

"He doesn't say anything," Malloy answered, "but I get the feeling that he hates it."

Kristin nodded. "That's just like my mother. I know that she misses my father like crazy even though she's not alone by any stretch of the imagination. My grandmother lives with her, and there's always someone coming or going in the house, like her sisters and my cousins. Plus there's a small bunch of grandnieces and nephews to occupy her time—but all she can focus on when I see her is when am I going to get married and make her a grandmother. I don't think she realizes that that's liable to just drive me away."

"You could bring her to one of Andrew's get-togethers to distract her," he suggested, finishing his beer.

Kristin rolled the offer over in her head. Turnabout just might be fair play in this case, she mused. Maybe being subjected to something like that would finally make her mother cease and desist trying to match her up with her "soul mate."

"Maybe," she said, letting the matter drop for now.

He found the word very hopeful. He'd made progress with the ice princess. "Maybe" was a great deal better than a flat "no."

"Maybe," he echoed, toasting the possibilities behind the word.

Chapter 11

Folding her used napkin and neatly placing it on her empty plate, she put the near-depleted mug of beer on top of it, then looked up at Malloy.

"I'd better be going home," Kristin told him, rising to her feet.

Her limit was one beer. Anything more and she felt obligated to take a cab home, even though she had the ability to imbibe several without feeling its effects. It was far better in this case to be safe than sorry.

"Okay," Malloy said, rising himself. The check had already been taken care of, and he left a couple of bills now as a tip.

Was this going to be a problem, she wondered. "Just because I'm leaving doesn't mean you have to," Kristin pointed out.

"Yeah, I do," Malloy replied, saying it as if it was a given.

"Why?" she asked.

They'd discussed coming here, but neither one of them had said anything about what was to happen after they'd had that drink he'd wanted to buy her. Served her right for letting her guard down.

"Because I'm following you home," Malloy told her simply.

She should have known. Still, she really felt disappointed. He had been going up in her estimation, now he was back down to tomcat level.

"Look, just because you sprang for a cheeseburger—which I offered to pay for twice," she reminded him, "doesn't mean that you—"

"Have to follow you home to make sure that spare tire holds up to get you there?" he filled in quickly. "Yeah, I do."

That caught her off guard. "Wait—what?"

"The tire I put on," he reminded her. "Remember, you had a flat?"

If he was talking down to her, he was *really* going to regret it, she thought fiercely.

"You said it would last for fifty miles. I don't live fifty miles from here," she pointed out. She was still more than half convinced that he was just using this concerned Good Samaritan act as an excuse to follow her home and then talk his way into her house.

"*Ideally* it should last for fifty miles," he emphasized. "But if our line of work has taught us nothing else, it's taught us that the world is not a perfect place where things go perfectly according to plan."

She wasn't some dewy-eyed innocent, and she resented him treating her that way. "Well, I'm *perfectly* capable of taking care of myself," she informed him in a no-nonsense voice.

He glanced toward the window where he noticed sheets of rain coming down. "It's still raining," he pointed out.

What did that have to do with anything? "And I don't melt."

"It's a lot easier to skid in the rain if you have a blow out," he told her. "I'd still feel better knowing you got home safe. Look, if you're worried about me being the one who follows you home, I can get Bryce to follow—or Kelly, if you prefer."

She paused for a moment, trying to connect the name to a person. "You mean your brother?"

"Or my sister," he added. "Take your pick."

"I don't know either one of them," she protested. The idea of asking a stranger to follow her seemed ridiculous.

Malloy sighed. Nobody could accuse this woman of making things easy. "You don't have to 'know' them, all you have to do is drive to your home. Safely," he underscored. "They'd just be following to make sure that happens."

She scrutinized him, looking for some telltale sign that would give away his true intentions. She didn't find any.

"You're serious?" she asked uncertainly.

"As an autopsy," he answered.

Kristin frowned. "You could have picked a better simile."

The corners of his mouth slowly curved. She had difficulty looking away, even though she knew she really should.

"I don't think so," he replied, his eyes shining with humor.

Kristin sighed, giving in. The last thing she wanted to do was cause a scene here in the bar, and she had a feeling if she continued opposing him, this was going to wind up turning into a scene. *He* might not wind up losing his temper, but she had a feeling that she would.

"You're my penance, aren't you?" It wasn't a question, it was an accusation.

"For what?" he asked, curious.

"I don't know, but it must have been something really bad I'm blocking out," she told him, giving up. "Okay, you can follow me home." Kristin's eyes narrowed as she told him in no uncertain terms, "But I am *not* inviting you inside."

"Didn't ask you to," he told her as they walked out of the bar.

Their departure was noted and followed by more than a few pairs of eyes.

Once outside, still standing beneath the bar's eaves, Kristin opened her umbrella. "Once we get to my car," she told him, raising her voice to be heard above the noise generated by the wind and the rain, "you can take the umbrella to where you parked."

Malloy had no comment one way or another. With his hand beneath her elbow to guide her, they made their way together to the first row of vehicles where Kristin had parked.

When she opened her door and slid into her seat, she offered the umbrella to Malloy.

"You hang on to it," he told her. "And wait for me to pull up before you take off."

"Take it," she insisted, thrusting the umbrella handle at him.

But Malloy had already taken off, running, without it.

"He has *got* to be the most infuriating man," Kristin muttered under her breath as she tossed her umbrella onto the passenger seat.

By the time she had buckled up, put her key into the ignition and turned on her lights, she saw the headlights of Malloy's car as he approached her row.

"Boy, that man moves really fast," she murmured to herself, then laughed dryly. "But then, we already knew that."

Backing out of her parking space, Kristin drove out of the lot.

She told herself she wasn't going to, but she wound up glancing up into the rearview mirror a number of times to assure herself he was still there.

Why she even did that, she hadn't a clue. She was certain that he wasn't about to lose her. Undoubtedly, Malloy had a great deal of practice following women to a variety of destinations. The man was probably part bloodhound.

The unexpected rain made traveling the slick streets less than smooth. She'd noticed that whenever it did rain, California drivers did one of two things, they crawled as if fearing that doing anything over thirty miles an hour would lead to their certain, untimely death. Or they flew, traveling well over the speed limit in an effort to outrace both death and raindrops.

Either way, traveling on freeways and thoroughfares during the rain was definitely a challenge.

But finally, it was over, and she was pulling into the driveway of her modest, two-bedroom townhouse. Kristin hit her garage door opener although she would have really preferred to keep the house sealed up until she could watch Malloy's car drive past her home and off to his.

Parking in the garage, she got out of the vehicle just in time to see Malloy pulling up behind her and then parking his vehicle.

Damn.

She held her breath, waiting and watching him. Now what?

For a brief second, she thought about closing the garage door and just going into the house. But his car was positioned so that the nose of his hood was in the direct path of the garage door's descent. If it detected anything in its way, the door's safety feature wouldn't allow it to come down and crush something.

Besides, abruptly closing the garage door would be running, and she didn't run. She sent others running— and if he made just one wrong move, Detective Malloy Cavanaugh was going to be joining that group shortly, she promised herself.

She never took her eyes off him as he came closer.

"Yes? Did you forget to say something?" The way she asked, she was clearly issuing a challenge to him, daring him to say anything in his own defense rather than just getting back into his car.

He wondered if the woman had any idea just how damn appealing she looked right at this moment, with her eyes blazing that way. She would never know the intensity of the control he was exercising.

"As a matter of fact," he replied, "yes, I did."

Suspicion entered her eyes. "What?" she asked.

Malloy made no effort to get any closer even though standing where he was caused him to get progressively wetter. "Don't forget to call in tomorrow morning to tell my uncle you're going to be coming in late."

All sorts of red flags were going up in her head. "Why? Because we'll be having so much fun in bed?" she asked sarcastically.

"I was going to say because you had to stop by the tire store to get a 205/65r15 tire to replace the flat you have, but what you just said is definitely not an unappealing idea, either."

The look he gave her was sexier than sin, and she could feel her temperature going up by the microsecond.

"Oh." Heat was climbing up her neck, turning her face a bright shade of pink. "I thought that you—I mean that I—I'm sorry."

"Don't give it another thought," he told her. "On second thought, judging from the color on your cheeks, maybe you should." His grin was boyish and wicked at the same time. "I'll see you tomorrow sometime," he said just before he got back into his car.

As if someone had snapped their fingers, Kristin magically came to as the car began to pull away.

"You make me crazy," she shouted after it.

Despite the wind and the rain, he'd heard her.

"The feeling," Malloy said to the reflection he saw in his rearview mirror, "is mutual."

He came in early, intending on going through the rest of the missing person flyers he'd flagged and reviewing the little they knew about the cold case so far.

When the phone on his desk rang, he didn't hear it at first. By the time he did, he yanked the receiver up impatiently. He wasn't getting anywhere, and it frustrated him.

"Cavanaugh," he bit off.

No one responded. For a moment, he thought that whoever had called had hung up. But then a rather faint female voice asked, "Are you the detective who came to the campus the other day, looking for information about Abby Sullivan?"

Malloy snapped to attention. "Yes, I am. Who am I talking to?"

"This is Rachel McNeil," the woman told him. "I had several classes with Abby."

"Were you friends?"

"Not really, but I knew her. And Zoe."

"Zoe?" he asked,

"Zoe Roberts," the woman on the phone said, supplying the girl's last name. Something stirred in the back of Malloy's head, but it was gone before he could grab hold of it.

"Zoe and Abby met in college," Rachel went on to tell him, "and they got pretty close from the way it looked. Studying together, that kind of stuff. I don't know if this means anything," she said apologetically.

"Go ahead," he coaxed. "Sometimes the slightest small thing breaks a case."

"When Abby didn't turn up in her classes, Zoe became really worried. She was certain that Abby hadn't just dropped out or taken off. She told anyone who'd listen that something bad had to have happened to Abby, and she was going to find out what."

"And did she?" he asked in a calm, restrained voice. He didn't want to frighten the woman off.

"I think Zoe disappeared, too. At least, I never saw either one of them again."

As he listened, Malloy made notes to himself. "How did you happen to hear that I was looking into Abby's disappearance?" he asked.

"I teach at UCA now. Teachers talk," she added almost as an apology.

He took down her phone number and thanked her for coming forward. "I'll be in touch," he promised.

"Please, let me know if you find out anything," Rachel requested. "I always wondered what happened to them."

"I'll get back to you," he promised just before he hung up. His mind was already racing.

"Did you get your tire replaced?" Malloy asked as he walked into the morgue some time later.

She'd gotten in over an hour ago, having bribed the man at the tire store to put her at the head of the line and get her back on the road within the half hour. That and flashing her medical examiner credentials had her out the door in twenty-two minutes.

"You mean you haven't already checked my car out in the parking lot?" she asked. When he said nothing but continued to look at her, Kristin sighed. "You do realize that you're treating me like a two-year-old."

"Two-year-olds don't drive," he pointed out, still obviously waiting for his answer.

"Yes," she told him through gritted teeth, "I got my tire replaced. You really didn't have to come by to check on me."

"I didn't," he answered honestly. "I came by to tell you that I think I might have identified another one of the victims."

She forgot about being annoyed at the way she felt he was treating her. "When? How?"

"That victim you identified, Abby Sullivan," he said by way of setting up the background. "I went to the college she was attending when she disappeared and talked to the teachers she had who were still there."

This wasn't anything new, she thought, disappointed. "I know, you told me. Nobody remembered her."

"Well, it seems that word got around the college that someone was asking questions about her and that Abby might have been killed by a serial killer."

"Okay," she said. He still wasn't saying anything new. "How does that get us the identification for a second victim?"

"Seems that one of the current professors at UCA was a student at the same time that Abby was and they shared a few classes. According to her, they weren't close, but they were friendly enough."

Kristin stopped pretending she was working. "How do you know this? Did she call you?"

Malloy nodded. "She called me this morning, saying that maybe Zoe Roberts was another one of the killer's victims because Zoe and Abby were pretty close, and after Abby disappeared, Zoe tried to find out what happened to her."

This was definitely good news. It could get them one step closer to finding out who was responsible for the murders, but at the same time, Kristin could feel her stomach turning in protest. "Let me guess, Zoe went missing, too."

"I pulled her flyer," Malloy said, producing the photocopy he made off the database. He handed it to Kristin. "Now all you need to do is see if you can match her dental records to one of the eleven skulls you have left." He saw the stunned, somewhat dazed expression on Kristin's face as she reacted to his news. "What's the matter?"

Looking away from the flyer, she raised her eyes to his. "Didn't you notice?"

"What? That she and Abby looked enough alike to be sisters? Yeah, I noticed." But there was more to it than just an unexpected coincidence. It meant that the killer had been going after a certain type. "It's not all that unusual," he told her. "Lots of serial killers have a 'type.'"

"And we just found his," Kristin said excitedly. She looked at him again. "This is a real breakthrough, isn't it?"

"Yeah, I guess it is." For a moment, he allowed himself to absorb the genuine excitement he saw on her face. The look transformed her, made her appear softer and even more appealing than she already was.

The next moment, he shook himself free of that train of thought. There was a serial killer to find and other young women to identify and finally lay to rest. His reaction to Kristin was just going to have to be put on hold for now.

"I'd better go back to my desk and start pulling all the twenty- to twenty-five-year-old missing persons flyers for twentysomething blue-eyed blondes." He laughed dryly at the thought. "This being California, I've got a feeling that's still going to be a sizable pile."

"But less than before," she told him.

The comment had him looking at her. "Are you turning optimistic on me?" he asked, amused.

"No, I'm being scientific—or, more to the point, mathematical," she said, a bit defensively. "Bring me half the pile once you're done pulling flyers."

Now she really had his attention. This seemed like a turning point for their association. "Are you offering to help?"

Maybe she'd gone too far. Kristin retreated. "You said you're working alone, that your partner's out on sick leave. I thought you could use the help. If you don't want it—"

"I never said that," he interrupted quickly, honestly glad of the offer. Granted, the woman was exceptionally easy on the eyes, and this gave him more of a legitimate excuse to be around her, but he actually could use the assistance and told her so. "I need all the help I can get."

The comment made her laugh. "You said it, I didn't."

He cocked his head ever so slightly, as if that helped him absorb the sound better.

"You've got a nice laugh, Doc."

"Go." She waved him away. "I've got work to do."

But as she heard him walk out of the morgue and into the hallway, Kristin smiled to herself for no definite reason.

"It's a match!" Kristin declared excitedly, making the announcement to the skeletal remains on the exam table.

She had just matched Zoe Roberts's dental X-rays to the dental impressions she made of one of the remaining eleven skulls. It had been her sixth try with as many different skulls.

Malloy had picked that moment to walk back into

the morgue carrying a stack of some forty-three missing persons flyers under his arm.

"What's a match?" he asked, immediately caught up in Kristin's uninhibited exclamation of triumph.

Startled, she swung around to face him. She was so excited, she forgave Malloy for scaring her half to death. "I just found Zoe Roberts, or what's left of her, thanks to these dental X-rays her dentist faxed over. Actually, it was the dentist who took the original dentist's place, but that doesn't really matter. What matters is that we've got our second victim's name."

"Oh, Lord, we've got our second victim's name," Kristin repeated in a voice that was far more subdued and shaken.

"Mixed feelings?" Malloy guessed, reading between the lines.

"If they were any more mixed, I'd be pouring them straight out of a blender," she admitted. Kristin looked up at him as she suddenly remembered something. "You'll take me with you, right? When you go to break the news to her family, you'll still take me with you?"

Why would she think that he'd change course now? "Why wouldn't I? A deal's a deal."

"Right." And then, still riding the emotional roller coaster she was on, Kristin allowed herself another moment of triumph. She felt almost giddy. "We've put a name to our second victim!"

She was overcome with a real sense of elation and triumph at the same time that she was battling a wave of sadness over the fact that a family would be grieving all over again for a final time once the news was broken to them. Kristin found herself turning toward Malloy and throwing her arms around him, half in celebration and half because she felt a sudden, overwhelming need for human contact and comfort at the same time.

And what happened next took her even more by surprise.

Chapter 12

It felt like the entire world had shrunk down to the very small, intense sphere that contained just the two of them.

Kristin was exceedingly aware of every single nuance that made up the man she had so spontaneously thrown her arms around. Aware of his hard chest, his muscular biceps, his warm breath along her face and very, very aware of the way he looked at her.

As if she were the last woman on earth and he was glad of it.

She was aware, too, that there was nothing more on this earth that she wanted to do at this moment than to kiss him and be kissed by him.

Her heart hammered wildly in her chest.

Desire lanced all through him, permeating every single space—large and small—of his being. The thought traveled through Malloy's head that this was neither the time nor the place for this.

It was a first for him.

Ordinarily, *anytime, anyplace* was the right time and place for him to kiss a willing woman, to hold her and make her his before the actual act ever took place. For as far back as he could remember, Malloy had thrived on stolen moments, stolen kisses and, most of all, on stolen trysts.

But not this time.

Not with this woman.

As the thoughts played themselves across his mind, he felt that he had to be losing either his grip or his mind, possibly both.

This wasn't like him.

But then, she wasn't like any other woman he'd ever encountered.

She was special, even though, if pressed, he couldn't quite define exactly why.

So, rather than leaping in and making the most of the opportunity that had just presented itself to him, Malloy forced himself to loosen his hold on her. And then he dropped his hands to his sides and stepped back from quite possibly the most tender trap that had ever tempted him.

Struggling for some semblance of control, not to mention normalcy, he said casually, "I guess we make a pretty good team at that."

Oh, God, what had she almost allowed herself to do?

In a moment of complete insanity, she'd all but thrown herself at him, and the only thing that had saved her was *him*. Not any feelings of self-preservation on her part, not her own common sense, but *him*.

Up was down and down was up, and now that she thought about it, there was a very good chance that she might very well never get her bearings again.

Braced, Kristin looked into the cocky detective's eyes, waiting for him to taunt her or at least tease her about what had almost happened.

She held her breath.

Okay, in the scheme of things, a kiss was no big deal, but *she* would have been the one doing the kissing—this after she had let Malloy know exactly what she thought of his happy-go-lucky, carefree-bachelor attitude—and of him, neither of which was flattering.

Shaken, she had no choice but to clutch to the line Malloy had just tossed out to her about their so-called "teamwork."

"I guess we do," she agreed in a stilted voice. Clearing her throat, wishing fervently that she could clear away the haze in her mind as easily, or better yet, just disappear, Kristin forced herself to focus on the case. Maybe it would distract him and make him forget about what had almost happened.

And complicating everything was the nagging little question: *Why* hadn't he kissed her? Didn't he find her attractive? The man had a reputation of romancing every woman under eighty, yet when the opportunity to kiss her had presented itself, he hadn't.

Why?

C'mon, Kris, back to the case. Don't let him mess with your head. That's probably exactly what he's trying to do.

"I guess this confirms it then," she said, doing her best to block out every other stray thought. "Our killer did have a type. He definitely went after blue-eyed blondes."

"Now all we have to do is figure out why," Malloy concluded.

"What do you mean, why?" She didn't understand where he was going with this.

"Well, did she remind him of a girlfriend who'd jilted him—or who he thought had jilted him? Did she remind him of his mother or maybe an aunt who tortured him as a child? The more we know, the more we can figure out why he targeted who he did and, with luck, it'll lead us to him."

When Kristin groaned, he laughed. "Nobody said this was going to be easy." He watched her for a long moment, temporarily regretting his more chivalrous instincts. "None of it."

Another wave of warmth suddenly undulated through her.

The case, think about the case.

"That woman who told you about Zoe. Did she have anything else to add, maybe another name?"

"No, but I told her I'd get back to her if we could confirm that one of the victims turns out to be Zoe. Maybe she'll remember something by then," he added hopefully.

"Don't you have to notify the next of kin first before you tell a victim's friend?" Kristin asked. She was only vaguely aware of the proper protocol.

"Haven't found any yet," he told her. "But I just did a cursory search. I figured I'd do a more thorough one once I get back from the funeral."

"Funeral?" Kristin questioned. Ordinarily, she didn't ask personal questions, didn't pry into the lives of the people she worked with. But this, this had been different right from the start, and she heard herself asking him, "Whose?"

"Abby Sullivan's." In wanting to maintain contact with the man who had connected him with his daughter after all this time, Henry Sullivan had called him at the precinct to let him know where and when the funeral was being held. "I feel that since we were the ones to break the news to him, it's only right that I attend the funeral."

This was definitely going over and above what she thought Malloy was capable of. She looked at him as if she'd never seen him before.

"You really are sensitive, aren't you?" she asked, part of her still waiting for him to say or do something that would negate what she'd just said.

"Only partially," he told her. "I'm also going in case, for some perverted reason, her killer turns up to watch the ceremony. Serial killers are a weird bunch, and they all have their odd quirks that in some way enhance their kills. Who knows? This one might need to see the grieving faces and know that he was responsible for putting them there."

"The bodies have all been in the ground at least twenty years. You don't think he's stopped killing?"

"There are a lot of reasons why he might have stopped for a period of time—for instance, he could have been in prison—or a mental hospital all this time. Or maybe he just went to another state to satisfy his bloodlust, and nobody's made the connection. In either case, he's been damn lucky and not gotten caught."

"So you do think he's still alive?" she asked, trying to pin down his mind-set.

"Let's just say I don't want to arbitrarily rule it out," he told her. "And if he's out there, I want to catch him."

"You really think, if he is alive, that he'll show up?"

The possibility filled her with horror, and yet, Malloy was right. If there was the tiniest chance that the man was alive and brazen enough to watch the funeral play out, he had to be apprehended.

"Tiny chance," Malloy admitted. "But even if he doesn't show up for one reason or another, maybe one of the mourners might be able to tell me something that'll lead to our next identification." He glanced at his watch. He still had a couple of things to do first. "I have to get going if I'm going to be leaving on time."

"What time's the funeral?" she asked.

"One o'clock," he answered, wondering why she'd want to know.

Kristin nodded. There had been a shooting early this morning, and she had promised Sean Cavanaugh that she'd perform the autopsy as soon as she could. She was going to have to get cracking herself if she was going to finish up before she left.

"Come by and get me at twelve fifteen. We'll go together."

To him, funerals were something to be avoided if at all possible. He didn't want her to feel obligated to attend just because he was going. "There's no need for you to go, too."

"Cavanaugh, I'm the one who decides what I need or don't need. Now, are you going to pick me up, or do I go by myself?"

She really was the most stubborn woman he had ever encountered, Malloy thought.

"I haven't told you where it's being held," he reminded her, curious as to what she'd say.

Kristin shrugged indifferently. "I can find out," she replied.

For a second, he leaned against the exam table that was between them, studying her. "Okay, got another question for you. Why would you *want* to go?"

"Out of respect for Mr. Sullivan's loss and his grief. The man waited over twenty years to find out what happened to his daughter. The way I see it, he can use as much emotional support as he can get. I don't know if he has a large family or not, but I got the impression of loneliness when we were at his house."

"Good enough for me," Malloy said with a shrug. "Okay, I'll pick you up at twelve fifteen," he told her. "As long as you clear it with Uncle Sean. Don't want him thinking you've run off to play hooky with me," he said teasingly.

"Hooky?" Kristin echoed. "What are we, in high school circa 1960?" She laughed. And then she became serious. "Would you actually expect your uncle, my boss, to say no to my attending the funeral?" she asked incredulously. "Chief Cavanaugh has to be positively the sweetest, most understanding man on the face of the earth. He'd be the first one to appreciate why I'm attending. He might be surprised that I'm attending it with you," she qualified, "but he'd definitely understand *why* I'm attending."

"Okay then," Malloy agreed. "Twelve fifteen." He glanced at the body on the next table. Unlike what had been on all her exam tables recently, this body was still a unified whole. "I'll leave you to your work."

With that, he left the morgue.

* * *

True to his word, Malloy returned to the morgue at twelve fifteen. He was dressed exactly the same as when he'd left her, one of the advantages of coming to work every day wearing a suit, he thought as he entered the building on the north side. Forgoing the elevator, he took the stairs and went down to the basement, where both the morgue and part of the crime scene investigation lab were located.

For once, Malloy knocked on the door before entering despite the fact that it was open. "Sure you want to do this?" he asked her as he crossed the room.

"Go to a funeral?" she asked. "No. Comfort that poor man? Yes. This funeral is all going to bring it home to him, you know. Just in case he doesn't have a friendly face in the crowd, he's going to need one." She realized that he was grinning broadly. "You're laughing at me, why?"

"Medical examiner by day, comforting angel of mercy by night. Has a nice ring to it," he told her. "And I'm not laughing at you, Doc," he contradicted. "I'm laughing with you."

"Which might make sense if I were laughing—but I'm not," she pointed out. Shedding her lab coat, she placed it on the back of the leather office chair that was by her desk.

"Give it time," he told her significantly. "It'll make sense to you."

"If you say so." Grabbing her purse, she closed her desk drawer. "Ready," she announced.

His eyes met hers. "Me, too."

As she left with him, Kristin couldn't shake the feeling that they were no longer talking about attending the funeral.

* * *

Abby Sullivan's funeral had a small turnout. Malloy deliberately remained in the background, doing his best not to call any attention to himself as he attended first the service at the church, then the ceremony at the gravesite.

Besides himself and Kristin, only a handful of people attended. The way they gathered around Henry Sullivan made Malloy think that the people at the services were either the man's friends or his family. No one at either location looked to be a contemporary of the deceased woman.

Apparently, Malloy thought, the woman who had called him, alerting him to Zoe Roberts, hadn't known about the service or had chosen not to attend.

Henry Sullivan remained standing beside his daughter's freshly dug grave after the others who had attended the service had left the area. It was around that time the man noticed Malloy as well as the young woman who had come with him. By the look on his lined face, he recognized them both. It was also obvious that he was surprised to see them.

The moment they came closer, he asked in a voice that was both eager and weary, "Did you come with any news, Detective? Did you find out who killed my little girl?"

"Not yet, sir," Malloy replied. "We just came to pay our respects."

A tired smile passed fleetingly over his thin lips. "Thank you for that. I know you have to be very busy." He hesitated for a moment, then said, "If it's all the same to you, I'd rather have the name of her killer than any words of respect." Taking hold of Malloy's arm, he added urgently, "I need to know who did it. And I need to know—if I can't kill him with my bare hands—that he's made to pay for what he did."

The way Sullivan said it, Malloy could see the man actually acting as the killer's executioner.

"As I told you, I won't rest until I find him, Professor Sullivan," Malloy said in a quiet, firm voice.

There were tears in the man's eyes as he shook Malloy's hand again. "Thank you for that." Sullivan shifted his cloudy brown eyes to the young woman standing beside the detective. "Thank you both," Abby's father said, his voice breaking as he took Kristin's hand and shook it, as well.

Being here had vividly brought back her father's funeral to her. There had been a lot more people attending, but the pervasive feeling of sorrow was the same. In total empathy with the man, Kristin struggled not to let her own tears flow.

"There's nothing to thank us for yet, Professor Sullivan," she told him.

"You brought my girl back to me. Not the way I would have liked," he added sadly, then had to pause for a moment to keep his voice from breaking. "But at least I know where she is now."

Nodding his head as if completing some private conversation in his mind, Henry Sullivan slowly walked away.

Malloy took one last look around the cemetery to see if perhaps someone was attempting to keep out of sight while viewing the proceedings. As far as he could ascertain, there was no one.

"I'd better get you back to the morgue before someone notices that your toe tag is missing, along with the rest of you," he quipped.

The words sounded frivolous to her and hit Kristin the wrong way. She shook her head. "Just when I think that there's actual hope for you, you start acting like an idiot, and I'm left wondering how I could possibly have given you any points at all."

"I'm on the point system?" Malloy asked, amusement curving his mouth. "How many points do I have to get in order to win?"

"There aren't that many points in the whole world," she informed him, doing her best to sound distant and resurrect the crumbling barriers that just refused to remain up between them. There was something about the way he looked at her that kept creating fissures in those walls no matter how hard she tried to keep them in place. "At least, not where you're concerned."

He was doing it again, watching her as if he could see her thoughts. Kristin couldn't get away from the feeling that she was waiting for a shoe to suddenly and irrevocably drop.

Although they were standing in the cemetery, alone for all intents and purposes, he still leaned in and whispered, "I do love a challenge, Kristin."

Kristin, he'd called her Kristin. Not "Doc" the way he usually did. Kristin couldn't help feeling that somehow, she'd just been put on notice.

The question still remained, notice of what? He'd had a perfect opportunity to take advantage of her rather emotionally vulnerable state earlier at the morgue. She'd actually thought that he was *going* to kiss her—and he hadn't. He'd been the gentleman she didn't think he was. Now, had he done that for an honorable reason—

or because he was carefully laying the groundwork to completely disarm her and then do exactly what she'd thought him capable of doing all along?

A couple of weeks ago, she would have never even wavered in her thoughts, but now she felt torn, leaning first this way, then that. And all the while, she felt herself being drawn closer and closer to this man whose reputation to "love 'em and leave 'em" was well-known throughout the entire precinct.

Drawing on all the bravado she could pull together, she looked at Malloy and asked, "How do you feel about losing?"

"I don't know," he answered after what seemed like a moment's reflection. "It's never happened."

She straightened her shoulders, drawing herself up to her full height and trying to appear just a wee bit taller and more formidable than she actually was. "Well, then, Detective Cavanaugh, brace yourself for a brand-new experience."

Damn, but she felt as if his eyes were totally undressing her as Malloy replied in a quiet voice, "I'm counting on it."

Kristin decided that it was wiser if she just said nothing further, not until she managed to sufficiently rearm her defenses against this silver-tongued devil in a suit.

Chapter 13

As soon as he got back to his desk, Malloy began searching for Zoe Roberts's next of kin. It took some extensive digging, but because he'd managed to pick up a few computer tricks from Valri, he was finally able to learn that his second identified victim was a product of the social services system.

According to what he uncovered, there had never been a father in the picture, and her mother had died of some unspecified disease when Zoe was eleven. With no other identifiable relatives to be found, Zoe Roberts was turned over to social services.

Once absorbed into the system, she went from one foster home to another—he counted eight in total—until she finally aged out at eighteen. Throughout those turbulent seven years, she had somehow managed to keep her grades up and had, apparently through sheer determination, earned a full scholarship to UCA.

Malloy closed the file and rocked back in his chair for a couple of moments. He stared at the blank screen, thinking.

It just didn't seem fair to him.

"All that potential, just to wind up in an unmarked grave for the past twenty years," he said to himself. "Who the hell did this to you, Zoe?"

"So now you're talking to yourself, Detective?"

Malloy didn't have to turn around to know who belonged to the melodic voice coming from behind him. He did, anyway.

"What are you doing in my part of the building, Doc?" he asked.

An odd restlessness as well as an unrelenting curiosity had brought Kristin here to the cold case squad room. She wasn't the type to remain idle, especially when there was something to do.

"Well, I sent the autopsy report in to be transcribed, and until you give me another name to match up to the remaining nine skulls, or homicide sends me another body, I really don't have anything to do. By the way—" she dropped the stack of flyers he'd left with her on his desk "—for what it's worth, I separated the blondes from the rest."

But Malloy's attention was focused on something she'd just said. "Nine skulls?"

"Yes." Why was he questioning that? He knew how many had been dug up as well as she did.

"We started out with twelve and identified two. Wouldn't that leave ten?" he asked.

"It would—but you're trying to identify women, and if you recall, one of those skulls turned out to belong to a man."

"Right. I guess I lost sight of that." Rocking back in his chair, he scrutinized Kristin for a moment. He had a feeling there was more, but he didn't want to come right out and ask, so he led up to the subject and let her fill in the blank. "You didn't have to come all the way up here to bring me the flyers. I would have picked them up. All you had to do was give me a call."

"I didn't come here to bring you the flyers," she clarified. "I came to find out if you managed to locate Zoe's next of kin."

"She didn't have any." Even as he said it, it sounded so pitiful to him. Having grown up in what was tanta-mount to a crowd scene, he couldn't begin to imagine how lonely Zoe Roberts's upbringing had to have been. "She was an orphan long before she attended UCA."

If there was no next of kin, that left only one per-son to notify about finding Zoe's remains. "Have you called her friend yet? The one who initially gave you Zoe's name?"

"Oh, you're talking about the UCA professor. They weren't really friends," he reminded her. "According to Rachel McNeil, they were more or less acquain-tances because they attended the same classes, and no, I haven't called her yet. Why?"

Kristin had to admit that even though she wasn't sup-posed to get caught up in this aspect of her work, the mystery was beginning to consume her. "Well, she's definitely had some time to think since she called you, and I just thought that she might remember something more about either Abby or Zoe that could help solve the case."

He'd been thinking along the same lines, but he was

curious to hear just what Kristin's exact thoughts were. "Like what?"

Kristin shrugged. These were all vague thoughts that had been slipping in and out of her head. "Like the names of mutual friends Abby and Zoe had at the time, or maybe the names of boyfriends if either of them had any—or just anything unusual that might have been going on at school at the time Abby and Zoe disappeared. Something has got to lead to a breakthrough," she insisted.

Malloy read between the lines. "Feeling a little claustrophobic in the morgue?" he guessed.

For a split second, Kristin's back went up. "I am *not* claustro—" And then she relented. "At least I wasn't until this case came along." With a sigh, she came totally clean. "I'd like to help move the case along, and there's no more insight to be gotten from those bones that were dug up. I've matched and assembled them as best I can, gleaned approximate height and weight from all twelve remains, and like I said, I've gotten caught up in this."

She saw Malloy opening his mouth, and she second-guessed what he was about to say. "And before you say anything, yes, I ran it past the chief. He's always encouraging the team to exercise independent thinking, so if this helps wrap up this case somewhere down the line, he's fine with my coming along with you."

"And you have no problem being my sidekick?"

"I'm not your sidekick," she corrected with just a touch of indignation. "You're Cold Case, I represent the medical examiner's office as well as the crime scene investigation unit."

"Well, that's a mouthful," Malloy commented. "Just

for the record, I have no problem with you coming along—as a sidekick or as a representative of whatever you just said. But just so we're clear, this *is* my case and my field, so you follow my lead."

"Do you want me walking two steps behind you, too?" Kristin couldn't help asking.

"Only if we happen to be on the side of a steep mountain road," he quipped. He rose to his feet. "You ready to go?"

She hadn't sat down since she'd entered the squad room, looking for him. "Absolutely."

He grinned at the sound of that. "I'll remind you of that later," he said.

His comment made her wonder at first, and then she decided that she was better off not knowing exactly what the detective had meant by that.

Having transferred her number from the phone on his desk to his cell, Malloy called Rachel McNeil from the road. He told her that he had some information for her and that he wanted to meet with her at the earliest opportunity.

"I just taught my last class for the day and was about to go home," the English professor told him. "Is this about Zoe?"

"Yes."

He didn't want to say any more than that until he saw her. Sometimes, his older brother, Duncan, had taught him, you could learn more from the way someone said something than from what he or she said.

"All right, I'll wait for you," the woman agreed. "How soon can you get here?"

Malloy glanced at his mileage. "I'm about fifteen minutes away. Where can I meet you?"

"I'll wait for you in front of Paul Klapper Library," Rachel replied, apparently assuming that he was as familiar with the campus as she was. "There're several benches out front," she went on. "We can talk there."

"Public place," Kristin commented once he terminated the call. He'd had it on speakerphone. "Did you frighten her last time?" she asked, curious.

"I doubt it." He took a left turn at the end of the block. "I'm harmless."

Kristin refrained from laughing, but not from commenting. "You, Cavanaugh, were never harmless. Not even when you were born."

He eased to a stop at the light and spared her a look. "Why, Doc? Do I frighten you?" he asked.

"Just making an observation," Kristin answered evasively.

He tabled that for a future discussion. They were almost at the campus. "Right now I need you to pull up a map on my GPS and locate Paul Klapper Library on the UCA campus."

She looked at him in surprise. "You don't know where it is?"

"Not offhand," he admitted. He was catching all the lights now, and the entrance to the campus was coming up soon. "I found the administration building. I didn't memorize the layout of the entire campus."

"So you didn't go to UCA?" Kristin concluded in surprise.

"I'm not a local boy, no."

"I thought all the Cavanaughs were local."

"Most of them are, but some of us came from Shady

Canyon," he told her, mentioning a city some fifty miles away. He could see that she had more questions. "Long story. Maybe I'll tell it to you some time—after we solve this case."

"You say it like it's a sure thing."

"What? Solving the case or my telling you the story?"

This time, she did laugh. "Both."

"That's because I only know how to approach things one way," he explained. "From a positive perspective. The college is coming up just ahead," he told her, interrupting himself. "Which way do I turn?"

Caught up in the conversation, Kristin barely had time to type in the school's address and then enlarge the map that materialized.

"Left," she said quickly. "Make a left at the end of the winding road."

Because of the last minute instruction, the turn he made was sharp—and jarring. It wasn't the way he normally drove.

"Remind me not to let you navigate next time," he said dryly as he pulled into an empty space some distance away from the actual library.

"What makes you think there'll be a next time?" Kristin challenged cryptically, unbuckling her seat belt.

He slanted just the briefest glance her way. "Just a hunch."

The mild answer got under her skin for more reasons than just one.

Without another word, Malloy got out of the vehicle and hurried up the handful of stairs that took him from the compact parking lot to the front of the library. Kristin was right behind him.

Rachel McNeil was sitting on the bench closest to

the stairs. The moment she saw him, she instantly rose to her feet.

"Was I right?" the slender, conservatively dressed woman asked before he had even reached her. "Was Zoe one of the bodies you found with Abby's?"

Before he answered her, Malloy took a moment to make the necessary introductions. "Doc, this is Professor Rachel McNeil. Professor, this is Dr. Alberghetti. She's the medical examiner who matched Zoe Roberts's dental X-rays to one of the bodies we found."

Rachel covered her mouth. A tiny sound of dismay still managed to escape. For just a moment, the years melted away from her face, and she was an undergraduate again.

"I knew it. I had a feeling. I just had a feeling they wouldn't have just run off that way," she said to Malloy. "Especially not Zoe. She was determined to prove herself."

Malloy studied the woman for a moment. "I thought you said you didn't know either of them that well," Malloy said as they all sat down on the stone bench.

Kristin sat down next to him and edged out a little in order to have a better view of the woman they had come to question as well as notify.

"I didn't, really," Rachel explained. "But we studied together in the library. That library," she emphasized, indicating the building behind them. "It was a lot smaller back then," she remarked. "A few of us would get together to study and pick each other's brains before tests. Zoe was always the most intense, even though she was like a walking encyclopedia."

Malloy took out a small, well-creased notepad and a pen from his pocket. "Can you remember any of the other people in the study group?" he asked Rachel, opening the notepad.

But she shook her head. "No, I'm sorry. That was two decades ago. I just remember Abby because of that police detective who came to the campus to question us. And Zoe because she was so sure something bad had happened to Abby. She said she was going to go looking for her—"

"Did she say where she was going to look?" Kristin asked.

Rachel shook her head again. "I was going out with this junior, and I didn't pay any attention. Not until Zoe went missing, too." She sighed. It was obvious that she felt somehow responsible because she hadn't been paying attention. "That's something that stays with you," she added quietly.

"You just mentioned a police detective," Malloy said. "Do you remember his name?"

Rachel thought for a moment. "Monahan or Mulroney, something like that." She offered an apologetic smile.

Malloy made a notation. The name was easy enough to obtain. The investigative detective would be a matter of record.

"You just mentioned a boyfriend," Kristin said, picking up on the woman's narrative. "Do you remember if either Abby or Zoe had a boyfriend?"

This, Rachel seemed rather clear on. "All Zoe had time for were her books—and Abby," she added. "I had the impression that Zoe didn't have any friends, and from what I heard, she latched on to Abby when they hit it off as freshmen."

"Did Abby have any boyfriends?" Malloy asked, following Kristin's lead.

Rachel thought for a moment. It was obvious she was attempting to remember that far back. "I saw her talking to this guy a few times, but I wouldn't have called him her boyfriend."

Any crumb was better than none. "Do you remember *his* name?" Malloy asked. So far, it didn't seem as if names were Rachel's long suit.

By the frustrated expression on her face, she really tried to remember the student's name—and failed.

"Sorry." But she did have something to offer. "I do remember he was in her botany class, or some class that had to do with plant life. I remember thinking that was kind of odd because most guys that age weren't into things like growing plants—except maybe the kind they could smoke. Abby did say that he'd told her that he was only taking the class to please his father, because the old man was really into plants."

Nodding, Malloy made another notation. "Anything else?"

But Rachel shook her head. "Sorry. That's all I can remember." She hesitated for a moment, then timidly asked, "They didn't suffer, did they?" She paused, as if the words were sticking in her throat. "Abby and Zoe, they didn't suffer when they died, did they?"

"Death was instantaneous," Kristin told her, quickly answering the woman's question before Malloy had the chance.

Rachel exhaled a shaky breath. "I'm glad. I mean, I'm not glad that they died," she corrected quickly, "but if they did die, I'm glad they weren't tortured." She pressed her lips together. "Am I making any sense?" she asked the couple.

"Yes," Kristin answered with understanding.

"Here's my card," Malloy said, handing it to Rachel. "It has my cell number on it as well as my work line. If you can remember anything else, *anything* at all, call me," he instructed.

Rachel nodded. "I will."

They left the college professor still sitting on the bench in front of the library, looking at Malloy's card.

It wasn't until they were back in his car and he had buckled up that he turned to Kristin and said, "You didn't tell me that death was instantaneous."

"That's because I don't know," she admitted, securing her own seat belt.

He put his key into the ignition. Her actions caused questions to arise in his mind.

"But you just told that professor it was instantaneous. Did you lie?" He wouldn't have thought her capable of that, no matter what the reason. The woman was obviously a lot more complicated than she seemed to be at first.

Rather than look at Malloy, Kristin stared straight ahead. "I told her what she needed to hear. Why should she have to suffer visualizing images of those two young women having their last breaths wrenched from them? It's better if she just believes that they died quickly and painlessly. There's no need for the woman to torture herself."

Starting the car, he pulled out. "You're a fraud, Dr. Alberghetti. You do realize that, don't you?"

Kristin instantly took offense. "What are you talking about?" she demanded.

His mouth curved. "You pretend to be this tough, hard-nosed woman, but on the inside, Doc, you're just this big softie."

Was he mocking her? "I wouldn't go betting the farm on that."

"I don't need to," he told her. "I just witnessed it with my very own eyes. Don't be embarrassed, Doc," he told her. "You just did a good thing. I like it."

Did he think that was the only thing that mattered to her? His approval? "And I don't care *what* you like," she retorted.

She heard him laugh softly under his breath. "If you say so."

She'd never met anyone who could make her so angry so fast. "Yes, I say so."

"Uh-huh." He kept his eyes on the road, as did she, but she could hear a smile in his voice.

She opened her mouth to say something twice, and shut it twice. There was no point in talking to the man. He had a gift for twisting words.

Dead silence accompanied them the rest of the way back.

Chapter 14

"Can I come?"

Malloy looked at the woman in his passenger seat quizzically. Not a single word had passed between them for almost ten minutes, constituting the rest of the ride from the UCA campus back to the police precinct. And then, just as he had pulled into one of the numerous spaces available in the lot at this late time of the day, Kristin had suddenly deigned to ask a question.

A rather obscure question at that, as far as Malloy was concerned.

"You're going to have to be more specific than that, Doc," he told her as he pulled up his hand brake. "Come where?"

Taking a short breath, Kristin began from the beginning of her request.

"When you go to interview the detective who investigated Abby Sullivan's disappearance, can I come with you?"

Kristin was well aware of the fact that Cavanaugh was within his rights to refuse to let her come along. After all, she was a medical examiner, not a police detective. But at this point of the investigation, she really felt invested in this cold case they were piecing together, and waiting on the sidelines for Cavanaugh to get in contact with her with any bits and pieces of information he found was frustrating as well as totally unacceptable, as far as she was concerned. Aside from the remains that had been dug up at the nursery—remains that were still waiting to be identified—things at the morgue had ground to a halt. She really had nothing to do at the moment now that the last autopsy was completed for that unrelated case. That gave her the option to go out into the field if the opportunity to do so suddenly came up—and it most obviously had.

"It's late. I'm not going today," he told her, evading her question.

Kristin was not about to be sidelined. "I rather thought you wouldn't, but when you do go, I'd like to come with you." She decided to skip asking for his blessings outright.

"And I'd like to be police chief," he replied flippantly, "but we don't always get what we want." Getting out of the car, he looked at Kristin over the roof of his vehicle. Her expression looked stern to him. "You're serious, aren't you?"

"I wouldn't have asked you if I wasn't." Didn't he know that by now? "Maybe you haven't noticed, but it's hard for me to ask for a favor."

He laughed dryly. "Oh, I've noticed." He paused,

playing the moment out a tiny bit longer. "All right, once I find out who the investigating detective was, I'll let you know."

This was all before his time. Twenty years ago, he was just entering middle school and setting his sights on Jenny Gallo, an eighth grader.

"The man's definitely retired from the force by now—for all we know, he might be dead or living somewhere in the Caribbean—but if he's breathing and accessible, I'll let you know," he promised. And then he smiled. "Now you have to do something for me, Doc."

"What?" she asked warily.

The guarded tone in her voice did not go unnoticed. "Are you always going to look at me as if you expect me to drag you into an alley and have my way with you?"

"I know you wouldn't drag me into some alley and have your way with me."

"Thank you for that."

"Because I know martial arts."

He raised a quizzical eyebrow. "And that's the only reason?"

"No," she told him rather flatly. "You don't drag, you seduce." She drew a breath. "But I still know martial arts."

He laughed, getting a kick out of the fact that she never gave up. "Fair enough, I guess."

"What was it?" she asked him suddenly.

"What was what?" Malloy asked, locking his car's doors. He'd lost the thread of whatever it was that she was saying.

She pressed her lips together, certain he was deliberately drawing this out for his own enjoyment. "The 'something' you wanted me to do for you."

Again he paused, aware that she was building this up in her mind, not knowing what to anticipate. And then he said simply, "I was going to ask you if you felt like grabbing a bite to eat with me after we clocked out. I could use the company."

She wasn't sure if she believed him. There had to be more. "And that's it?"

"Yeah." And then his eyes shone with humor. "Unless you want to top off the evening with hot sex after dinner."

"No." She said the word so quickly, he could have felt the breeze it created.

"Then grabbing a bite to eat it is," he announced simply.

Cavanaugh was assuming things again. The detective seemed to really enjoy wrenching control out of her hands, she couldn't help thinking. "When did I say yes?" she asked.

"Well, I didn't hear 'no,'" Malloy countered.

Kristin frowned. He had her there. "I guess you have a point."

The wicked smile was back.

"I usually do." Malloy glanced at his watch, doing a quick calculation. "I clock out in less than half an hour. You?"

Kristin didn't need to look at her watch. "I could already be gone if I wanted to be."

Malloy nodded. "All right, we'll meet out here in half an hour. Any place special you want to go?" he asked, politely leaving the choice of the restaurant up to her.

Kristin had nothing to offer. She didn't frequent restaurants in general. She either prepared something on the simple side for herself at home or, more than likely, she either ate at her mother's or had meals that her mother—on occasion her grandmother—had made and then sent home with her.

Kristin shrugged. "Wherever you were going to go is fine."

"You're on," he told her as they walked into the precinct.

Against her better judgment—not because she didn't want to, but because she *did*—half an hour later found her back in the parking lot, sitting in her car, waiting for Malloy to show up.

When she saw him coming down the steps that led to the parking lot, her survival instincts made one last rather urgent plea for her to run.

She didn't.

Instead, she got out of the car and waited for Malloy to cross to her.

"Part of me didn't think you'd show," he told her honestly once he was close enough to her not to have to shout.

"Part of me didn't want to," she freely admitted. "But I said I would, so here I am."

Malloy already knew that her word meant a great deal to her. It was one of the things he really liked about her.

Glancing at the car she was leaning against, Malloy said, "I can drive us to the restaurant and then bring you back later."

She made him a counteroffer. "I can just as easily follow you to the restaurant, and when we're done, we can both drive home—to our separate homes," she emphasized deliberately.

Malloy pretended to be wounded. "When are you going to trust me, Doc?"

"When you make me feel safe," Kristin answered without hesitation. "Right now, you make me feel like I'm walking on a tightrope stretched out across Niagara Falls on a very windy day."

His eyes held hers. His were unfathomable. "The smart thing to do in that case," he told her, "would be *not* to walk the tightrope."

"Exactly," she agreed. She refused to look away, even though she wanted to.

And then, ever so slowly, the corners of his mouth curved again. He'd never had anyone resist him before, let alone to this extent. He began to wonder things about Kristin in earnest.

"You have nothing to worry about, Kristin," Malloy told her, his voice low, sultry. "I'd never do anything you wouldn't want me to do."

He sounded earnest, but Kristin wouldn't allow herself to believe him. "Said the man with the hypnotic eyes."

"Really?" he asked, amused. "You think my eyes are hypnotic?"

She sighed. She was not about to stand here and say things that he took as compliments. Kristin shook her head. "Let's just go before they start serving breakfast at this restaurant you picked."

"We'll save breakfast for another time."

She opened her mouth to say, "In your dreams," then realized that if she did, she would be guilty of reading things into his statement. After all, he never said that the breakfast he was referring to would follow a night of lovemaking. That was *her* imagination that had put that interpretation to his words.

So she pressed her lips together and said nothing. Instead, she got back into her car and, after he'd given her the address in case they were separated, she followed him to the restaurant he'd chosen.

A few short miles later, Malloy turned into a parking lot. He'd brought her to a restaurant that looked as if it had once been someone's home.

The faded sign out front told her they were stopping at "Jerry's."

"Are you sure they're open?" was the first thing she asked as she emerged from her car after parking it next to his.

"All these other people seem to think so," he told her, gesturing toward the other cars that were parked around them. "And the lights are on, so I think that the odds are pretty good that Jerry's is open."

With reluctance, she locked her car. Looking at the building, she still had her doubts as to the wisdom of this venture she'd agreed to. The building appeared somewhat run down.

"What kind of food do they serve here?" she asked.

"Good food," he answered, preceding her up the three steps to Jerry's front doors.

She followed him up the stairs, but then she went no farther, stubbornly stopping by the door and placing her hand over it to keep him from opening it, as well. She wasn't about to take another step until he stopped playing games and answered her.

"Let's try this again. What kind of food do they serve here? It's a legitimate question," she said pointedly.

Did she think he was taking her to someplace other than what he'd just said? "And this is a legitimate restaurant. You can look it up on your smartphone. It comes with a high rating, and as to what they serve, they serve mainly steak and seafood. Anything else?" he asked gamely.

He made it sound as if she was being paranoid, but she decided not to comment on that. "No. Was that so hard?" she asked, then, unable to refrain, she had to put another question to him. "Why is it you want to play games all the time?"

"Games can be fun," he told her with what could have only been referred to as a sexy leer.

Kristin knew she should be annoyed or indignant— or both—and probably should just walk out now, while she still had the chance. Cavanaugh, she knew, was way too charming for her own good.

But they were in a public place, and as long as they were, Kristin knew she was safe enough to relax a little and just have dinner with the man. She didn't want him thinking she was being a coward. And, she reminded herself, there quite possibly might even be some informative conversation on the agenda.

Besides, if things did start to go south on her, her car was within sprinting distance. She was confident that she could get to the vehicle quickly in order to make her getaway.

But, in all honesty, she had to admit that she doubted it would come to that.

Oh, God, she realized, she was beginning to actually trust him.

"At times," she allowed, repeating what he'd just said

before she added her own footnote to the words. "I don't think that this is one of those times."

She was surprised to see him smile in response. The detective's smile told her that he knew more than she did about what she'd just said.

"That remains to be seen," Malloy replied.

Holding the door for her, he waited until Kristin walked inside, then followed her in.

The interior of Jerry's was not so dimly lit that patrons had trouble making out the faces of the people sitting across from them, yet definitely was not bright enough to detect any flaws, both with their food and with the person sitting opposite them.

Malloy felt it was the perfect compromise and said as much to his companion.

Kristin was quick to catch the contradiction. "I thought you said the food here was good."

"I did and it is. But nothing's perfect," he said matter-of-factly.

"Will this be all right?" the hostess asked, bringing them to a booth.

Rather than answer, Malloy looked at Kristin, waiting for her to respond. "It's fine," she replied, surprised that Malloy had deferred to her. After all, the man was nothing if not a take-charge personality.

Once the hostess had withdrawn and Kristin had taken her seat, Malloy followed suit and then asked, "What's your pleasure?"

Caught off guard, Kristin could only stare at him. He wasn't blatantly saying what she thought he was— was he? "What?"

"What's your pleasure?" Malloy repeated, his smile growing just another shade wider.

The gleam in his eye made her think that she was right. So much for subtlety.

"You're asking that now?" she demanded. "Here?" She didn't bother hiding her annoyance.

"I'm talking about food," he pointed out mildly. "What are you talking about?"

She felt like an idiot. What was wrong with her? She was usually far more in control and put together than this. She kept anticipating him putting moves on her, and he was being nothing but polite. Was this the real him—or just part of his game to get her off her guard?

"Steak," she told him between clenched teeth. "I like steak."

"Must be hard to chew if you keep your jaw locked like that," he observed. Closing the menu that the hostess had given him, Malloy leaned over the table. Lowering his voice so that he wouldn't be overheard, he said, "Relax, Doc. We're just here to eat—and maybe talk a little more about the case if you'd like. Nothing else."

The last sentence sounded as if he was giving her his word.

Even so, Kristin still looked at him uncertainly. "Nothing else?" she repeated.

"Nothing else," Malloy said again, his voice mild as he straightened in the booth. "Just two colleagues, grabbing a bite to eat, discussing a cold case they're working."

The waitress came by then to take their order, and he paused, looking at Kristin politely.

"Steak, please."

"How would you like that?" the waitress asked.

"Rare."

Out of the corner of her eye, she saw Malloy smile

to himself. She had to stop doing that, she told herself. She had to stop trying to figure out what he was thinking. Whatever it was, it didn't matter, Kristin silently insisted.

The waitress went on to ask her what kind of side dishes she wanted and how she liked them prepared. As Kristin responded, Malloy's smile deepened.

And then she knew why.

"And what would you like, sir?" the waitress asked, turning her attention to him.

"I'll have the same," he answered, giving her his menu. "Guess we have more in common than we thought," he said to Kristin.

As the waitress withdrew with their orders, he asked, "You've really never been here before?"

"No, why?"

"Because, from your order, you obviously like steak, and Jerry's has the best steak in the city. The place has been here for the past forty years," he told her. And although he'd only lived here a short while, it wasn't as if he hadn't come here on more than one occasion before he'd relocated.

"When you don't go looking for something, then you won't find it," Kristin told him. "Whenever I have a craving for steak, I usually buy one in the grocery store and make my own."

The sides of his eyes crinkled. "I love a take-charge woman."

She thought they weren't going to do this now. She just wanted to enjoy dinner. "Cavanaugh," she said in a warning voice.

"Sorry," he apologized, then repeated as if it was

some kind of a mantra, "Just a friendly dinner, just a friendly dinner."

"Which could turn very unfriendly very quickly," she reminded him.

Kristin had to admit that she was surprised when he looked directly into her eyes and said, "You really don't mean that."

She wanted to say yes and that he had no idea what she meant. He didn't know her. But somehow, the words just refused to materialize.

Instead, what she did manage to say was, "Let's not put it to the test."

His eyes were smiling at her, as if he knew she was all talk and nothing more.

She was exceedingly tempted to show him how wrong he was, but she had to admit that he was being nothing but polite, and she couldn't very well repay him for that by being nasty to him.

Taking a deep breath, she told herself to relax. Never mind that he had given her the same advice a few minutes ago. She wasn't trying to let go of the tension she was harboring for his sake; she was trying to let go of it for hers because at the moment, her nerves had taken over and were literally making her feel as if she was going to shatter into small pieces at any moment.

She couldn't put her finger on the exact reason why she felt this way—or maybe she could but felt safer if she didn't.

The trouble was, she didn't want to live life in the safe lane.

Slow and steady might very well win the race, but she didn't want to win it that way. Because even if you did win the race that way, where was the passion, the sense of victory and fulfillment that went with a win?

A win wasn't a win until it was actually felt in every part of your being.

It was official, she thought, looking into Malloy's green eyes; the man was making her crazy.

Chapter 15

The minutes seemed to speed by, and they wound up talking longer over dinner than she thought they would.

The most surprising thing about that was Kristin found it easy. Not just listening to him, because she was fairly accomplished when it came to listening—or at least *looking* as if she was listening—but talking to him, as well. That was the part that she really found surprising.

Because talking was trickier, especially when it came to talking about things that mattered. Mattered personally, rather than things like liver temperature and approximate time of death, which were in the realm of her job, not her *life*.

Before Kristin knew it, almost two hours had gone by, they'd eaten their meals, had dessert and the waitress had come by to refill their coffee cups for a third time.

Shifting somewhat self-consciously—how had she managed to go on like that?—she glanced at her watch for confirmation.

It was even later than she'd thought.

"I didn't realize it was getting so late." She should have left an hour ago, she upbraided herself, if not before.

Malloy shrugged casually. "For some people, the evening hasn't even started."

"Those people probably don't have to get up early to go to work." She made it a point to arrive at work each day before she was supposed to, catching up on whatever might have happened after her shift.

Kristin picked up her purse and opened it. "What does my half come to?"

"You don't have a half," Malloy told her.

She wasn't about to get into the habit of having him pay for her. That constituted a debt, and she made it a point not to feel as if she owed anyone anything except her best efforts.

"We ate exactly the same thing, right down to the chocolate cream pie and the coffee. It's only fair that I pay for half," Kristin insisted. "Now what is it?"

She reached for the receipt that the waitress had brought back after Malloy had put the amount on his credit card. It would be a simple enough matter to divide it in half.

But he pulled the receipt away before she could get it.

"Sorry, none of us Cavanaugh boys were raised that way," he told her, affecting a Southern twang. "The male of the species pays. Even if he's going out with his sister," he qualified when he saw her begin to protest. "It's just the way things are. Live with it," Malloy added pleasantly.

The hell she would. "I don't like being in debt to anyone for anything."

He should have known she was going to give him a hard time over something he viewed as routine behavior. "Okay, you want to consider debts and their payments— just consider this my payment for the pleasure of your company."

It was a line and she knew it was a line, but he said it with such sincerity and conviction that she could have very easily bought into it.

And that, she reminded herself, was the man's gift.

Frustrated, she wasn't about to argue in public. Instead, she said, "I pick up the next check."

His eyes instantly gleamed. "The next check, eh? Gives me something to look forward to."

Too late she realized that she'd said exactly what he'd wanted her to say. She'd just given validity to the notion that there was going to be a next time for them. Another meal, another several hours where very little about work was aired.

She needed to be on her guard more, Kristin thought, shaking her head. "You are a very devious man."

His smile seemed to unfurl like a flag on a windy day. "I'll take that as a compliment."

"I'm not sure I meant it that way," she told him as they walked out. It was a criticism more than anything else—for him as well as for herself.

"So what did you think of the place?" he asked her as they each reached their respective vehicles and came to a full stop.

Kristin glanced over her shoulder at the building

they had just left. "Quaint. Nice. Homey." She paused after each word, giving herself time to think of the next one. She would have preferred to have found it lacking, but she hadn't, and she couldn't lie, even to him. "I like it," she concluded.

He looked genuinely pleased, and she couldn't help wondering why it would make a difference to him if she liked the place or not.

"Thought you might," he told her.

She was lingering, Kristin realized. Lingering and maybe waiting for something she knew she shouldn't be waiting for. Taking a breath, she silently upbraided herself. She needed to make a quick getaway before she was tempted to go further.

"Well, thanks for dinner," she announced abruptly. "I'll see you tomorrow."

"Tomorrow," he repeated.

Malloy held her door open for her as she slid in behind the steering wheel, then closed it as she buckled up.

Taking a breath, Kristin backed out of the space and then drove off the lot. She allowed herself only one backward glance in the rearview mirror. Malloy was just getting into his car.

Eyes on the road, Kris, she lectured herself. *You don't need to watch him.*

She had driven a total of three blocks when she looked up into her rearview mirror again. The car traveling a couple of lengths behind her seemed vaguely familiar.

It was Malloy's car.

Keeping her eyes on the road, she reached into the purse she'd tossed in the passenger seat and rummaged around until she located her phone. Operating purely by touch, Kristin inserted her smartphone into the phone holder she had mounted on her dashboard. Once she was sure that her phone was secure, she tapped out his number on the keyboard.

In less than half a ring, Malloy answered.

"Cavanaugh," he responded whimsically.

She could almost feel his eyes boring into the back of her head. It made her angrier. "Yes, I know. What I don't know is why you're following me home." She remembered the reason he'd given her last time. "This is a brand-new tire, so it can't be to make sure that it doesn't blow before I get home."

"You're right, it's not. The reason's far more old-fashioned than that," he told her.

She glanced up into the rearview mirror, even though she knew he really couldn't see her, and at this distance, she couldn't see him, either.

"Okay, I'll bite. What is it?" she asked.

"A gentleman always makes sure a lady gets home safely," he told her.

A gentleman, eh? "You have someone else in the car with you?" she quipped.

He took no offense. He'd come to expect her parrying and would have been disappointed if she hadn't made a crack.

"Nope, just me. Now stop talking on the phone, Kristin," he said, "or a cop's liable to pull you over and give you a ticket for that."

A lot he knew. "I'm not using my hands," she told him.

The pause before he spoke was long and thoughtful. "Now there's an image."

Biting back a few choice words, Kristin disconnected the call.

He followed her all the way home.

And, just as the first time, when she parked in her garage, he pulled up into her driveway. But this time, she walked out to her driveway as well and electronically closed the garage door.

"Mission completed," she declared when he stepped out of his vehicle. "You saw me home safely."

"Technically, the 'mission' isn't complete until I see you walk into your home and turn on the lights to make sure everything's secure."

The way he said it made her think of the manner in which police secured a building. "Is that going to entail you coming in, gun drawn and clearing every room, one at a time?"

She did have a flair for the dramatic, Malloy thought, amused. "I hadn't thought of that, but now that you mention it, that would definitely complete the mission."

"Let me put your mind at ease," she said with a touch of sarcasm. "I have very nosy neighbors. If anyone was seen breaking into my house, they would have lost no time calling 911, and we would have seen the house surrounded by squad cars when we pulled up. Nobody's here," she guaranteed.

He wondered if she had any idea just how strongly attracted he was to her and how much it took for him not to act on that attraction.

"You can never be too careful," he told her, although he remained standing exactly where he was. He wasn't about to push. He didn't believe in it. Things either happened naturally, or they didn't.

"You're not going in," she observed, stating the obvious. Her stomach had been churning ever since she'd spotted him in her review mirror, following her home. Right about now, her fingertips had joined the act, growing icy as her palms did the exact opposite, sending heat through the rest of her.

His eyes met hers. His voice was almost seductively low as he asked, "Do you want me to go in?"

His question was reminiscent of what he'd told her the other day. That he would never do anything she didn't want him to do. He was waiting for an invitation, she realized. All she had to do was say no, and she'd be out of danger. He'd leave.

Just one little two-letter word, that was all it would take.

She took a breath.

And then she heard herself saying, "Get it over with."

Malloy arched one eyebrow, puzzled. "Get what over with?"

There was almost defiance in her eyes as she continued looking up at him.

"Kiss me," she told him. "Kiss me so that we can both get it out of the way and get on with our lives."

He was trying hard not to laugh. "I don't think I've ever heard it put quite that romantically before."

She'd almost doubled up her fists then, wanting to pound him on his chest.

Instead, Kristin managed to keep her hands at her sides as she retorted, "I'm not trying to be romantic, I'm trying to be efficient."

Well, that was a new one on him. "Oh, is that what you call it? Efficient? Never heard it referred to as that before."

Her chin was raised in that defiant way he'd come to recognize.

"*This* is in the way for both of us for different reasons," she retorted, feeling almost desperate because of the havoc that was going on inside of her.

She knew that he wanted to kiss her in order to prove to her that he could turn her world upside down. As for her, with increasing frequency, she'd been catching herself wondering what it was like to be kissed by him. It was now at the point that it was a part of every hour of every day. She wanted it to stop.

"And I don't think we can really continue productively working together until we resolve this—this—*issue*," she cried for lack of a better word, "and move passed it."

"Okay," he said gamely, "if that's what you really want." Malloy took her into his arms. "Just remember that this was your idea."

There it was again, she thought. That grin of his. That wicked grin that was half sin, half redemption. She still fought it, still tried to seal herself off from its effects, but it was a losing battle.

"What I really want is not to have it cropping up on me all the time, taking my thoughts prisoner like some kind of guerilla soldier on a mission."

"So let me get this straight," he said, doing his best to keep a straight face. "If I kiss you, then this will all be over? The wondering, the anticipating, all of it would be over? Finished?" The way he posed his question made her feel that he highly doubted that would be the outcome.

"God, I hope so." The words rushed out, riding a heartfelt sigh.

Malloy deliberately leaned in as if to kiss her, then drew his head back at the last possible moment. When she widened her eyes, looking at him both surprised and confused, he said, "Maybe we should take this inside," then explained, "Nosy neighbors," reminding her of what she'd just told him about her neighborhood.

Inside.

He wanted to take this inside.

This was a step she hadn't quite thought out. A step that was certain to instantly make everything twice as intimate as before.

But she couldn't very well back out now, not when it had been her idea to do this in the first place. He was counting on that, wasn't he? she thought, seeing the confidence in his eyes. It made her resolve twice over to be immune to him no matter how torrid the kiss turned out to be.

So she murmured something akin to agreement and put her key into the lock. The *click* that resounded as the lock was released echoed and magnified itself in her head.

Malloy reached behind her and turned the knob, opening the door for her.

Like someone who was caught up in the remnants of a dream, Kristin crossed the threshold and walked inside her house.

The next moment, he followed her steps and eased the door closed behind him. She expected him to take the lead, but he didn't. Good, bad or neutral, whatever was going to happen next would be entirely up to her.

She felt her heart pounding hard.

"Oh, all right!" she cried out loud in something that resembled terrified frustration.

The next moment, she threw her arms around his neck and brought her mouth up to his.

She'd just meant to complete the act. Lips against lips, skin against skin. The promise of the act was supposed to be far more enticing and fulfilling—at least on the mental level—than the actual execution of the act itself.

Supposed to be.

But reality had a way of playing havoc on expectations, good or bad. And in this case, the expectations paled in the face of reality. Because it wasn't lip against lip and skin against skin. It turned out to be lightning and thunder, wind and gale and, in all likelihood, a little hurricane and earthquake thrown in, as well.

The latter because Kristin could have sworn, as the kiss kept deepening and deepening to the point that she thought she was in danger of falling off the edge of the world, that the earth had moved beneath her.

Definitely moved.

Not just a tiny bit that would have caused her to doubt her perception, but moved with a mighty jolt. So mighty that she was surprised she was still standing.

Had his arms not tightened around her the way that they had just then, she was certain that she would have fallen. Especially since her knees had somehow been obliterated, taking on the consistency of cotton after it had been left out in the rain for three days.

She wound up clinging to him for dear life even as her mouth remained sealed to his, and something akin to ecstasy riding a lightning bolt darted through her entire body, leaving no part of her untouched.

Chapter 16

Okay. She'd done it.

She'd kissed him, and yes, it had turned out to be a great deal more than she'd bargained for, Kristin realized. But even so, she actually *did* bargain on that in her own way.

Because this was Malloy Cavanaugh, and countless women couldn't be wrong.

But she'd satisfied her curiosity. So now was the time to push him back, declare "Done. Finished. Moving on with my life," and then do it.

In a second.

One more second.

Just one more second.

This was never going to happen again, so she needed to have it last a little longer in order to create that firm imprint in her mind that wouldn't immediately fade at first light.

Oh, who the hell was she kidding? In a heartbeat she'd gotten a ton more than she'd bargained for, and if she lived to be two hundred and twenty-four, this was *not* an impression that would fade, not at first light, not at *any* light.

Ever.

She was just using that as an excuse. She didn't want this to stop.

This was insane, and Kristin knew it, but the rush had seized her. Her heart was pounding so hard and so loud, she was certain she would go deaf.

It didn't matter.

She didn't care.

Malloy had wanted this from the very first moment he'd seen her, looking so stern and professional as she was bending over that mismatched pile of bones that had been dug up. But the longer he waited, the longer he'd wanted to wait, because somewhere inside his head, a little voice had whispered that if he proceeded the way he'd always proceeded, he would get what he'd always gotten, which in the end were just very pleasant memories and an empty space beside him as well as inside of him.

Kristin was different.

He'd sensed it, knew it, and winning her would mean winning not the brass ring but the gold one. The one that carried a great deal of weight with it, not the least of which was commitment, *real* commitment, something he'd never really considered.

In all honesty, he didn't even know if he was capable of it.

And Kristin wasn't the kind of woman meant for a

fling or a tryst or two. She was a woman of substance, a woman for all time.

And maybe, just maybe, a woman who was too good for him.

But all that belonged in his cerebral realm.

Physically, emotionally, it was a completely different story.

Every fiber of his being wanted her, wanted to kiss her, to touch her, to make love with her until he was too tired, too worn out to breathe.

The rest of it he'd sort out later. He had no will left, no strength to deny himself what he wanted so supremely.

The actual lovemaking began on her doorstep the second their eyes met. Once inside the house, he started to make love to her in earnest. With his hands, softly touching, caressing, worshipping and, all the while, moving the cloth obstacles away from her body.

With each pass of his hands and each inch of skin that was exposed, he heard Kristin's breathing growing ever so slightly more pronounced.

Heard his own breathing increasing in tandem. Felt his heart pounding harder as he drew closer and closer to his goal.

She excited him more than any woman he had ever wanted. Any woman he had ever had.

From the beginning, she'd been so cool, so reserved, yet in his heart he'd been certain that a wildcat lived beneath all that icy control.

And he'd been right. He found that exciting beyond words.

The word "Stop!" echoed in Kristin's mind, growing weaker and weaker because she really didn't want him to stop.

As Malloy advanced, she moved back, but not because she was trying to create a chasm between them, but because she wanted to lead him farther into her house, into her living room.

Into her life.

Losing her bearings for a moment, Kristin stumbled backward when the back of her calf encountered the light tan sofa that was against the far wall of the room.

Caught off guard—every fiber of her being completely consumed by the onslaught of his lips—Kristin fell onto the sofa, and he fell with her.

His body pressed hard against hers.

That only further ignited her desire, all but setting her body on fire in every single place that his had touched.

Whatever articles of clothing were still left between them—and they were few—were quickly, impatiently, dealt with and discarded.

And all the while, he continued bathing every inch of her with ardent, openmouthed kisses that were swiftly becoming her entire undoing.

She arched her body in a silent offering as his lips and tongue continued to hold her hostage, making her quite possibly the most willing prisoner in history.

Kristin felt her head spinning, mimicking the rhythm of her heart. Shaken to the core, she half sat up, seeking his mouth and then sealing hers to it.

Her breathing was so ragged, so labored she was in danger of either hyperventilating or suffocating. She did neither. All she wanted, all she focused on, was doing whatever she could to hang on to to this wild, dizzying roller-coaster ride that had become a free fall through space for her.

She clung to Malloy harder.

* * *

Kristin was making him crazy, and he couldn't hold out much longer.

By his own reckoning, he'd already gone past all human limits that he'd thought himself capable of attaining. And then, unable to maintain the last shred of restraint any longer, Malloy moved until their bodies were perfectly aligned and, pausing for just one split second so that he could look into her eyes, he sank into her and united them.

Not with a driving force that had taken over his being, but slowly, like the calm within the center of a turbulent squall. He didn't want Kristin to remember this as a sudden storming of her body, but as a passion-laden union of two equal beings. He had nothing to prove, no conquest to triumph over. He just wanted to be with her and have her want to be with him.

Once he'd entered her, Malloy began to move with rhythm and purpose, increasing both with each heartbeat, each complementing movement he felt on her part.

She didn't just follow, she led.

They each did, taking turns until the rhythm reached an overpowering crescendo, and the final ecstasy found them, wrapping them both in its breath-stealing shower of fireworks.

He held her as if letting go meant certain death. And if death did come right at that moment, then it came. He was where he wanted to be.

With her.

The shower that had enshrouded them retreated by slow, saddening increments. He went on holding Kristin, not wanting to acknowledge the change, the feeling of loss.

His heart was still pounding, as was hers, he noted with secret satisfaction. Slowly, both hearts returned to a semblance of their former states. Still, he didn't want to let Kristin go, even as he wondered how much longer he could go on holding her.

When he felt her stir against him, he knew his time was almost up. The rest of life was waiting. He wanted it to wait a little longer, but he knew that was asking for too much.

He took a few more subtle breaths, waiting for the world to return to normal—if that was even possible.

"I don't know about you, but for me, that was a surprise," he admitted quietly.

Kristin could feel every word he said rumbling against her skin as she lay there with her cheek pressed against his chest.

She raised her head now to look at him, wondering if, now that it was over, he was mocking her. "What do you mean, a surprise?"

He brushed his lips against her hair. "Just that."

She tried to make sense out of what he was telling her and couldn't. It was still all too vague. "You didn't think I was capable of passion?" she guessed. Her eyes unaccountably stung as she said that.

"Oh, I had a feeling that you were," he assured her. Feeling her breath along his abdomen was definitely having an effect on him. He tried to concentrate on what he was saying. "I just didn't think it was to that level. I didn't think *I* was capable of reaching that level, either."

Malloy took a breath, trying to steady his pulse, trying to clear his brain.

"So, did this settle things for you?" he asked, referring to what she'd said on her doorstep. "Can you move on now?"

This was the part where she said yes. Where she added some kind of sophisticated words that would make Malloy think that this meant no more to her than it did to him. All she had to do was say it and be free of him.

But what came out was a question, one that, if she had an ounce of self-preservation running through her veins, would have never seen the light of day.

"Do you want me to?" she asked him.

Ordinarily, he would have said something to the effect that she was her own person, that she could do whatever she wanted to do. That whatever she chose was good with him.

Instead, he breathed, "Oh, hell, no," and shifted her so that his body was leaning into hers with his *really* feeling the effects of wanting her all over again, as if he'd never had her—as if he'd *always* had her and just wanted more.

His voice was almost ragged as he told her, "I want to make love with you all over again, bit by bit, until we're both too tired to breathe. And then I want to make love with you one more time."

"Are you always this insatiable?" she asked, already feeling her excitement heightening in anticipation of what was to be.

A giddiness was bubbling inside of her like a newly uncorked bottle of champagne.

"There is no 'always,'" he told her quietly. Earnestly. "This is different. I can't explain it. Not to you, not even to myself," he said with sincerity, almost worshipfully framing her face with his hands. "I can only tell you what I'm feeling right this minute."

Kristin was trying very hard not to let herself be swept away. Not to allow herself to believe that out of all the women Malloy had ever known, not to mention the ones he had been with, he felt that she was the one who stood out. The one who was *different*.

She knew better.

And yet, when she looked into his eyes, she knew nothing except that she wanted him to make love with her again, wanted him to take her to the very pinnacle of the world, to the very top of the mountain and then, holding her hand, jump off so she could feel that wild, heart-racing rush consuming her again.

Trying very hard to keep Malloy emotionally at arm's length, to keep him from getting through the last plate of her swiftly cracking armor, she said, "They said you were good."

"'Good' has nothing to do with it," Malloy told her, pressing kisses first to one shoulder, then the other, before moving on to the hollow of her throat where the very touch of his lips created tidal waves in the core of her body.

She could feel herself throbbing, wanting him.

If she had an ounce of integrity left, she would have said something flippant, pushed him away and then called it a night, sending him on his way. She knew, *knew* deep in her bones that this was just a fling for Malloy.

But rather than terminate the evening on her own terms, she wanted to absorb as much of what was happening as she could so that she could store it and, months from now, comfort herself with the thought that she had at least had this one perfect evening in her life—even if she'd never admit it to him. Because until now, she hadn't realized that she was capable of this level of feeling, this level of joy and ecstasy. Malloy had brought her not just to the threshold of a world she hadn't known existed, he'd made her realize that there was such a thing as paradise.

With the right man.

Or the wrong one, depending on a person's view of Malloy Cavanaugh, she thought, her mouth curving despite herself.

He felt her mouth curving beneath his and drew his head back to look at her. "Something you'd like to share with the class, Kristin?"

She looked at him uncertainly. "What?"

"You were just smiling," Malloy told her. "And I was just wondering why."

"I'm not about to flatter you, Malloy."

"I'm not asking you to flatter me," he told her simply. "I just wanted to know what I did to make you smile."

Suspicion flickered in her eyes. She wanted him, but trust was a completely different issue. He was up to something. "Why?"

"So I could do it again." He touched her face, brushing his fingers along her cheek. "Make you smile like that again."

"Shut up and kiss me," she all but ordered.

It was his turn to smile—and he did. Teasingly. "Is that all it takes?"

Her eyes were dancing, and she had no idea what prompted her to say what she did, all but giving him carte blanche. "You can make it up as you go along."

"Whatever you want." He shifted and pressed a kiss to her temple. "Your wish is my command."

That kiss, small as it was, vibrated all through her. The man had a gift all right, there was no denying that.

"For now," she murmured.

Malloy pulled her to him, about to kiss her. But he stopped for a second, his eyes meeting hers as he said, in all seriousness, "That's all we have, Kristin. All we have is 'now.'"

He was right. There was no way to guess at what tomorrow held. Those young women whose bodies they had unearthed at the nursery had never thought their lives would be so brief or end so abruptly.

Every second of life was precious and shouldn't be wasted.

She wasn't going to waste another second of "now" because "later" most likely wouldn't work out.

With that thought echoing in her brain, Kristin passionately sealed her mouth to his and lost herself in Malloy's embrace.

Chapter 17

Malloy stayed the night.

Part of Kristin felt that she should have called it a night and sent him home at some point, but that part was at war with the one that just wanted to hang on to the moment, the interlude that had been created and had, in all likelihood, the life expectancy of a large, glistening soap bubble. All too soon it would burst, and then it would be as if it had never existed at all. All too soon.

So Malloy stayed.

In her house.

In her bed.

Stayed until first light crept into the darkened room, lightening it with tiny, delicate, baby steps until darkness was just a memory.

Kristin woke up first.

He seemed to be so soundly asleep that, although

she knew she should take advantage of the moment and quickly slip away, she allowed herself to linger for a moment, just looking at him.

Asleep, his hair unruly, Malloy appeared almost innocent. She knew better, of course, but if she hadn't, if she had no idea who he was, if his reputation hadn't preceded him, she would have said that he looked almost boyish and adorable, rather than roguishly sexy and possessing an utterly lethal mouth.

And if he were the former rather than the latter, she definitely could have—

Could have nothing, Kris, she upbraided herself, mentally pulling back. She couldn't give in to the temptation, to the things that she was feeling—that she *shouldn't* be feeling, she warned herself fiercely. Not even for a moment. This was *Malloy Cavanaugh*, playboy nonpareil. *Proceed at your own risk and prepare to have your heart ripped out of your chest if you let your guard down again*, she silently warned.

Taking a breath, Kristin began to slowly ease out of her bed. And as she did so, she never took her eyes off Malloy in case her movements, careful as they were, began to wake him.

She could have saved herself the trouble.

No sooner had she put her bare feet on the floor than she heard Malloy ask—in a voice that was definitely *not* sleepy, "So, do I look better in the dark, or in morning's first light?"

Startled, she froze. "You're awake?"

The second the words were out of her mouth, she realized it was a stupid question, but he had caught her completely by surprise.

There it was again, that sexy grin. "No, I'm talking in my sleep."

Annoyed, Kristin curbed the very strong urge to punch him. Thank God she hadn't said anything that she was thinking out loud. She knew he'd never let her live it down.

"How long have you been awake?" she asked.

"Doesn't matter," he told her, this time opening his eyes. The moment he did, she felt as if she was the only person in the immediate world. His eyes held her prisoner. "So, do I pass inspection?" he asked teasingly.

She didn't know what he was waiting to hear. She felt awkward and was, at this moment, desperately searching for some sort of footing. Last night had set fire to the rule book she'd been trying to abide by, and she was back to square one.

She'd let her guard down and allowed him into her world. For the *whole* night. There was no way she could erase that.

"This doesn't change anything," she informed him, trying to sound indifferent.

"If you say so." His expression was completely straight—except for the telltale curve in the left corner of his mouth. "Of course," he added loftily, "you might sound a bit more convincing if you weren't standing there, nude, as you were saying it."

"I'm not nude," she retorted. "I've got a blanket against me." A blanket she was clutching so hard, her fingers felt as if they were in danger of breaking off.

Malloy playfully tugged at the blanket's edge. "We've got a little while before we need to be in. Why don't you drop that thing—" he tugged on it again "—and we'll make the most of the time we have."

She wanted to. More than anything, she wanted to. But then he would see just how entrenched he'd become in her world after just one night. She couldn't allow him to know that. She needed to maintain some shred, however small, of dignity. Otherwise, he'd think of her as needy, and that had never been her.

Besides, men ran from needy women unless they were insecure and abusive, and whatever else he might be, Malloy was neither insecure nor abusive.

He was unattainable, and she had known that right from the start.

Kristin raised her chin, entering self-preservation mode.

"I plan to make the most of it—by taking a shower and getting ready for work. You're welcome to take one, too," she said as matter-of-factly as she could manage as she walked away. "There's a shower in the guest bathroom down the hall."

With that, she went into the adjacent bathroom, closed the door and flipped the lock. Only when the door was locked did she drop the blanket to the floor and step into the shower stall.

Her heart was pounding as she started the water. She'd just barely managed to walk away from Malloy. He'd looked so damn desirable, lying there. The temptation to leap into bed and join him, make love with him all over again, had been almost overwhelming, but somehow, she'd been able to resist.

Kristin had barely had time to congratulate herself for her superhuman efforts when she felt a slight breeze directly at her back. Before she could turn to see if the shower door had opened for some reason, Malloy was slipping into the shower with her.

Stunned, Kristin stared up at him. "I flipped the lock," she cried.

"And I unflipped it," he told her.

"You picked the lock," she accused in disbelief.

"Maybe." Malloy shrugged casually. "I pick things up along the way. Pass the soap."

"I told you that you could use the guest shower," Kristin cried helplessly, doing her best to fight the very strong urges that were spinning and twisting throughout her entire body.

He was unfazed by her protest. "I thought this was more efficient. Despite the occasional surprise cloudburst, we *are* in the middle of a prolonged drought, and we all need to do our part in conserving water. This is my part," he told her, a mischievous smile playing on his lips.

His hand extending beyond her, Malloy reached for the soap that was resting in the dish on the shelf just above her head. In doing so, he was forced to move forward. His body brushed, then pressed, against hers.

"There *is* something to be said for close quarters," he told her, his eyes smiling into hers.

The next thing she knew, the soap, the shower and everything else was forgotten. Malloy was kissing her again, and her entire body was on fire.

Just before he took her into his arms, Malloy shut off the water.

"Conservation," he murmured against her mouth a second before he kissed her again.

Kristin forgot about getting into work on time.

The last time she could recall feeling *this* exhausted walking into work, she had pulled back-to-back all-nighters interning at University Hospital.

It completely mystified Kristin how she could feel this charged and this worn out at the same time. Malloy was turning her inside out.

The problem was, she liked it. Liked the way he made her feel, liked being with him.

And she was setting herself up for a huge fall.

You're a big girl, Kris. You'll bounce back.

Forcing her mind back on her work, Kristin quickly checked in at the morgue, making sure that there were no new cases, no new bodies that had been brought in overnight needing to be autopsied. That left her free to accompany Malloy when he went to question the detective who had investigated Abby Sullivan's disappearance.

To her surprise, Malloy had actually remembered that he'd agreed to that, to take her with him when he went to talk to the investigator who had handled the missing person case.

"I've got a name," Malloy announced, calling her on her cell five minutes after she had walked into the morgue. "We're in luck," he went on. "The guy's retired, but he's alive—which is definitely a plus—and he's in our part of the state, which makes him accessible, although it means a road trip. I'm driving out to his place in twenty minutes."

Habit had her glancing at her watch. "I'll be in the parking lot in ten," she told him. "I just have to sign out on the board so they know where to find me in case something comes up and they need me."

He didn't want to put her out, although the idea of a road trip with her was really appealing. Rather than slipping into a holding zone after having spent the night and morning with her, he found himself wanting her again. Wanting her even more than he had before. This was a new wrinkle in his life.

Still, he didn't want her facing a backlog when she returned. "You don't have to come if you have work," he reminded her. "I can tell you if I find anything out when I get back."

Was he trying to extricate himself out of her life so quickly? "Sorry, Malloy. You're not weaseling out of this," she said flatly.

"Why would I want to?" he asked. "I was just trying to make things easy for you."

"Easy doesn't interest me," she informed him.

"I am beginning to realize that." His laugh washed over her, warming her. "Okay, then. See you in the parking lot."

"Count on it," she told him.

"I am."

Kristin smiled to herself as she terminated the phone call.

Ten minutes later had them meeting in the parking lot. "We're driving to wine country," Malloy told her as they got into his car. "Mahoney retired six years ago to Sonoma. His wife came into an inheritance, and they bought themselves a little vineyard. What do you plan on doing when you retire, Kristin?"

"Being dead," she answered.

"Come again?"

"I plan to work until I die," she said simply. "I like my work, like finding pieces of the puzzle and putting them together to solve mysteries, or at least answer questions. If I can't do that, there's not that much point in going on. How about you? What are your big plans?"

"I don't plan," he told her. "I just go on, and life just happens around me, surprising me."

She could well believe that.

Retired Detective Dan Mahoney was a man who had worked in several different departments at the police station before he retired. It was only then, after he retired, he liked to tell people that he finally found his true element.

After years of conducting diligent police investigations, working cases that, for more than half of them, remained opened and unsolved, the still powerful-looking man with the round, beach-ball face looked to be at peace with the world he had chosen for himself.

"Put every last dime my wife and I had into buying this little gem of a vineyard," Mahoney was saying in a voice that over the years had been coated with a liquid that was stronger than the one Mahoney was now in charge of producing.

He looked around with marked pride at the land he was giving them a tour of. "We don't put out anything earthshaking that'll put us on anyone's map, but it's a respectable little chardonnay, and we make a fairly decent living at it. Our needs are modest at this point," he added.

Mahoney grinned, the lines about his mouth and cheeks deepening considerably.

"And the best part is, the bottles don't shoot at me. So," he said expansively, glancing from Malloy to the woman with him, "what is it you and the little lady here drove all this way out to talk to me about?"

Malloy got right down to it. He had a feeling that Mahoney could probably go on for hours about the vineyard if he was even the slightest bit encouraged.

"You worked a missing person case twenty years ago. A college student by the name of Abby Sullivan went missing when she came back to UCA her sophomore year. I've got the flyer for you to look at right here," Malloy offered, reaching into his pocket. After all this time, he didn't doubt that the detective's memory might need some help.

Mahoney waved the offer away. "Don't need it. I remember the case," he told Malloy. "Remember the parents mostly," the man went on, shaking his head. "The pain in their eyes when they talked about that girl, it was enough to make a rock bleed. I gave my best to each case I worked, but I worked harder than I'd ever worked before on that case, trying to get some kind of lead to find that girl," he admitted. "But it just wasn't good enough." He was talking to the past now, more than he was talking to them. "Finally had to just chalk it up to another runaway case."

"Why runaway?" Kristin asked. She'd kept quiet up until now, only giving the retired detective her name when they were exchanging introductions. But he had made her curious. "What made you think she just took off?"

The wide, slightly slumped shoulders shrugged haplessly. "I didn't find any evidence of foul play, not in her dorm, not in any of the usual student haunts at the time." He stopped walking and sat down in the shade. Despite the somewhat cool weather, he took off his wide-brimmed straw hat and fanned himself. "I remember some of the other students saying that she was a really friendly, outgoing girl. Only child, first time away from home. Trying her wings. That kind of thing," he said, looking at the faces of his visitors for acknowledgment. "You know the type."

"Do you remember if she had any boyfriends, any guys hanging around her?" Malloy asked.

The vineyard owner shook his head. "Not that I recall." And then something nudged at his memory. "Oh, wait, there was this one guy. I talked to him during the investigation. Seemed real concerned about her." He nodded his head as he spoke, as if confirming his own memory of the time in question. "He wasn't her boyfriend but said she had talked to him about wanting to get away from her parents because they were so strict. Asked him if he knew of any place she could go."

Mahoney looked at Malloy as he spoke. It was obvious that he considered the younger man the investigator. The woman he'd brought with him was window dressing. *Excellent* window dressing.

"Do you remember his name?" Malloy pressed.

"No," Mahoney admitted, but then his face became more animated. "But I know I wrote it down. I wrote everything down those days," he confided. "Memory wasn't worth a damn," he was forced to admit. "Just too many details to keep straight." Turning from the field, he gestured for them to follow him to his house in the distance. "Come with me."

Once they got to the house, Mahoney led them to a room on the first floor that was located at the rear of the structure. The door was locked. Mahoney fished through his pockets until he found the key he was looking for.

Opening the door, Mahoney didn't stand on ceremony. He walked in first.

From the looks of it, Kristin thought as she was the last to enter the room, the man's wife wasn't allowed in at all. There was dust absolutely everywhere, and the top of the scarred desk was a disaster area. It was obvious that the business end of his winery was *not* run from this room.

Mahoney pulled open the bottom drawer of a rusty, battered-looking metal file cabinet, and after rummaging through it for a long while, he finally found the file. Since there really was no flat surface available to him, he spread the pages on top of the miscellaneous papers on his desk.

He murmured to himself as he searched. Three pages of torn sheets later, he declared, "Parker. Kid's name was Anson Parker." He looked at Malloy, pleased with himself. "Now that I think of it, the kid *was* kind of intense. He called and asked me how the case was coming along a couple of times. I got the feeling he cared about the Sullivan girl."

"And he was another student on the campus at the time?" Malloy asked,

This time, Mahoney didn't need to think about the answer.

"Yeah. Agriculture or botany, some kind of earth thing," he told them, waving his hand around vaguely as if he was trying to capture the thought. And then his eyes narrowed as he looked at Malloy. "Why all this sudden interest in the girl after all this time? Did you find something?" he asked, his voice growing more eager as he considered the possibilities.

"Yeah," Malloy answered. "We found her body."

"So she *was* killed," Mahoney said. The triumph

was short-lived and hollow. "Poor kid. You got any idea who did it?"

"That's what we're trying to piece together," Kristin said, but she doubted that the man heard her. His attention was focused on Malloy.

The retired detective was regarding the active one with almost an envious eagerness. "Can I ask where you found her?"

"She was buried along the perimeter of a cacti and succulent nursery," Malloy informed the older man.

He chose his words carefully. Because he was retired, Mahoney was the equivalent of a regular civilian and, as such, not entitled to any more information than what the average citizen might be privy to listening to the morning news.

"A construction crew was bulldozing the land, and they accidentally dug up her remains." He paused, watching the retired detective's face before adding, "along with the remains of eleven other people."

There was genuine surprise on the other man's face. For now, Malloy ruled him out as a possible suspect. But that didn't mean that the man was completely out of the running. Retiring from the force didn't automatically prove his innocence.

"You're kidding me," Mahoney cried, staring at him. "Twelve bodies? Do you have any names? Any further form of ID's?"

"Just Abby's so far." No, that wasn't right. He recalled the second name and watched the man carefully as he said, "And her friend's, Zoe Roberts. We're still trying to identify the others."

Mahoney might have tried to give the aura of a man

happily retired from the force, but it was easy to see that a part of him missed it. His questions were almost eager.

"You think that the Sullivan girl was the victim of a serial killer?"

"Right now, we're open to any working theory," Malloy told him. They had to be getting back. The drive wasn't a short one. Taking out his card, he handed it to the retired detective. "You think of anything else that might have slipped your mind about this case, give me a call. Anytime," Malloy emphasized.

Mahoney looked down at the card in his hand, then back at Malloy. The expression on his face showed that his interest was definitely engaged. "I knew an Andrew Cavanaugh back in the day. Any relation?"

Malloy nodded. "He's my uncle."

Nodding and smiling, the other man pocketed the card. "Small world," the detective said. "Small world. I've told you everything, but I'll call you if I do remember anything else. But you've got to call me if there are any new developments on the case."

"It's a deal," Malloy said, shaking the man's hand again.

One, he hoped as he and Kristin began to walk away from former Detective Dan Mahoney and his vineyard, that would bear useful fruit.

Chapter 18

"What's your next move?" Kristin asked once they were back on the road.

She was looking at Malloy's profile and she saw him smile just a little. "Well," he told her after a beat, "I was thinking along the lines of dinner and a movie."

It took her a couple of seconds to realize that Malloy was teasingly referring to their yet-not-quite-formed relationship, not the case.

"I'm talking about the investigation," she told him evenly.

"Oh, that. Well, other than hoping that you and your assistants get lucky, matching those missing women from the flyers' dental X-rays to the skulls at the morgue—" he knew that was still in the really long-shot realm "—I haven't come up with any new avenues to pursue."

She heard the frustration in Malloy's voice. "What

about that nonboyfriend that Mahoney mentioned?" she asked. "The botany major or whatever he was supposed to be. I think the detective said his name was Anson something-or-other…"

"Parker," Malloy recalled, working his way over to the right lane on the freeway. "He said the guy's name was Anson Parker."

Now that Malloy said it, she remembered. "Right. Him. Both Mahoney and that UCA professor we talked to mentioned Parker, although she just remembered his major." As she talked, her idea took on shape. "Maybe there's a reason this Anson Parker stuck out in both their minds," she suggested.

"I suppose it's worth a shot," Malloy agreed, adding, "We're not exactly going anywhere with this right now. The cacti nursery's new owner's lawyer is still unreachable on that damn cruise he's on—"

"Still?" Kristin questioned. "Where is this cruise, the Bermuda Triangle?"

"I have no idea," he retorted, the frustration level in his voice rising. "All I know is that I can't reach him by phone or carrier pigeon—I tried the former just before I met you in the parking lot for our road trip—and the upshot of that is that I can't ask him questions about the sale—or the former owner's name."

Something wasn't right here, Kristin thought. "And you can't get your answers from the new owner?" she asked. "I admit that the guy didn't exactly strike me as being friendly and cooperative." The truth of it was he had been positively rude to her when she'd arrived and stated her business at the nursery. "But he didn't strike me as being a village idiot, either."

"He's not a village idiot," Malloy agreed, taking advantage of the open road and bearing down on his accelerator a little harder than he normally would have. "Just not the type who wanted to be bothered with any details. According to him, that's what he 'pays other people to do.' He has them iron out all the minutia so that all he has to do is bask in the spotlight and take all the final credit when the time comes."

Kristin fell silent, thinking, as he continued making excellent time and zigzagging through openings in the traffic as it began to build.

"How about the county registrar?" Kristin finally asked.

The line of conversation had been dropped a good ten minutes ago. "How about him for what?" Malloy asked.

"It's a she," Kristin stated matter-of-factly. "The county registrar's name is Barbara Allen. And her name is on every property tax bill that gets sent out every year," she told him, answering the unspoken question she saw in his eyes as to how she knew the woman's name. "And what I was getting at was how about going to the county office to find out the chain of ownership?"

"I'm listening," Malloy told her, waiting for her to continue.

"Every time the property changes hands, the sale and the name of the new owner has to be registered," she told him.

For some reason, he'd forgotten all about that. Rather than be embarrassed by the oversight, Malloy took it from there now. "If we find out who owned that piece of property approximately twenty years ago, maybe we can finally start finding out just what the hell was going on at that nursery that caused all those bodies to be buried there."

So far, a cursory check of the local news stories from that time frame had yielded absolutely nothing that would have allowed him to make a connection between the bodies and the nursery.

"So what are you going to do?" Kristin asked, eager to help in any way she could. She'd come to think of this as her case, as well. It was a definite first for her.

"What I'm going to do first is get you back to the morgue," Malloy answered.

She sighed. She wasn't in the mood to be teased. "That was a given," she informed him. "And then?" Kristin asked, turning in her seat to get a better look at his face.

The whimsical curve of his mouth told her that his first thoughts weren't exactly focused on the case. She had to admit, albeit only to herself, that she was having the same problem. She would have also had to have said that she'd be lying if she didn't admit that her first priority—work—kept slipping into the background in light of this new development in her life.

"And again, I'm talking about the case," she underscored.

Since she was obviously being serious, Malloy grew serious himself.

"I'd thought I'd get someone in tech support to go through the DMV database to see if Anson Parker still lives somewhere in the state. If we can find him, maybe he can enlighten us about who Abby associated with back then and if she actually talked about dropping out of college and running away, or if someone just arbitrarily thought that up."

"According to Mr. Sullivan, that was news to him and his wife," she reminded him.

"Parents are usually the last to know anything about their kids," he commented, discounting the man's statement.

"Are you speaking in generalities?" Kristin asked. Or was he basing it on personal experience, she couldn't help wondering.

"Why, you have a rebuttal to that?" Malloy asked, curious.

"Not a rebuttal, just a personal experience," she corrected. "Except for one glaring bone of contention, my mother and I were usually pretty much on the same wavelength when I was growing up."

"Glaring bone of contention," Malloy repeated, intrigued. "Let me guess. Your mother hated the guys you dated." That was usually the classic reason for mother-daughter conflict. He could remember specific examples of that within his own family of three sisters.

Boy, was he wrong, Kristin couldn't help thinking. The exact opposite had been true, which was why she'd kept her sparse dating life to herself.

"I'll have you know that my mother was prepared to literally *adore* any guy I brought in through the door as long as he wasn't Jack the Ripper," she informed him.

"So, then what was the glaring bone of contention?" he asked.

Kristin laughed shortly, mainly to herself. "The fact that I didn't bring in any guys through the door," she stated simply.

"You snuck them in through your bedroom window?" he guessed, trying to decide whether or not the younger version of Kristin would have been rebellious enough to pull something like that off.

"I didn't bring them in at all," she told him. She could see that he wasn't following her, and she really couldn't blame him. She hadn't mentioned the key component in all this. "My mother wanted to be—and still *wants* to be—a grandmother in the worst possible way."

He was still waiting for the fly in the ointment. "But?"

They'd made love and he'd seen her naked, but baring her soul was something else entirely. It was difficult for her. But because he was looking at her, waiting, she forced herself to tell him.

"But there's never been anyone I was willing to take that risk on."

Okay, still not clear, Malloy thought. "Risk?"

"That one evening he just wouldn't walk in through the door." He was part of a cop family. He had to understand *that*, Kristin thought. "I don't ever want to be in that place that my mother was in when my dad was killed."

"What place?"

"Devastatingly alone," she answered grimly, recalling what her mother had been like back then. "Even with the family all around her, she was still alone."

"So, just so I have this straight," he said slowly. "To avoid being alone, you're choosing to be alone, is that right?"

Kristin frowned at him, exasperated. "When you say it that way, it doesn't sound like it makes any sense."

Malloy called it the way he saw it. "I don't think that there *is* any way for it to sound like it makes any sense."

Kristin took offense. "I wouldn't talk if I were you,"

she pointed out. "In case you haven't noticed, you're alone, too."

"I've noticed," he told her, sparing her a look. There was no point in sparring with one another over this. Things would work themselves out, he silently promised. All it would take was time—and patience.

"How about two loners grabbing a bite to eat on our way back to the precinct?" he suggested, deliberately changing the subject.

She glanced at her watch. This was the height of lunchtime. "Might be getting crowded right about now," she told him.

He knew that, and he had no desire to continue any conversation with her in the center of a teeming mass of humanity.

"I was thinking along the lines of takeout."

"That's a better idea," she agreed.

Being around her, Malloy thought as he took an off-ramp that led them away from the freeway, had caused him to entertain a lot of "better ideas" lately.

"You're getting to be a regular fixture around here lately, Malloy," Sean commented good-naturedly. He had just almost walked into his nephew as the latter turned a corner, hurrying to the morgue at the same time that the CSI chief was coming from there.

"Still working on the same cold case with your ME," Malloy replied, getting his bearings.

Sean paused for a moment. "How's that coming along?" he asked with interest.

Malloy tried to sound upbeat, but at the moment that was getting increasingly difficult. "I was just coming to tell her that another potential lead we thought we had has just vanished on us."

Sean nodded. "Keep at it. You'll find an opening," he said with far more confidence than Malloy was currently feeling. "By the way, this has nothing to do with work, but Andrew's having another one of his get-togethers Saturday afternoon."

"Any particular reason for this one?" Malloy asked.

Sean laughed softly. "Andrew always has a reason, but he doesn't always share it with the rest of us. I do think he's got something up his sleeve, though."

"Why?"

"When he told me to spread the word, he said to make sure you were coming and bringing Kristin with you. And her mother," he added as if the woman was an afterthought.

Malloy had a feeling he knew better. "And her mother?" he repeated, intrigued. Waiting for a reason.

He wasn't given one. "The man moves in mysterious ways," Sean said. "Do us all a favor and ask Kristin to come and bring her mother."

Malloy didn't get a chance to attempt to refuse—not that he was inclined to. The next second, Sean retreated, turning down another hallway.

She looked up the moment Malloy stepped into the morgue. It was almost as if she could sense his presence even before he crossed the threshold.

He seemed a little down, she thought.

"Any luck?" she asked, hoping that she wasn't reading his expression correctly.

But as he drew closer, Kristin knew that she had guessed it.

"Yeah," he answered her question. "Bad. I had Valri double-check my findings. My sister's beginning to regret having such a technical aptitude for computers," he commented dryly. "But we both wound up coming to the same conclusion."

"Which was?" she asked, unable to wait until he set the proper stage for this.

"Anson Parker hasn't renewed his California driver's license in the past eighteen years."

She tried to think of all the different things that could actually mean, other than the obvious.

"Did the license just expire, or did he move and apply for a new license in another state?" she asked. If his sister was the computer whiz kid he'd said she was, then Valri could definitely track that piece of information down.

And, it turned out, she had tried.

"Val couldn't find any evidence of a new application anywhere. Parker could have just decided to drop out of society," Malloy went on to suggest. "Or he could have gotten a new identity for some reason."

"Or he 'couldn't' do any of those," Kristin suddenly guessed.

"What do you mean by 'couldn't'?" Malloy asked.

Rather than answer him, Kristin swung around and hurried over to one of the long metal drawers that were built into the far wall. The metal drawers in the morgue stored the bodies.

"Kristin, what are you thinking?" he asked, following her.

Grabbing the handle, she pulled it open in order to get to the drawer behind the door and the body that was lying there. Or rather, the piles of bones.

"One of the bodies we found belonged to a male victim," she reminded him.

Kristin pulled the drawer out, displaying the collection of bones she had determined formed the skeletal remains of the lone male body they had found.

"What if," she began, throwing out what in all likelihood was an outlandish theory, "you can't find where Anson Parker went because he didn't 'go' anywhere? What if he's right here?" she asked, gesturing at the bones lying on the slab she'd just pulled out.

"Do you have his dental X-rays?" he asked, looking at the remains in a new light.

"Until just now, I didn't think we had *him*," she reminded Malloy. Sparing the victim on the slab between them one last look, Kristin told Malloy, "It's going to take a little digging to find the name of Parker's dentist, but at least we have another possible victim's name."

"Even if this does turn out to be Parker, what we still don't have," Malloy said more to himself than to her, "is a reason for all these dead people in the first place. Having Parker—if it *is* Parker—in the mix just muddies up any working theory we have now."

And then Malloy took a deep breath, as if to organize his priorities.

"Identifications first, working theory last," he told Kristin. "And while you're trying to locate X-rays for our mystery guest's less than pearly whites," he commented, looking down at the skull's rather uneven, yellowish teeth, "I'm going to see if I can get the lowdown on that nursery's previous owner."

Malloy made it all the way to the doorway before he stopped and turned around to look at her. In the mounting excitement, it had slipped his mind—until now. "Oh, I almost forgot."

Kristin was already trying to gain access to a dental database that had begun being compiled years back. She glanced up when he'd crossed over to her again.

"What?"

The only way to get through this was to bluntly state it, he told himself. "You and your mother are invited."

Kristin stared at him. "Back up, Cavanaugh," she ordered, terminating the call she was in the middle of placing regarding the database. "Invited to what and by whom?"

"I ran into Uncle Sean in the hallway."

The man had just left the morgue after talking to her. So far, Malloy wasn't telling her anything new. "Go on."

The way she was watching him, he had a hunch he was not dealing with the sort of woman he'd been accustomed to. Those had been accommodating above all else.

Malloy pushed on. "And he happened to mention that Andrew hadn't thrown one of his famous get-togethers in a while."

Her eyes narrowed suspiciously. "Define 'a while.'" Was this going to be some kind of a blowout? Her mother hated noise.

"A couple of weeks," he admitted with a dismissive shrug. "That's not the point."

Kristin instinctively braced herself, although she couldn't really logically explain why. "What is the point?"

"That Uncle Andrew is throwing one now—this Saturday—and that you and your mother are invited."

"He said that specifically?" she asked, a little thrown.

"He said to invite me *and* my mother?" That didn't make any sense, she thought. "And you know that for a fact?" she pressed, as if taking the offensive. "How would he even know about us?" she questioned. So far, she hadn't allowed Malloy to take a deep breath and circle the wagons, something she knew he was good at.

She wasn't letting him answer.

"He's Andrew Cavanaugh. He's all knowing. Your mother will enjoy herself," he promised, handling two sets of questions at the same time.

Kristin shot him an exasperated look. "I wasn't thinking about her, I was thinking about me." Her mother was not going to be happy meeting a whole slew of strangers.

"I'll take care of that part," he said, a gleam entering his eyes.

"Not with your usual flair you won't," she informed him. "My mother's progressive, but she's not *that* progressive."

He laughed, thoroughly amused. "Parents have a way of surprising us," he told her.

"Not *that* much," she assured him. "Trust me." She could just hear the thousand and one questions that would precede this event.

"But you will come." It wasn't a question, it was an assumption.

"We'll see," she replied vaguely.

"I might have given you the impression that there was a choice," he told her now. And then he set the record straight. "There isn't. Not really. On the plus side, nobody's ever had a bad time attending one of Andrew's gatherings."

It would be a house full of strangers. Her mother did

best in situations where she knew most of the people. "My mother might feel funny."

"Not from what you told me."

"Okay, *I* might feel funny," she corrected.

That was one excuse that wasn't going to fly. He grinned at her.

"You'll get over it."

Then, before she could offer any more arguments, Malloy made himself scarce.

Chapter 19

The County Registrar's office was given to red tape and endless waiting. Going there was not something Malloy was even remotely looking forward to. Since he still hadn't been able to reach Harrison's lawyer regarding the purchase of the nursery, the registrar was his only available option.

Busy psyching himself up for the task ahead, Malloy was preoccupied when he stepped off the elevator on the ground floor. It almost made him miss the exchange between the desk sergeant at the reception desk and the tall, thin, somewhat greenish-looking man looming over her. The latter was definitely peevish and losing what little temper he had left—fast.

"I said I'm looking for a Detective Cavanaugh," the visitor said irritably, raising his voice.

Sergeant Ellen McNally was known for her easygoing manner, which was probably why she'd been given this position in the first place. She laughed good-naturedly at the man's request.

"Well, you've certainly come to the right place, I can tell you that. We've got a whole array of those in practically all the different departments. Any particular Cavanaugh you'd like to see?" the young blonde asked, thoroughly amused.

"I didn't come here to play guessing games," the man snapped as he mopped his brow with a well-creased handkerchief. "I want to see the one who left me twelve messages on my phone, none of which I can make out," he complained, holding his cell phone aloft to display the number of missed calls. "Look, I've just been on a ten-day cruise from hell where everything that could go wrong *did* go wrong, including a rip-roaring case of dysentery, something I thought I'd eluded until just now. Now, where is this guy so I can answer his questions like a good, upstanding citizen and then go home, crawl into my bed and die?"

"Sir, I really am going to need a first name from you," Sergeant McNally told him. "As I said, we do have a great many Cavanaughs on the force, and I don't want to waste your time—"

"Too late," the man snapped curtly.

Malloy crossed the lobby and made his way to the sickly looking man brow-beating the desk sergeant.

"I'll take it from here, McNally," he told her. He was rewarded with a very relieved smile.

"Who the hell are you?" the man asked. He held on to the desk, most likely for balance, as he turned to look at whoever was talking to him.

Malloy gave the man his most congenial smile. "I'm

sorry, I couldn't help overhearing," he began. "Would you happen to be Roy Harrison's lawyer?"

Now very obviously holding on to the desk for support, the man regarded him with nonexpressive brown eyes. "William James," he said, identifying himself. "And you are?"

"Probably the Detective Cavanaugh you're looking for. Malloy," he added since the lawyer didn't seem to know his first name. He examined James more closely. "If you don't mind my saying so, you don't look so good."

James's breathing was becoming somewhat audible, as if he'd been running. Except that he hadn't. "Tell me about it," the man moaned.

"Do you want some water?" Malloy offered, about to ask McNally to get some for the man.

But James was quick to refuse the offer. "I think that's what started this whole thing in the first place. There was something wrong with the water," he complained. "Almost everyone on the ship came down with this except for a few of us. I thought I'd lucked out—if you could call it that—until I was on my way over here in a cab." There was perspiration gathering on his brow. "What I want is to clear up whatever's going on. Harrison was almost incoherent when I got his call a few minutes ago. Something about it costing him a fortune because work couldn't continue because of the bodies that were found." His eyes were growing watery as he turned them on Malloy. "What bodies?"

Malloy moved to take the man's arm and lead him to an elevator. "Why don't we go upstairs and talk in one of the conference rooms?" he suggested.

"You mean one of the interrogation rooms?" James

countered. "I've got a better suggestion. Why don't we just sit out here in the lobby, and after I answer your questions, I'll have a shorter walk to the outside of the building."

Malloy gestured to one of several chairs in the lobby. "Take your pick," he told him.

The lawyer dropped into the chair that was closest to him. He looked as if he'd barely made it.

"Now, what's this about finding bodies on my client's property?" he asked, struggling to maintain a professional air.

Malloy quickly told James as much as he felt the man needed to know in order for the lawyer to volunteer the necessary information. "We're trying to identify who these women are, and we need to know the name of the previous owner, the person who sold the property to your client."

Rather than volunteer the name, James shook his head, or attempted to. "That's not as straightforward as you might think."

Why should this be any different from the rest of this case? Malloy thought wearily.

Out loud Malloy said, "Mind if I ask why?"

Sweating and beginning to radiate heat, James still had a counteroffer. "Not if I get to ask my question first."

Malloy curbed his impatience. "Go ahead."

"Why would you need the previous owner's name?" he asked.

Looking as if he was fading fast, James was still every inch a lawyer, Malloy thought.

"These murders all took place at least twenty years ago. So unless your client was using that part of the property as a killing field back then and suddenly decided he wanted to take actual possession of the land—"

"No, of course not," the lawyer protested. And then he held up his hand as he covered his mouth with his handkerchief. The next moment he was coughing almost violently into it. His eyes were considerably more watery by the time he stopped and looked up.

"Sure I can't get you anything?" Malloy asked. He wasn't much of an expert on sick people, but the man appeared as if he was going to pass out at any moment.

"Other than a gun to shoot myself with, no," James answered, clearly miserable.

Taking out his smartphone, the man proceeded to flip through several sections before he found what he was looking for.

Exhaling a ragged breath, he said, "I didn't deal with the actual owner, but I can tell you who I did deal with in order to buy the property." He squinted as he read the name written on one of his calendar entries. "An Enrique Montoya." James swiped the phone closed, but he continued clutching it in his hand, as if it somehow helped to keep him sitting upright in the chair. "Montoya was the last of the original owner's employees. In this particular case, he was given power of attorney by the owner of the nursery to conduct the sale. Montoya was the one who signed all the legal papers. Everything's aboveboard," he emphasized sharply, as if he had just been challenged.

"That seems rather odd," Malloy commented. "Where's the original owner?"

James shifted, not because the questions made him uncomfortable, but because his mounting illness did.

"Don't remember," he confessed. "Montoya showed

me all the proper documentation, so I dealt with him. I saw no problem with that."

"All right," Malloy said gamely. "Can you tell me where I can find this Enrique Montoya?"

Malloy waited for a response, eyeing the other man. The latter's complexion was growing progressively greener, and he had a feeling that it was just a matter of time before the lawyer would become too miserable and sick to talk.

James was apparently struggling to remember details now. "Montoya said he was moving down to San Diego to live with his daughter and her family the second the ink dried on the deed."

"And you have that number?" Malloy asked.

James took offense at the question. "Of course I have that number. What kind of a lawyer do you think I—" Another coughing fit interrupted the question.

Malloy glanced over to the sergeant at the desk. The latter was already dialing a number. Hopefully, McNally was calling for an ambulance, Malloy thought.

Rather than tell Malloy the phone number, James turned on his smartphone again and jabbed an index finger at the screen.

Malloy looked and quickly committed the name and number he saw to memory even as he took out the notepad he carried in his pocket. His memory was excellent, but he'd learned that it never hurt to back up everything, whether they were computer files or ones that were in actual memory.

He heard one of the elevator doors opening as he finished writing. Putting away his notepad, he registered the sound of high heels hitting travertine. The sound grew louder.

"What are you feeling?" a soft voice asked.

Kristin.

Startled, Malloy turned around to look at her. Kristin was obviously the one who had gotten out of the elevator.

The next moment he realized that she wasn't talking to him. Her question was directed at the man sitting in the chair beside him.

The man who looked as if he was going to pour out of his chair and onto the floor any second.

"Who are you?" James asked weakly, vainly trying to project his voice and remain in control.

"I'm Dr. Alberghetti. Tell me your symptoms," she urged, even as she took his pulse.

"Nausea, fever, ringing in my ears…" He was about to continue when his own labored breathing cut him off.

"You need more than I can do for you here," Kristin said gently.

Within another minute, she had the desk sergeant calling for an ambulance.

"That's what I was going to tell her to do," Malloy said. And then he asked, "What are you doing here?" Her sudden appearance seemed like far too much of a coincidence.

"The sergeant called me," Kristin said, nodding at the woman behind the desk. "I am a doctor, you know," she reminded him.

Because the fire station was only, literally, down the block, the ambulance arrived almost immediately.

Malloy stepped back as the two attendants strapped James onto the gurney. "Here's hoping he doesn't wind up like all your other dead patients," he quipped.

William James's eyes grew huge as he stared at Kristin while the attendants wheeled him away.

Kristin waited until the attendants were gone and McNally went back to her desk. "Learn anything useful?" she asked Malloy.

Malloy turned away from the doors. "Actually, I did. The person acting on the former owner's behalf is currently residing with his daughter and her family down in San Diego."

That seemed like a rather sweeping statement. "San Diego's a big place," she commented, fairly certain that Malloy was playing this out for effect. For the moment, she went along with it. "Do you happen to have an address or a phone number?"

A Cheshire cat-type grin took over his mouth. "I have both," Malloy replied.

So, there was another possible lead again. "When are you planning on going?"

He looked as if he was seriously considering her question. And then he innocently asked, "Are you and your mother coming to Uncle Andrew's party?"

She couldn't believe he was doing this. "You're kidding. Are you trying to blackmail me into coming to this party and bringing my mother along?"

"*Blackmail* is such an ugly word," he told her. "Why don't we just call it a trade? Remember, technically, since I don't expect to find any dead bodies down in San Diego, there's no reason for you to come with me. Bringing you along is all strictly up to my discretion."

Kristin's eyes narrowed. "You don't play fair," she accused.

Malloy was the picture of complete innocence. "Never said I did."

She *needed* to be included in this investigation. She was certain the solution was out there, just within reach, and she hated the idea that it *could* be reached without her. She was far too invested in this to just docilely drop out now.

This *was* blackmail, pure and simple, and she didn't want to give in because of the principle of the thing. But she really did want to be included, and her relationship—if it could be called that—with Malloy had gotten complicated. She didn't want it to end yet, and if she really refused this invitation, it just might.

Wavering, Kristin chewed on the inside of her cheek for a moment, then grudgingly bit off a single word. "Fine."

"Fine, what?" he asked innocently.

"Fine, we'll come. My mother and I will come," she spelled out in case there was any misunderstanding or he accused her of being fast and loose with rhetoric.

He peered into her eyes, as if he could see if she were lying. "I have your word?"

Okay, enough was enough. "You'll have my fingers around your throat very quickly if you keep this up."

"Hot temper." He grinned broadly. "I like that in a woman."

"I wasn't hot tempered until I met you," Kristin accused.

He nodded his head, pleased. He knew her well enough now to realize that she wouldn't go back on her word no matter how much she wanted to.

"Even better." He began to move to one side for privacy. "Let me give Mr. Montoya a call and tell him we'd like to talk to him about his former employer." But even before he stepped to one side and started pressing the keypad, he paused to look at Kristin. "It's going to be a really long drive down to San Diego. Are you sure you want to go?"

There was no way that he was leaving her behind. "I'm sure."

He glanced toward the elevator and the rest of the building it symbolized. "Won't they need you in the morgue?"

"For the moment, 'Death' seems to have called a moratorium since we started working this cold case. A couple of my assistants are working today, and besides, I have some vacation time coming if I need to go that route. One way or another, I'm coming with you. We are going to solve this case," she concluded with conviction.

"Never doubted it for a moment," he told her. "Just let me make this call to Montoya."

With that, he placed a call to Prickly Gardens' last-known employee.

The trip from Aurora to San Diego took more than four hours, even using little traveled roads that were, for the most part, mercifully free of traffic.

During the trip, radio stations came and went, depending on the strength of the signal. But, strong or weak, it merely provided background noise. Malloy used the time to bounce various theories about the case and its heretofore still unknown victims off Kristin.

"You do know that this Montoya might turn out to be your murderer," she said out of the blue.

She saw him grin and realized she wasn't telling him something he hadn't already thought of—and, from the look of it, disregarded.

"The thought did occur to me," Malloy admitted.

He was being awfully cavalier about this. After all, they were trying to find someone who'd killed twelve people *that they knew of.* There could still be more victims out there.

"If that's the case, shouldn't you be going in with backup?" she persisted.

Malloy spared her a glance. "I have backup. You," he told her after a beat.

She blew out an annoyed breath. "Be serious."

"I am being serious," he argued. "If this retired nursery man attacked me, you wouldn't jump right in to my rescue?"

"I'd probably help him attack you. Besides, you're not his type. If he was the killer, he'd sooner attack me than you." And suddenly her words played back in her head, and she looked at him, startled. "Wait, am I supposed to be bait?"

He didn't answer her right away. Instead, he laughed. "Are you aware that you have a habit of overthinking things?" he asked her. "And to answer your question," he went on, growing serious, "I'd never use anyone as bait, least of all you. As for backup, I've already notified the San Diego PD that I was going to be coming to their city—it's known as a courtesy notification," he told her before she could ask. "If I run into trouble, all I have to do is give them a call.

"At this point, we're just on a fact-finding trip. I've got a hunch that this Montoya *isn't* our killer."

She'd heard the term "hunch" bandied about ever since she'd joined the medical examiner's office. It didn't seem like a very scientific way to operate to her.

"Why? Because he's moved in with his daughter and her family?"

"That's part of it," Malloy said with a vague shrug. "But mainly it's because the man's as clean as a whistle. In the past forty-five years, he hadn't gotten so much as a parking ticket. He files his taxes regularly. Attends church faithfully and, until last month, he donated his spare time at a rescue mission twice a month."

Kristin could only look at him incredulously. They'd only gotten the man's name shortly before they set out on this trip. "How do you know all this?" she demanded.

"Background check," he replied simply.

"When? You just got the man's name a few hours ago," she stressed. Malloy hadn't had the time to look any of this up. "And we've been on the road for most of that time."

He wanted to tease her a little longer but decided that was being cruel. "Sometimes having all that family on the force comes in handy," he told her. "*Really* handy."

She'd grant him that, but she hadn't heard him calling anyone. "I still don't—"

Okay, so maybe he *was* enjoying playing this out a little, he allowed. He knew that if he were in Kristin's place, he wouldn't have appreciated being strung along like this.

"We pulled into that rest stop halfway here, remember?" he said.

"Yes." He'd been out of her sight for maybe five minutes during that time, probably less. Was that when he'd tracked down his information? If so, she'd clearly underestimated him.

"I got a couple of texts filling me in," he told her, putting the mystery to rest. "I owe both Valri and Brenda steak dinners," he said, tapping the cell phone in his pocket. The second woman he'd referred to was the

Chief of D's daughter-in-law and the head of the computer lab. "Maybe some lobster thrown in, as well. In any case, it's definitely money well spent."

Growing serious, Malloy looked at her as he took an off-ramp, which brought them to the heart of San Diego. "And just for the record, I wouldn't have brought you along if I thought Montoya was a dangerous man. I would have found a way to get you to stay behind at the precinct. Much as I like your company, nothing's worth risking your life."

Despite the warm shiver that swept over her, Kristin had no idea what to say to him after that, so she said nothing.

Chapter 20

Leaning into a winding turn as he drove, Malloy glanced in Kristin's direction. That was when he observed the slight trembling movement just at her left hip.

"Either you're cold, which doesn't seem possible, given the temperature outside, or you've got a call coming in," Malloy said, nodding toward her hip.

Out of habit, Kristin had set her cell phone on vibrate, which was what it was presently doing in her pocket.

Her mind focused on the man they were on their way to see, Kristin momentarily debated not taking the call. The debate was a short one. It wasn't in her nature to ignore anyone. In her opinion, if someone was calling her, they deserved her attention.

Taking her phone out, Kristin swiped it open and placed the device close to her ear, leaving it off speaker. She liked maintaining an illusion of privacy. "Alberghetti."

His curiosity piqued, Malloy waited for her to say something further so that he could begin piecing together who was calling her and why. Unless he found out otherwise, he assumed the call had something to do with her work, possibly even this case. The last he'd heard, Kristin had left her assistants searching through a dental database.

Kristin remained silent, apparently listening to whoever was on the other end of the call. And then he heard her say, "You're kidding…Really?…You're sure?…No, of course. Thanks for calling me. I'll see you when I get back."

Terminating the call, Kristin tucked her smartphone away and stared out the windshield.

"Wow," she whispered under her breath, more to herself than to him.

His attention was totally captured. "Would you like to expand on that?"

As if suddenly realizing that he was there, Kristin shifted in her seat, the seat belt digging sharply into her lap.

"You know that male victim that we found buried with the other bodies? Well, that *did* turn out to be Anson Parker. Rich just called to tell me that they managed to find Parker's dental records, and they *did* turn out to be a match," she said, referring to one of her assistants.

He'd been under the impression that her assistants were going to be trying to match dental X-rays to the female skulls that had been found. "I thought you said that you didn't know who Parker's dentist was."

"I didn't," she answered. "I had Rich call every dentist within a twenty-mile radius who was in practice twenty to twenty-five years ago and run Parker's name past them. Apparently he got lucky," she said, awed, then amended, "Doubly so, because that male victim *did* turn out to be Anson Parker."

"Now all we have to do is figure out if Parker was collateral damage because he was in the wrong place at the wrong time—or if he had some kind of connection to all these other victims and the serial killer." Stepping down on the accelerator, Malloy just made it through the intersection before the light turned red.

"I don't think the word *all* is big enough to fit this situation," she commented.

"Tell me about it," Malloy agreed with a dry laugh. The next minute, right after turning down a residential street, he began to slow the car.

"What's wrong?" Kristin asked. Was he stopping because he wanted to discuss this latest turn the investigation had taken, or was there something else on his mind?

"Nothing," Malloy answered. Stopping the car beside the curb, he pulled up the hand brake. "We're here."

"Here" turned out to be a rather pleasant-looking two-story forty-year-old house with what appeared to be guest quarters located on the rear of the property.

There were a variety of imposing-looking succulents planted all throughout the front yard. The plot itself was a decent size, and there were all sorts of fledgling plants in the front struggling to spread their roots and get their bearings.

"How can you tell?" Kristin cracked, then went on to complain, "I feel itchy just looking at those things." She struggled not to shiver.

"I suppose that means getting a part-time job at a

cacti nursery is out of the question for you," he guessed
dryly.

The moment he got out of the vehicle on his side, the
front door opened. A friendly-looking older man with
a mane of silver-gray hair and kind eyes came out to
meet them. Almost square in build, the man appeared
powerful despite his age.

"You are Detective Cavanaugh?" the man asked. The
question was directed at Malloy, but the man's sweeping
gaze took Kristin in as well and rested appreciatively
on her for a good thirty seconds.

"That's right, I am," Malloy confirmed, taking the
wide, powerful hand that was being offered in greeting
and shaking it. "And this is Dr. Kristin Alberghetti, the
department's medical examiner."

"So attractive for such grim work," Montoya lamented in sympathy, shaking her hand, as well. "I am
Enrique Montoya," he said, introducing himself to
her. "Come into the back," the older man invited. "My
daughter has prepared refreshments. We can eat and
drink while we talk."

Offering his arm to Kristin, Montoya led them into
the backyard. Aside from a gazebo and a child's elaborate swing set and slide, the backyard was meticulously
landscaped and completely drought friendly, Malloy
observed.

"The garden's beautiful," Kristin told the man. She
had a feeling that he had selected every specimen that
was planted there.

Montoya's smile deepened with appreciation. "I had
time on my hands, and I do not like being idle."

He waited until his guests were seated and offered

them both iced tea and slices of a pie that had very obviously only recently been removed from the oven.

Satisfied that their needs were attended to, Montoya sat back and asked, "Now, what is it I can do for you, Detective?"

Malloy got right down to it. "You were recently in charge of handling the sale of the nursery where you worked. Prickly Gardens," he added, watching the other man's expression.

"Ah, yes, the Gardens," Montoya said fondly. "I enjoyed working there," he confessed. "But sadly, I am not the young man I used to be, and the plants insisted on becoming heavier," he added with a laugh. "When I finally told Miss Agnes that I was retiring to go live with my daughter and she was going to have to find someone else, she asked me for one last favor.

"I said of course. I thought she wanted me to find my replacement, but instead she asked me to find someone to buy the nursery." There was a touch of pride mingled with humility in his voice as he told them, "She said that without me there to run the Gardens, she was no longer interested in keeping the nursery going."

"Tell me," Malloy began, sliding a bit closer to the older man on his seat, "Why didn't she handle the sale herself?"

"Miss Agnes is not a well woman. She had not worked at the Gardens for a few years, and she told me that she was confident I would be able to deal with any questions a buyer might have better than she would."

"So you worked there a long time?" Kristin asked.

Montoya's smile seemed to go up another hundred watts as he answered her. "Oh, yes. A very long time. Mr. Bruce was the one who hired me."

"Mr. Bruce?" Malloy repeated.

Deftly refilling Kristin's partially empty glass, Montoya continued with his narrative. It was easy to see that the man enjoyed talking and liked having an audience listening to him.

"Mr. Bruce bought Prickly Gardens two years before I went to work for him. It was small back then, but Mr. Bruce, he had a vision. And I was happy to help him achieve it."

Malloy was feeling his way around, trying not to make it seem as if he was interrogating the former employee. "Did 'Mr. Bruce' want to sell the nursery, too?"

Montoya's expression lost some of its sunny demeanor. "Mr. Bruce died more than ten years ago."

Malloy was still trying to identify the players. "And Miss Agnes was his wife?" he guessed.

"No, she was his older sister," Montoya corrected. "She was also his partner, working beside him everyday, going on trips to look for new specimens to sell at the Gardens." Judging by the man's tone, it was easy to ascertain that, in his opinion, those constituted the better days. "Miss Agnes was the one who kept things running at the Gardens after Mr. Bruce lost interest."

"Was there a reason he lost interest?" Kristin asked, wondering if they were finally on the right track to learning the circumstances that led to all those young women being murdered and mutilated.

"Oh, yes, a very sad reason," Montoya said. Pausing as if to collect himself, he went on to give it to them. "One day Mr. Bruce's son just disappeared. No note, no reason, he just did not come home when he was supposed to. Mr. Bruce got angry, then he got frightened. He hired private detectives to find the boy.

"When they could not," Montoya sighed, "Mr. Bruce started drinking. Miss Agnes tried to get him interested in the nursery again—it was his passion, you see—but all he cared about was numbing his pain. So he went on drinking. She tried everything to make him stop. One day, Mr. Bruce, he just drove the car over the side of one of the winding roads. He died before they could get him to the hospital."

As he spoke, Montoya cut second slices of pie and placed one each on their plates. "Eat, please," he urged.

And then he continued. "Mr. Bruce had left the nursery to her, so Miss Agnes ran the business until she became sick. She is in a wheelchair now, poor lady," he explained. "She asked me to keep the Gardens going, but well, it was getting harder and harder to do the potting and the shipping, not to mention the day-to-day things that have to be taken care of. I had some help, but..." He shrugged.

The older man's smile was rueful as he admitted, "It takes a young man to run this business, and I no longer am that. So when I told Miss Agnes I would be retiring, she asked me to sell the Gardens for her. I was surprised," he admitted.

"Why's that?" Malloy asked.

"I thought she would keep it in case Mr. Anson ever came back. But she said no, he would not be coming back after all this time, and she needed the money to stay where she was. It is expensive to be old and alone," he told them sadly. "So, what could I say? I told her I would stay on until I found someone to buy the nursery. Fortunately, that did not take as long as I thought."

Malloy exchanged looks with Kristin. By the expression on her face, he knew she'd caught it, too. "What did you say the owner's son's name was?" he asked Montoya.

"Mr. Anson." He nodded as if he understood why he'd been asked to repeat the name. "It is a strange name, I know."

"What did you say the owner's last name was?" Malloy pressed, just to get everything right.

"Miss Agnes? Her last name is Parker. The same as her brother. She never married," he added, even though there was no need to. "The poor lady had a good heart, but she was a very plain-looking woman. She did not try to make herself look prettier." It was obvious by his tone that he felt for the woman he was talking about. "I think that is why Miss Agnes liked the cacti and succulents so much. Many people say that they are ugly, but she thought they were beautiful."

"Was she close to her nephew?" Kristin asked.

She felt as if they were staring at all the pieces in this puzzle, but they still needed to make sense out of them somehow. So far, they were all just a mishmash of parts.

"Mr. Anson's mother died when he was a little boy, and Miss Agnes tried to be a mother to him, but I don't think that ever really worked out for either one of them. Mr. Anson was difficult for her to handle. He could be nice one minute, not so nice the next."

Montoya stared into the bottom of his empty iced tea glass. His expression was solemn.

"They were not a happy family, although Mr. Bruce tried to be a good father. He bought his son everything he asked for, but 'things' do not take the place of a mother, or love." Rousing himself, Montoya shook his head. "So much sadness."

"Are you still in touch with Agnes Parker?" Malloy

asked. It was clear that he was going to need to speak to the woman. Maybe she could shed some more light on things.

"If you mean have I seen her recently, no. We spoke on the phone when I sold the Gardens for her," Montoya answered. "She told me to have the check deposited into her bank account."

"When was that?" Malloy asked. He had his notepad out and was making notes accordingly now.

Montoya didn't have to pause to think. He remembered exactly. "Four weeks ago." He looked from the detective he was talking to to the woman sitting beside him. "Is something wrong?" he asked, then immediately jumped to the only conclusion that he could. "Did Mr. Anson come back?"

Malloy was tempted to tell the man the truth. Montoya had been straightforward with them and answered all their questions, not to mention that he'd been hospitable when he could have just as easily been hostile. But the case was still open, and the investigation was ongoing. That meant that details had to be kept secret until the crime was solved.

"Not exactly," was all Malloy could say. "But we need to get in touch with Miss Parker. Would you have her address as well as her phone number handy?"

"Yes, of course. Let me give it to you." Montoya reached into his pants pocket and, after a moment, tugged out a cell phone. "My daughter, she wants me to be part of the modern world as she calls it. Half the time, I forget where I put this thing, so now she makes me carry it with me."

He shook his head, as if the whole concept of having a cell phone still mystified him. "I like holding something in my hand that *feels* like something," he said. "This is like a toy," he complained, opening the phone. Muttering something under his breath, he swiped through pages, attempting to get to the right section.

It took him several tries. His fingers were undeniably thick. He kept hitting the wrong keys by accident.

Finally, he opened the window he was looking for. "Here it is," he declared, holding the phone out to Malloy for his perusal.

Malloy took the cell from him and keyed the phone number and the address onto his own phone.

"Thank you," Malloy said, putting his phone away. Then he offered the cell phone back to the older man.

Montoya shoved the cell phone back into his pocket.

What the man said next surprised Malloy. "I realize that you are not able to say anything right now—" Montoya smiled brightly when they both looked at him. "I watch television," he explained. "I know about investigations. But when you are able to tell me what is going on, will you?" he requested with genuine sincerity. "I would appreciate getting a call from either of you explaining why you are so interested in the nursery and the people I worked for. I can assure you right now that nothing exciting ever happened at Prickly Gardens. Not in all the years that I worked there."

Malloy restrained himself from exchanging glances with Kristin. Instead, he told Montoya, "For now, let's just call it tying up loose ends."

"And later?" Montoya asked, curious. "What will you call it later?"

"We'll let you know," Kristin promised.

It was time to wind this up. Malloy had a feeling that the man had told them everything he knew.

"Thank you for the information and for your hospitality," Malloy said, rising to his feet. Kristin instantly followed his lead and rose to hers. "But we need to be getting back."

"Yes, of course," Montoya agreed, quickly standing up, as well. "It is a long drive back to Aurora."

He accompanied them through the backyard and then, taking the side yard, he walked them out to the front.

"When you see Miss Agnes," he requested, "please, give her my best."

"When *was* the last time you saw her?" Kristin asked, her curiosity aroused.

"More than a year ago. I helped her move her things from the old trailer, where she used to live, to the new place. I think they call it a 'bed and board.' It is really a warehouse for old people, but it is a nice warehouse," he added tactfully.

Montoya stopped by their vehicle, and after a moment, he confided in a lower voice, "Miss Agnes did not look well."

Kristin had a feeling that the man was referring to something other than just the natural progression of old age and the aches and pains that it ushered in.

"Do you know what was wrong with her?" she asked the man.

The broad, wide shoulders rose and fell in a vague movement. "If you mean what the doctors called it, it was something with a name I don't remember. But I think it was more than that."

"Oh?" Kristin urged him on.

"I think something was eating away at her, from inside." Montoya tapped his chest with his fist for emphasis. And then he shrugged. "But maybe I am just imagining things," he added.

"What do you think it was?" Malloy prodded him, wanting to get the nurseryman's take. Right now, every little bit could either add to the puzzle or help to solve it.

"When we get older," Montoya said, "we have regrets. Things we didn't do. Things we did. Who is to say?" The next moment, his reflective mood was gone, and his warm smile had returned. "I hope I have been helpful."

"That you have," Malloy said as they got into his car. "Thank you," he repeated.

A moment later, they were pulling away from the curb. Montoya stood by the curb, thoughtfully watching them until they disappeared from view.

Chapter 21

"Thoughts?"

The sound of Malloy's voice slipped into the silence in her darkened bedroom, competing with the elevated beating of her heart.

Kristin raised her head from his chest, just enough for her eyes to meet his.

The trip back from San Diego had been nothing short of exhausting.

Traffic on both ends of the journey, first in San Diego, then in Aurora, had been far heavier than they'd anticipated. Consequently, they had agreed, long before they entered the city proper, that paying Agnes Parker a visit should be moved to their next day's agenda.

Because it took so long to get back, it was far too late to pay the older woman a call at this hour of the evening.

What hadn't been touched on was how the evening

would end. She had just assumed that they would each go to their separate residences, get whatever sleep they could and resume the investigation—hopefully bringing it to some sort of a conclusion—in the morning.

But when Malloy had brought her to her car in the police parking lot, he didn't just drop her off, then pull out and continue home the way she thought he would. He waited for her to start up her car, and then, as he had done twice before, he went on to follow her home.

She knew better than to presume *anything* when it came to Malloy, so after she'd parked her car in her driveway and got out of the vehicle, she'd approached his, prepared to ask questions.

She might have been prepared to ask them, but she'd never gotten the chance to voice them because the second Malloy had gotten out of *his* car, he'd swept her into his arms and kissed her. Kissed her until her head was spinning.

And *that* had answered all the immediate questions that never got the opportunity to make it off her tongue.

There'd been no verbal exchange between them as Kristin had somehow managed, while still locked in his embrace and her lips very much sealed to his, to unlock her front door so that they could get into her house.

Once the door was closed, separating them from the rest of the immediate world, they lost no time in separating one another from their clothing.

Things escalated from there.

Passion and heavy breathing effectively took the place of words.

Satisfaction was met not once, but twice, until exhaustion finally resurfaced again, and they collapsed in one another's arms.

Thoughts?

The single word that Malloy had just uttered—in the form of a question—was the first one she'd heard from him in what seemed like hours.

"Regarding anything in particular?" she asked him, playfully running the tip of her finger along the outline of his lips. She wasn't fooling herself. This was Malloy Cavanaugh, and however intense this time between them felt right now, she knew it would end. But for now, she intended to enjoy it. "As in my thoughts as to whether or not you're the world's greatest lover?"

He was almost too tired to laugh.

When he tucked her against him, Kristin thought she could feel laughter rumbling within his chest, but the sound didn't fully emerge. Malloy apparently was shoring up his energy.

"Nice guess—we'll revisit that thought later," he promised. "But what I'm asking you is what your thoughts are about what we found out from Montoya today."

He wasn't being totally clear, Kristin thought. "You're not asking me if I think Montoya killed all those girls, are you?"

Malloy tucked one arm under his head as he reflected on their visit to the former nursery employee. "No. I don't think he did. But we've got three more players in this thing we really didn't know about before.

"What if," he began, drawing her even closer against him, "Parker Senior was the serial killer? He was killing these young girls all along, burying them on an undeveloped section of his property. Then one night, Junior stumbled across his secret. He threatened to go to the police and, panicked, Senior killed Junior to keep him quiet. Then, when he realized what he'd actually done, Senior went through the motions of reporting his son missing. Playing the grieving father, he pretended to try to locate him. It didn't take long for his guilt to get to him—after all, he'd killed his only son and heir— and Senior started drinking until he eventually wound up killing himself."

"That would definitely explain why we found Anson's body with the others," Kristin agreed. "The problem is, how do we go about proving this?"

"Hey, I can't do everything," Malloy pretended to protest. "I came up with the theory."

"*A* theory," she corrected. "You came up with *a* theory. We really don't know if that's the right one," Kristin reminded him.

Malloy suddenly pulled her down so that in one short movement, she was beneath him again. "Hey," he asked, pivoting himself on his elbows as he looked down at her face, "have you always been this picky?"

She laced her arms around his neck. "Always," she whispered, her eyes alluding to things that she refrained from putting into words.

"Oh. Okay, then."

And then the room fell into silence again as Malloy took full advantage of the invitation that he saw in her eyes.

Agnes Parker's advanced infirm condition had forced the once active, strong-willed woman to finally surrender her principles, as well as her desire for independence, and accept the assistance she needed in her day-to-day life.

Since a personal caregiver came with a prohibitive

price tag in her region, she had opted to move into a board-and-care facility in Shady Canyon, a city located some fifty miles from Aurora and the nursery where Agnes had spent a good part of her adult life for almost the past forty years.

The board-and-care facility was another name for a regular two-story house that had been converted to a six-bedroom home in order to follow certain state guidelines. Agnes Parker resided in one of the larger bedrooms. It came with its own entrance to the patio and afforded her a view of the garden.

Agnes kept her curtains drawn, leading Kristin to speculate that the woman had had her fill of gardens. She couldn't help wondering why.

"What do you mean I have visitors?" Agnes demanded sharply of the young male caregiver who had brought them into the old woman's room. "I never have visitors. There's nobody left to visit me now that Enrique's moved away," she declared, stating the rather sad fact without any accompanying emotion.

Showing emotion, the woman had been heard to say, was a waste of time and effort.

Malloy was quick to introduce himself and Kristin to the former nursery owner. "I'm Detective Cavanaugh and this is Dr. Alberghetti," he told her. In addition to stepping forward, he had also raised his voice in case the woman had trouble hearing. "We're from the Aurora Police De—"

He got no further.

Agnes's long, thin, blue-veined hand spread out like a fragile spider web, covering her heart. For a moment, she appeared to turn even paler than she already was.

"I knew it," she cried, her voice going up. "I knew

this day would come." Regaining control over herself, Agnes's bright blue eyes swept over her visitors. And then, in a resigned voice, she asked, "You found them, didn't you?"

Under ordinary circumstances, Malloy would have asked the woman to elaborate on that question by asking one of his own, specifically, "Found what?" But in this case, he had the impression that he would get further if he allowed the woman to believe that her worst fears had been realized.

"Yes, we did," he told her.

Agnes took in a long, deep breath and then shook her head. "Finally. It's over." Her eyes shifted back to Malloy. "All the bodies?"

Feeling that specifics actually were called for, Kristin spoke up.

"We found twelve," she told the woman. "Were there more?"

Agnes sighed. The sound seemed to come from deep within her soul.

"No, that's all of them. God forgive me," she murmured to herself. "That's all of them."

Agnes was seated in her wheelchair. Malloy pulled up the lone chair in the small, furnished room for Kristin. He was more than prepared to stand, but the aide who had showed them into Agnes's room had returned with a folding chair and offered it to him.

"Thanks," he told the man, taking the chair from him. He then closed the door behind the caregiver as the latter left the room.

When Malloy turned around toward the woman in the wheelchair, he saw that Kristin had taken Agnes's thin hands into her own in an obvious gesture of comfort, just as she had done with Professor Sullivan.

Pulling up the folding chair close to Agnes, he asked, "Would you like to tell us about it?"

"Confession is good for the soul, is that it?" Agnes asked. She appeared to be growing steadily wearier. "Well, the soul that could have really benefited from that never had the chance to confess, and that's on me," she told them sadly. "That's all on me."

"What happened, Agnes?" Kristin prodded gently.

Agnes's eyes were bright with anger—and exasperation—because she hadn't been able to right the wrong.

"I caught him, that's what happened," she stated flatly. "I caught him burying that poor girl."

Rather than question Agnes as to the "him" she was referring to, they allowed the woman to tell her story at her own pace.

"At first, I couldn't believe what I was seeing. I'd always felt there was something wrong with my nephew, but I kept hoping that he'd change, that he'd grow out of it. But he didn't," she said bitterly. "He just got worse. But I never thought…" She shook her head, still in shock even after all these years. "It didn't seem real…"

"What didn't seem real?" Malloy pressed, leaning forward and creating an air of intimacy.

"That he'd killed that girl and then looked so calm, burying her—burying *pieces* of her," Agnes underscored with a shiver. "When I came forward to demand to know what had happened, I saw that the poor girl's hands had been cut off. They were lying *next* to her in the grave he was digging.

"He laughed at me for asking. Then he told me to go home, that it was none of my 'damn business' what he was doing." Her face darkened with anger she had no way of channeling. "He killed another human being— a lot of other human beings it turned out—and it was none of my business," she cried incredulously. "He was a monster." There were unshed tears glistening in her eyes as she made the unyielding pronouncement.

"When you saw what he was doing, why didn't you call the police?" Malloy asked.

"I was going to," she answered. "I told him that. Told him he was sick and that he needed to get help. I remember the rage in his eyes when I said that." For a moment, she was lost in the long-ago event. And then she returned to the present and her narrative. "That was when he came at me. He was holding that shovel, swinging it around like it was a weapon, trying to bash me in the head with it."

Trembling, Agnes pressed her lips together and closed her eyes. She was reliving the scene. When she opened her eyes again, she seemed to be seeking, if not forgiveness, then understanding.

"He was really such a scrawny boy, little, like his mother. I was heavier than he was—and taller. I got the shovel away from him, and he started screaming at me." She ran her tongue along the outline of her mouth, trying to dispel the parched dryness that reliving all this had created. Her lips felt as if they were sticking together as she spoke. "I knew at that moment, scrawny or not, he was going to kill me with his bare hands." She paused to catch her breath, as if remembering the scene had stolen her breath from her.

"He came at me, and I hit him with the shovel with all my might. I only meant to stop him," she said with all sincerity, her voice hitching. "But he wouldn't wake up, and I couldn't find a pulse. I panicked then, and wound up burying Anson with the girl he'd killed."

She looked from Kristin to Malloy, as if searching for understanding. "I didn't know what to do. I knew it would just kill my brother if he found out that his son was a murderer, so I said nothing." She sighed, a prisoner of her own making. "The longer I kept quiet, the harder it was to say something. It was easier just not saying anything." Sadness entered her eyes as she admitted, "At least I thought it was."

She seemed to gather herself together before their eyes, ready to take her punishment for a crime she hadn't wanted to commit.

"All these years, I've been waiting for someone to find those bodies. I think I'm relieved now. Afraid, but relieved," Agnes admitted, a slight rueful smile on her thin lips.

"And you're sure that your nephew killed all those women?" Malloy asked, carefully watching Agnes's expression as she gave him her answer.

Agnes nodded. "I'm sure," she replied. "He went so far as to brag to me about it. He said—" Her voice broke for a moment. She paused until she could speak again. "He said it was all my fault." Tears shimmered in her eyes. "And maybe he was right."

"Why would he say such a thing?" Kristin asked gently, coaxing the rest from her.

"Because I was the one who found her, who hired her," Agnes told her. "I hired the babysitter who took care of him when he was eight, nine years old."

Agnes pressed her lips together again, trying to compose herself. She had never admitted any of this before, and it now just came pouring out of her, unchecked, like a spigot whose handle had broken off.

"Anson's mother, Cathy, had just died, and I didn't know anything about raising a little boy. His father and I were busy building up the nursery back then. So I hired this babysitter to look after Anson when we were both away, collecting specimens for the nursery." Her eyes were wild as she looked from one to the other. "I swear I didn't know she abused him—not until he told me that night I found him burying that girl."

Her voice cracked again, but she pushed on.

"God forgive me, I should have paid closer attention to the way he was behaving. He was so erratic, but I just thought he was acting out. That he was a bad seed. That happens sometimes, you know, someone goes bad no matter how good his life is, how well he's treated."

"What did this babysitter look like?" Malloy asked her.

Caught off guard, Agnes stopped to think. "She was blond. About twenty-two. She had blue eyes. Why? Does it matter?" she asked, confused.

"It explains a lot," Malloy told her.

Agnes shook her head, speaking more to herself than to them now as she lamented the events. "If I had paid attention, those girls would have been alive. They all would have been alive now," she sobbed.

"Maybe Bruce would have been alive, too, instead of drinking himself to death like that because he thought that he'd driven Anson away somehow."

Her shoulders appeared to be even more slumped beneath the weight of her confession. Agnes struggled to try to rise above what she had just told them. Pulling herself together, she raised her head and looked at Malloy.

"Are you going to arrest me, now, Detective? I'm tired, and I want this to be over with," she told him. "I'm ready to pay for my crime."

Heartsick for what the woman had been living with for the past twenty years, Kristin turned toward Malloy. She couldn't see what purpose would be served if the woman was arrested and taken to jail. Then again, they couldn't just ignore the law.

"Isn't this a case of self-defense?" she asked Malloy. "She was only defending herself."

Malloy agreed with her, but there were rules to follow. After all, Agnes had had knowledge of several crimes and hadn't come forward.

"That's not up to me to decide," he told Kristin, then went on to say, "But we've got an assistant DA and two judges in the family. One of them has to know the name of a good defense attorney who does pro bono work." His last words were addressed to Agnes.

But the woman shook her head. "I appreciate what you're trying to do, Detective, but I've been in prison since the night I killed that boy. No amount of fancy words are going to set me free," she told him. Offering the duo a smile, she said, "I'm just glad this is finally over. If you need any further proof," she went on, "I wrote all this down and put it in a safety deposit box in the same bank where I have my checking account. I wrote down every detail—in case I was too much of a coward to confess during my lifetime," she admitted. "The problem with a secret like this is that eventually there is nothing else *but* the secret. Keeping it is the only thing that matters. Life ceases to have any joy, any meaning. Any value." She sighed. "And now it's out.

"Don't look like that," she said, seeing the pity in their faces. "You've both done me a huge favor. And they *are* right in what they say."

"How's that?" Malloy asked.

"Confession *is* good for the soul," Agnes concluded, nodding her head. "Thank you for hearing mine—and for not judging me," she added, her eyes once more glistening with tears. "It means a great deal," she assured them. "A *great* deal."

Chapter 22

Because she had freely confessed that she was responsible for her nephew's death, even though it had been accidental, and because, in Malloy's judgment, Agnes Parker was not a flight risk, the woman was kept under house arrest. He told her that he would speak to the assistant district attorney about her case and that someone would get back to her.

"You do what you think is best, Detective," Agnes told him. "I'm not going anywhere."

Malloy lost no time in getting in contact with his cousin, alerting her to the surprise twist his cold case had taken.

"She's an old, sick woman, Janelle. I hope she's given some leniency in this case."

"Let me see what I can do. I'll call you later," Janelle said.

"Now what?" Kristin asked him when he terminated the call. They were still driving back to the precinct.

"Now I fill out a ton of paperwork—and we wait," he said.

True to her word, Janelle reviewed all the available evidence, including the confession that Agnes had written and placed in her safety deposit box. Phone calls were made, strings were pulled and a couple of favors were called in. The results were that Agnes Parker was allowed to remain in her present living arrangements, technically under house arrest, until such time as her arraignment could be scheduled.

Janelle called both her cousin and the medical examiner into her office and gave them the news in person.

"I read her confession. Given Miss Parker's age, her rapidly failing health and the fact that there aren't any witnesses alive to dispute her version of the events, she might not go to prison. It will probably be ruled self-defense and she'll be allowed to live out the remainder of her life where she is."

Janelle looked at Kristin. "The other victims still need to be identified, so technically, the case isn't closed yet. But Miss Parker's account of the events will help a lot of families experience closure, and I think at this point, that's what everyone is after.

"Let me know as soon as you can identify those victims," she said to Kristin. "And I'll be in touch about the details regarding the legal side of this. It'll be just a matter of dotting the *i*'s and crossing the *t*'s," she elaborated.

Malloy rose to his feet. He knew when it was time to leave. Kristin rose beside him. "Thanks, Janelle. I know how busy you are."

"Never too busy for family," Janelle assured him. They began to leave the office when she asked, "So, will I see you two at the next gathering?"

Rather than answer, Malloy glanced in Kristin's direction and raised an eyebrow, waiting for her to respond.

The gathering. She'd almost forgotten that she'd agreed to go in exchange for his taking her with him to question Montoya.

"Sure," Kristin answered automatically.

The moment they were in the hallway, walking to the elevator, she asked, "Is that still on?"

"The gathering?" Malloy pressed the down button for the elevator. "Sure. Nothing gets in the way of one of Uncle Andrew's gatherings."

She shook her head. "No, I meant my attending."

"Why wouldn't it be?" he asked. He leaned against the wall as he waited for the elevator to arrive. "We made a deal."

She was well aware of that, but circumstances had changed. "I know, but that was before the case was solved."

His eyebrows drew together. "What does that have to do with anything?"

She was trying to word this as delicately as possible. She knew he'd be moving on. "Well, there's no more need for us to be working together."

He laughed. "I'm a detective, and you're the department's medical examiner. I think it's far too optimistic to believe that there'll be no more dead bodies in my future. Besides," he said more seriously, "I don't need a dead body as an excuse to see you. Do you?" he asked.

Why was he making her spell this out? "I just thought, you know, a fling has a limited life expectancy."

The elevator arrived, and they stepped inside. "Were you having a 'fling' with me, Doc?" Malloy asked. There was nothing in his expression to hint at what he was thinking. "Was I just your boy toy?"

She blew out an exasperated breath. "No, you idiot, I meant you. You're the one who was having the fling."

"With who?" he asked innocently, as if this was all news to him.

"With me," she cried in frustration. Why was he putting her through this? They both knew he'd be moving on. She was surprised that he hadn't already done it.

Yet he seemed determined to continue with this charade.

"Why would I be doing that?"

Was he deliberately baiting her, or was he just trying to get her to lose her temper so he could point to a reason he was calling it quits? "Because that's what you always do."

His eyes held hers and it was probably her imagination, but it seemed to Kristin that the humor was missing from his voice as he asked, "Says who?"

"Everyone," she pointed out.

"Maybe," he said seriously, "everyone's wrong."

"Much as I'd like to believe that," she confessed, "you have a reputation that definitely doesn't make you out to be a saint."

His eyes crinkled as he smiled at the thought. "Full disclosure, I was never trying to go for sainthood," he admitted.

"Well, congratulations," she said, desperately trying to reconstruct at least part of the barriers she'd had in place when she'd first encountered him. Barriers that were supposed to keep her safe from feeling as if her insides had been hollowed out with a jagged, rusty spoon. "You didn't achieve it." Still, she had to be completely fair to him. "Except, of course, you did try to find a way to help Agnes Parker avoid a jail sentence."

They arrived on the first floor and the elevator doors eased open.

Rather than go down the hallway to the building's entrance, Malloy suddenly pulled her over to an out-of-the-way alcove. His body barring her exit, he placed his hand on the wall right above her head, creating a feeling of privacy within a building that stood for the exact opposite.

"Don't change the subject, Doc," he told her. "This isn't about Agnes Parker, or the cold case. This is about you and me. About us continuing to see one another."

She felt as if her breath was caught in her throat. She was infinitely aware of the heat generating from his body that was less than inches away from hers. "Consulting on other cases?"

Why did she keep coming back to that? "If that comes up, sure. But like I said, I don't need a dead body as an excuse. I want to go on seeing you, Kristin," he said, growing serious. "I don't know what it is about you, but the idea of being able to see you makes me smile. Makes me feel like my whole day's in sync."

He took a breath, and then confessed, "This never really happened to me before, and I don't know where it's going to go, but I know that I do want to find out. Now, if this isn't all right with you, let me know now."

"And if it's not, you'll back off?" she asked incredulously. Could he just turn it off like that at will? How could he have any feelings for her if he could do it that easily?

"No, but at least I'll know what I'm up against—and that I'll have to work harder at making you want me to be part of your life."

She already *did* want him to be part of her life, but she couldn't tell him that. The second she admitted that, she'd frighten him away and he'd be gone.

"Where's this headed, Malloy?" she asked him quietly. It felt as if everything was trembling inside of her, and she was struggling not to let him see.

"I don't know," Malloy told her honestly. "But I do know that we owe it to ourselves to find out. I don't want to spend my life wondering 'what if?'" He slipped his fingers into her hair, framing her face and tilting her head up to his. "Do you?"

Her eyes met his. "I guess I'm going to the chief's party."

He smiled then, his smile reaching his eyes and lighting up his face. "Good to know." He began to lower his mouth to hers and was surprised when she put up a finger, blocking contact.

"Are you *sure* you want me to bring my mother along?" she asked.

"Sure. You said you thought she needed companionship. She'll have a good time," he promised her.

"I'm sure she will. But you should know that she will also start thinking of us as a couple," Kristin warned. Given an inch, her mother would take the proverbial mile.

Malloy didn't take her warning the way she thought he would. She expected him to look like a man who was having second thoughts, a man who had suddenly realized the error of his calculations.

Instead, he said, "It's got to start somewhere."

She wasn't sure she had heard him correctly. "What did you just say?"

"It's got to start somewhere," he repeated. "Put your hands down, Kristin. I'm beginning to feel like I'm playing patty-cake with an octopus. And 'patty-cake' isn't what I want to play," he informed her, his mouth curving wickedly.

"What *do* you want to play?" she asked in a hushed tone.

"That's what I'm trying to find out. Now, stop talking, put your hands at your sides and kiss me," he instructed.

"How am I going to put my arms around your neck if my hands are at my side?" she asked innocently.

"We'll work out something," he promised. The next moment, to forestall another response from Kristin, he sealed his mouth to hers.

And effectively kept her quiet for a long while.

Epilogue

"We need to talk," Malloy announced, walking into the morgue.

Surprised, Kristin looked up from the autopsy she was performing. She hadn't expected to see Malloy until later, after hours. He'd mentioned something about wanting to go out for dinner.

Since they usually took their meals together at her place, occasionally at his—with her handling the cooking in both cases if they weren't having takeout—Kristin had instantly known that something was up.

More than likely, a bad "something."

Seeing Malloy suddenly making an appearance in the morgue had her thinking that she was right. Something *was* definitely up.

She braced herself, certain that it would be something she wasn't going to want to hear.

Things had been going well.

Too well.

And that had her concerned that an end was coming.

She did what she could to sound calm. "Right now?" she asked.

"Well, we're alone," Malloy pointed out, thinking that there was no time like the present. He wanted to get this out before his nerve deserted him.

"Technically," Kristin corrected, glancing at the body on the table.

Malloy followed her line of vision. "I don't think he's going to mind."

She didn't want to fall apart at work, and if he said what she knew he was going to say, she would. "This can't wait?"

Malloy shoved his hands into his pockets. "Not really."

She took a breath, wishing her heart would stop thumping against her rib cage like that. "Does this have something to do with you taking me out to dinner later tonight?"

He seemed to be on the alert, she thought as he answered, "Yes."

"I knew it," she cried. Stripping off her gloves, she put the digital recorder she'd been using on pause, leaving it next to the body.

"You know?" He looked at her in surprise. "Who told you?"

She wasn't going to cause a scene, Kristin told herself. She'd been bracing herself for this ever since that first moment when butterflies had taken up residence in her stomach, fluttering whenever Malloy was around her. And now it was here.

"No one told me," she retorted, then asked, "You don't think I'm bright enough to figure this out on my own?"

"Well, if you figured it out, you're brighter than I am, I'll give you that," he told her, succeeding in thoroughly confusing her. "Because it didn't fully hit me until last night."

Last night.

She'd been afraid of that.

After spending every evening for the past two months in each other's company, after having his family all but absorb her, and her mother practically adopt him, Malloy had opted for what amounted to a "guys night out" with a few of his friends.

His *single* friends.

When he'd showed up on her doorstep later that night, he'd been surprisingly quiet—which had led her to conclude that their days together were numbered. By going out with his friends, he'd been reminded of the life he'd previously enjoyed and had undoubtedly realized that he wanted it back.

That was what tonight was going to be about, she thought. A well-rehearsed speech containing the words, "It's not you, it's me," or sentiments to that effect. And then that would be that.

She felt sick.

"Look, we don't have to go through this," she told him resolutely. "I've got an autopsy to finish, and you, you've got whatever it is that you have to do."

"This won't take long," he promised.

"It's already taking too long," she shot back. And if he remained here any longer, she knew she was going to break down and cry, no matter what she promised herself to the contrary. "Just go. Just—"

Words froze in her throat as she found herself looking down at a small black box that Malloy was holding in the palm of his hand.

"What's that?" she asked in a shaky whisper, the question barely making it out of her all-too-dry mouth.

"Something I was going to give you tonight, but I just couldn't wait. I guess it's burning a hole in my pocket," he admitted. Since she continued staring at the box, he opened it for her.

Her eyes widened.

"It's a ring," she whispered.

"That's what they usually put in ring boxes," he agreed.

She raised her eyes to his. "Who's it for?" she asked in the same hushed whisper.

"Well, it sure as hell's not for the guy on the table. I was going to give it to you tonight, but I showed it to your mother after I picked it up, and I realized that she wasn't going to be able to keep this a secret. I wanted to give it to you before she spoiled the surprise, so I decided to bring it to you now."

Stunned, Kristin continued looking at him.

Why wasn't she saying anything? "You're making me nervous, Kris. Are you going to make me beg?"

"I thought you were going to break up with me," she finally confessed, her voice cracking.

"Break up with—" His voice almost evaporated, then came back in full force. "Why the hell would I do that?"

She took in a shaky breath. He deserved an explanation. "Because you got to see what you were missing out on last night, going out with your friends."

He couldn't help laughing at how wrong her interpretation of last night was. "What I was missing out on was an empty life. Those guys are out there, looking for what I have right here." He took her hand in his. "I love you, Kris, and I don't want to go back to that life. Marry me. Marry me, Kristin, so that I can go on having and living that full life. Marry me," he said, lowering his voice, "or I'll sic your mother on you."

She started to laugh then, with relief and with joy. "Good closing argument."

He took her into his arms, bringing her body against his. "So it's yes?"

Her smile encompassed her entire being. "For a bright guy, you can be so dumb—it's been yes from the first time you kissed me."

"Then I'll just have to keep on kissing you," he said. And to prove it, he did.

* * * * *

If you loved this novel, don't miss other suspenseful titles by USA TODAY *bestselling author Marie Ferrarella:*

CAVANAUGH OR DEATH
COLTON COPYCAT KILLER
SECOND CHANCE COLTON
HOW TO SEDUCE A CAVANAUGH
CAVANAUGH FORTUNE

Available now from
Harlequin Romantic Suspense!

REQUEST YOUR FREE BOOKS!
2 FREE NOVELS PLUS 2 FREE GIFTS!

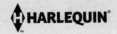

ROMANTIC suspense

Sparked by danger, fueled by passion

YES! Please send me 2 FREE Harlequin® Romantic Suspense novels and my 2 FREE gifts (gifts are worth about $10). After receiving them, if I don't wish to receive any more books, I can return the shipping statement marked "cancel." If I don't cancel, I will receive 4 brand-new novels every month and be billed just $4.74 per book in the U.S. or $5.49 per book in Canada. That's a savings of at least 12% off the cover price! It's quite a bargain! Shipping and handling is just 50¢ per book in the U.S. and 75¢ per book in Canada.* I understand that accepting the 2 free books and gifts places me under no obligation to buy anything. I can always return a shipment and cancel at any time. Even if I never buy another book, the two free books and gifts are mine to keep forever.

240/340 HDN GH3P

Name	(PLEASE PRINT)
Address	Apt. #
City	State/Prov.	Zip/Postal Code

Signature (if under 18, a parent or guardian must sign)

Mail to the **Reader Service:**
IN U.S.A.: P.O. Box 1867, Buffalo, NY 14240-1867
IN CANADA: P.O. Box 609, Fort Erie, Ontario L2A 5X3

Want to try two free books from another line?
Call 1-800-873-8635 or visit www.ReaderService.com.

* Terms and prices subject to change without notice. Prices do not include applicable taxes. Sales tax applicable in N.Y. Canadian residents will be charged applicable taxes. Offer not valid in Quebec. This offer is limited to one order per household. Not valid for current subscribers to Harlequin Romantic Suspense books. All orders subject to credit approval. Credit or debit balances in a customer's account(s) may be offset by any other outstanding balance owed by or to the customer. Please allow 4 to 6 weeks for delivery. Offer available while quantities last.

Your Privacy—The Reader Service is committed to protecting your privacy. Our Privacy Policy is available online at www.ReaderService.com or upon request from the Reader Service.

We make a portion of our mailing list available to reputable third parties that offer products we believe may interest you. If you prefer that we not exchange your name with third parties, or if you wish to clarify or modify your communication preferences, please visit us at www.ReaderService.com/consumerchoice or write to us at Reader Service Preference Service, P.O. Box 9062, Buffalo, NY 14240-9062. Include your complete name and address.

HRS15

ROMANTIC suspense

Tension wafted from Josie. "It's just like my father described—the tree, the carvings and the creek."

"Did he tell you what the carvings meant?"

She shook her head. "No, I'm not even sure he's the one who made them."

"Then, let's see if we can dig up an old watch," he replied.

They hadn't quite reached the front of the tree when a man stepped out from behind it, a gun in his hand.

Josie released a sharp yelp of surprise and Tanner tightened his grip on the shovel. What in the hell was going on? Did this man have something to do with whatever had happened to Eldridge?

"Josie Colton," he said, his thin lips twisting into a sneer. "I knew if I tailed you long enough you'd lead me to the watch. I've been watching you for days."

"Who are you?" Josie asked.

"That's for me to know and you not to find out," he replied. "Now, about that watch..."

"What watch?" she replied. "I—I don't know what you're talking about." Her voice held a tremor that belied her calm demeanor.

Tanner didn't move a muscle although his brain fired off in a dozen different directions. The man had called her by name, so this obviously had nothing to do with Eldridge.

Why would a man with a gun know about a watch wanted for sentimental reasons? What hadn't Josie told him? Was it possible to disarm the man without anyone getting hurt?

"Don't play dumb with me, girlie." The man raised a hand to sweep a hank of oily dark hair out of his eyes. "Your daddy spent years in prison bragging about how he was going to be buried with that cheap watch and then nobody would ever find the map to all the money from those old bank heists." He took a step toward them. "Now tell me where that watch is. I want that map."

Adrenaline pumped through Tanner. He certainly didn't know anything about old bank robberies, but a sick danger snapped in the air.

A look of deadly menace radiated outward from the gunman's dark, beady eyes. The gun was steady in his hands, and Tanner's chest constricted.

He tightened his grip on the shovel, calculated the distance between himself and the gunman's arm and then he swung. The end of the shovel connected. The gun fell from the man's grasp, but not before he fired off a shot.

The woods exploded with sound—the boom of the gun, a flutter of birds' wings overhead as they flew out of the treetops and Josie's scream of unmistakable pain.

Don't miss
COLTON COWBOY HIDEOUT by New York Times
bestselling author Carla Cassidy,
available July 2016 wherever
Harlequin® Romantic Suspense
books and ebooks are sold.

www.Harlequin.com

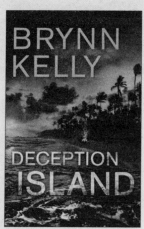

$26.99 U.S./$29.99 CAN.

EXCLUSIVE
Limited time offer!

$2.⁰⁰ OFF

BRYNN KELLY

A stolen boy
A haunted soldier
A cornered con woman...

DECEPTION
ISLAND

Available May 31, 2016.
Pick up your copy today!

H
HQN™

$2.⁰⁰
OFF

the purchase price of
DECEPTION ISLAND by Brynn Kelly.

Offer valid May 31, 2016, to June 30, 2016. Redeemable at participating retail outlets. Not redeemable at Barnes & Noble. Limit one coupon per purchase. Valid in the U.S.A. and Canada only.

52613467

5 65373 00082 3 (8100)0 12139

Turn your love of reading into
rewards you'll love with
Harlequin My Rewards

**Join for FREE today at
www.HarlequinMyRewards.com**

Earn **FREE BOOKS** of your choice.

Experience **EXCLUSIVE OFFERS** and contests.

Enjoy **BOOK RECOMMENDATIONS**
selected just for you.

PLUS! Sign up now
and get **500** points
right away!

Earn
FREE
REWARDS
Join
Today!
HarlequinMyRewards.com

MYR16R

JUST CAN'T GET ENOUGH?

Join our social communities
and talk to us online.

You will have access to the latest
news on upcoming titles and special
promotions, but most importantly,
you can talk to other fans about your
favorite Harlequin reads.

Harlequin.com/Community

Facebook.com/HarlequinBooks

Twitter.com/HarlequinBooks

Pinterest.com/HarlequinBooks

HARLEQUIN®

A *Romance* FOR EVERY MOOD™

Love the Harlequin book you just read?

Your opinion matters.

Review this book on your favorite book site, review site, blog or your own social media properties and share your opinion with other readers!

Be sure to connect with us at:
Harlequin.com/Newsletters
Facebook.com/HarlequinBooks
Twitter.com/HarlequinBooks